I0776440

"*CHISEL THE BONE* is a gruesome, gritty tale in which DeCamillis creates a stark, tense atmosphere of unease, dread, and pervasive and increasing madness. She shows evil in its big, bad, brutal glory, but also at its most insidious, often understandable, and inevitably tragic. Echoes of Laird Barron and Poppy Z Brite within a voice uniquely her own, DeCamillis flays the skin of polite society and exposes for all to see the sharp edges of desperation, need, and survival. This book will get under your skin in all the best ways."

— MARY SANGIOVANNI, AUTHOR OF *THE EVERYWHERE HOUSE*

"DeCamillis's writing is really fun, super descriptive, and highly entertaining in such a dramatic way. It recalls similar writers like Christopher Moore, Joe Lansdale, and Carl Hiaasen. This story would make a great play or movie. Definitely R-rated, but teenagers would love it!"

— MEG NORTH, AUTHOR OF *THE TRANSFORMATION OF CHARLOTTE POOLE*

"A fresh new voice in horror, Renee S. DeCamillis knows how to write tales that get under your skin. *Chisel the Bone* offers a macabre and unique brand of dark story-telling that will keep you turning the pages. This one is a fast-paced carnival ride that brings you on a wild journey full of twists and turns."

— MORGAN SYLVIA, AUTHOR OF *ABODE*

"For all the readers, including myself, who did not want to see DeCamillis' novella, *The Bone Cutters*, come to an end, we are in luck. The anticipated sequel comes to us in the novel, *Chisel the Bone*. And Renee DeCamillis does not disappoint. Dory finds herself in another nightmarish battle for survival. *Chisel the Bone* takes horrific things that can happen in real life and blends them with the supernatural. Follow the blood trail to the very end. You'll be glad you did."

— CINDY O'QUINN, BRAM STOKER AWARD-
WINNING AUTHOR

"*Chisel the Bone* by Renee S. DeCamillis is exactly the kind of book I'm putting in the hands of the next generation of readers who are just cutting their teeth on the horror genre. It is breakneck paced, and left me absolutely impressed with this clever twist on vampire fiction.

— PETER DUDAR, AUTHOR OF *THE GOAT PARADE* & *BLOOD CULT OF THE BOOBY FARMERS*

CHISEL THE BONE

Renee S. DeCamillis

Encyclopocalypse Publications
www.encyclopocalypse.com

To Josephine Salamone Young
1914-1983
Thank you, Nana Jo.

CONTENTS

CHISEL THE BONE

THE CARVER, THE COLLECTOR, AND THE STITCHER

The cloth secured in his mouth, knotted tight behind his head, prevents him from screaming. A blindfold stretches across his eyes. The white-hot sting of the blade slicing through the skin of his shin makes him grit his teeth.

Only a whimper escapes.

Buck knife in hand, The Carver gets down to the bone quickly. Twin serpent-like scars run up the outside of both of The Carver's forearms. They writhe and pulse as he uses the edge of the blade to shave and peel the flesh away from the outer layer of dense compact bone. After uncovering a large area, he reaches out and swaps the knife for a chisel and mallet. Like a modern-day Michelangelo, he begins whittling away at the victim's tibia, the bigger of the two shin bones, careful not to go too deep. Serpent scars slither around while he works.

Every hit of the mallet sends a shaking jolt through the restrained man. The chair legs rattle against the tiled floor with every jostle. Ankles zip-tied to the wooden chair legs. Wrists zip-tied to each side of the back of the chair. Tears soak the blindfold and leak down his cheeks from underneath. Snot bubbles at his nostrils. Strands of his shaggy brown hair stick to his sweaty forehead.

Rather than creating a work of art, The Carver extracts bone shavings. With the help of The Collector, who stands beside him, curls of shaved bone pile up on a sheet of tinfoil. These ribbons of victory will get dried and crushed to dust at a later time.

From behind The Carver, someone with gnarly scarred knuckles passes The Collector a second sheet of tin foil. They swap the filled foil for the empty.

The Carver reaches for a new tool. A small utility knife takes the place of the chisel and mallet.

Rapid shaving motions slide down the tibia over and over and over again.

More whimpering.

More chair rattling.

Sibling serpents shake and slither along with every movement of The Carver's arms.

Little bits of bone pile up on the tinfoil this time. This second batch is for immediate consumption. Mixed with blood, the pile of bone fragments looks similar to sticky black tar heroin. Bone Cutters call it Dark Heaven or Red Sugar or simply Dust.

Deal done, The Stitcher steps out of the shadows, thread and needle held in grotesquely scarred hands, to seal the wound.

The victim no longer whimpers.

The victim no longer cries.

The victim passed out moments ago, head hung low, chin to chest. Whether from shock or blood loss is of no concern to The Carver, The Collector, and The Stitcher.

They're only here for the Dust and the high that will come with it, as well as the money they'll make off what they don't smoke, snort or ingest themselves.

The Stitcher feels thankful. Not just for the high-to-come and the money they'll make.

It sure is easier to stitch the wound without all that shaking and blubbering from a few moments ago. The needle and thread zips back and forth through the flesh as smoothly as a whisper floating with the wind.

Wound now sealed shut, it's time to clear the scene. With two tips of the chair by The Collector and The Stitcher, The Carver carefully slides out the blood covered plastic tarp spread out underneath the victim and the chair. He rolls it up, preps it for disposal.

The zip-ties then get snipped from the victim's wrists and ankles and tucked securely into the tarp. Add in a few rocks from the park on the walk back to their den, and these Bone Cutters will send all remnants of this event down river.

All except the product and—

The buck knife.

The handle of the knife gets wiped clean. Hilt placed in the victim's hand with his fingers wrapped around it, assures only his prints appear on the weapon.

The Carver, The Collector, and The Stitcher cover their tracks well. Maybe not the tracks in their skin or the scars that double as their own living entities. Those they wear with pride, like badges of honor. But definitely the tracks from the assaults against all their unwilling victims.

Not *all* victims are unwilling.

Some enjoy the rush of the slice like a bite from a vampire.

The Donors.

Minions or Lackeys is what non-dust-users call them.

Some might even call them Renfields.

Many Bone Cutters (A.K.A. Dusters) also get a rush from the slice, but it sure does wear you down after a while. All that blood loss. All that pain. Much more satisfaction and stimulation comes from inflicting that pain on another. But when times get desperate—

They will again slice into themselves.

Scene all cleaned and sparkling, as though only the victim has been present, the three junkie-cutters vacate the premises. The tarp gets rolled up tight and worn like a backpack by The Collector. After one last wipe of the outside doorknob, the three practically skip down the hallway and out onto the sidewalk, as giddy as children approaching an ice cream truck.

While strolling away from the scene of the crime, as though nothing unusual has taken place, they hear the flapping of large wings overhead. The sound moves swiftly towards the house they just left behind.

They all look up, wondering if they'll see what they assume has risen. A glimpse of huge, black wings zooming past the beam shining from the streetlight confirms their assumption.

Grave Robberies Occurring Across the State

State Police report that numerous cemeteries throughout the state are experiencing gravesite desecration and exhumation. Not only have the caskets of the dead been robbed of all valuables contained within, but something else of import that has gone missing are the actual remains of the dead. The bones of over two hundred and seventy-five interred bodies across thirteen counties in the state have gone missing. Most recently, Howard Cemetery near Crystal Lake in Razorville was hit by graverobbers just last night. There is suspicion that these incidents may be the result of parties going on in the late-night hours, since drug paraphernalia was discovered at almost every crime scene. Police are asking that if you or anyone you know has witnessed any questionable activity in or around cemeteries, especially after dark, or if anyone has any information that can lead police to the violators, please call the State Police tip line at 1-800-555-7686.

CHAPTER 1
AT-HOME DORY

My eyes snap wide open from a dead sleep. I fling the covers off and bolt upright in bed. Covered in sweat from a recurring nightmare, I desperately try to catch my breath. Voices of all my previous therapists ricochet around in my mind: *Don't forget to breathe. Calm the mind; calm the body.* Remembering their training, I try deep breathing; breathe in for four seconds, hold for seven, release for eight.

It doesn't take long.

Rapid, shallow breathing soon takes over the 4-7-8 "relaxing breath" technique. A splash of cold water on my face will help snap me out of this.

As soon as my feet hit the floor, a *scraping* sounds out against my window. I freeze.

With the curtains closed, I'm unable to see if it's just a bird on the sill. But my curtains always remain closed, especially at night. City life doesn't offer much privacy. One must create it themselves.

Scraping sounds again.

I flinch, then ease myself out of bed. Slowly and quietly, I move toward the sound. At the window, I reach for the edge of the curtain and pull it open just enough to peek out.

Nothing on the sill.

I lean so close to the glass I feel the coolness of the October night on the tip of my nose. Streetlights illuminate the dark outside. A disturbing amount of artificial light fills the city sky, masking the glow of the full moon.

Nothing appears down in the driveway that could've made the sound. Nothing from the apartment building next door. Suddenly, a large shadow at the mouth of the driveway grabs my attention. It moves in waves, like the flapping wings of a huge bird, past the lamp post at the front of my building. Then it swoops down the length of the driveway. I crank my neck to look up and get a better view.

A loud *crash* makes me jump. I drop the curtain closed, a safety reflex. Then I realize—

That sound came from *within* my apartment.

It's almost three in the morning! What the fuck could that be?

I rush for the baseball bat by my door, then remember I'd already broken it when I flipped out on Jill's last fly-by-fuck, trashing the apartment in the process. Not my finest seeing-red moment. I grab the collapsed high-hat stand next to my bureau and stumble, half awake, into the kitchen.

Jill's half-bare ass stares me in the face as she's bent over in her itty-bitty boy shorts undies, picking up the stainless-steel bowl she must've dropped on the floor.

Why does this bitch run around half naked all the time?

"Hey there, Miss Paranoid. What's with the cymbal stand raised up over your head? Are you sleepwalking? News flash— that is *not* your hairbrush." Jill laughs at her own bad joke as she straightens up. She places the bowl on the counter and steps back over to the stove where she's frying up some plantains and eggs.

"What's with such an early breakfast?"

"My bartending shifts are wearin' me thin. No time for dinner between the office and the bar. I need some fuel."

"What gives? Still no raise at your day gig, huh?"

A loud, sarcastic laugh bursts out of Jill. "Yeah, I'm not

counting on *that* to happen at my testosterone-filled work-place." She huffs as she adds, "I *really* need a new job. I've got a fucking master's degree, and I still need to work two jobs to pay rent *and* my student loans. And if this full-of-itself-city keeps hiking up the rent..." She slams another pan on the stove. "Well, then I guess I'll have to switch to strippin' in the evenin' rather than tending bar." She sways her hips side to side as she stirs a pan of beans and rice.

Three hip sways later, she grabs the newspaper off the counter and tosses it at me.

"What's this for? It's too damn early to read." Ditching the high-hat stand, I replace it with a cup of coffee, black and bitter, and sit at the table. I don't bother asking why she brewed coffee at this hour. I assume it's to put in the fridge for iced coffee. Whatever. Works for me.

"Check out that section I left folded open. You'll never guess what's going on across the state. Makes me think of those psycho Dusters that were after you in the nuthouse."

Back to stirring the grub she's cooking up, she laughs. "Can you believe there's actually a Razorville, Maine?"

"What?!" My voice hits a high note I never thought possible this early in the morning. "Cut it out. No there is *not*."

"No joke. There *is* a Razorville. It's in the article. *And* it gets better."

Gulping my coffee, soaking in the warmth of the hot steam drifting across my face, I wait for this *better* part, as she dramatically waits an extra couple beats to deliver it.

She grabs some dishes out of the cupboard, utensils out of the drawer, stirs the grub a bit more before finally turning to face me. "There's also a Crystal Lake in Razorville." She's staring right at me, awaiting my reaction.

"Yeah, now I *know* you're full of shit. Nice try." Laughter bursts out of *me* this time.

"That's what *I* thought, too. I had to Google it to believe it. Turns out, Razorville is *actually* a village not a town, but it *is* real. Oh, and Crystal Lake is actually called Crystal Pond today. But, of course, a Crystal Lake in a town called Razorville grabs more attention for the article."

"It *all* sounds like a fucking horror movie to me." I huff. "I *wish* that's all it was. Waking up sweat-drenched from nightmares on a regular basis…that shit can fuck right off."

The article stares up at me, begging me to read, but I'm just too tired. Dealing with potential Duster news at this time of day makes my skin crawl just considering it. This is no movie. It's *my real* life for fuck's sake. I slide the paper aside.

"Is that why you're up so early again? Another nightmare?" Jill twists around, sits the coffee carafe on the table and throws me an inquiring look.

I nod.

"Were you back in the psych hospital again? Or was it one of the other ones this time?"

"Hospital…and unlike real life, I didn't get away. I woke up just as Git Girl and Toodles, both jonesing for a high and literally drooling like a rabid beasts, were getting ready to slice me open, chisel my bones." Shivers run through me. I shake it off. "But I'm fine. It's over."

"So great to hear you can just brush it off so easily, like a seasoned pro." She flashes her wiseass smirk.

"You know what they say, practice and all that jazz." I throw the smirk right back at her.

Jill hands me a bowl of black beans and rice and fried plantains, topped with a fried egg. "Hope you're hungry."

The way I woke up, I hadn't thought about food, but it all looks and smells so tasty. I pop the yoke and watch the yellow fluid bleed out all over the darkness underneath.

"What's up with the eggs? I thought you were a vegan."

"I am a vegan, silly," she says as she sets down a half-filled bowl for herself and pulls up a chair across the table from me. "But sometimes I crave an occasional aborted chick. What, are you the vegan police now?" She reaches her hands across the table toward me. "Cuff me and take me in, Officer, but don't you even *think* about getting frisky." Giggling, she flips her long blonde hair over her shoulder and stuffs half an egg into her mouth. "Mmm, dead baby chick tastes splendid on this beautiful ink-black morning." She licks her lips seductively.

"You really are one sick bitch. You know that, right?"

"I sure do, sweet and chipper Dory. Would you have me any other way?" Her breathy tone sounds way too porn-perfect.

"Not at all. If you were normal, I wouldn't have had a place to live after getting released from that cray-cray joint." As I'm forking the beans and rice around my dish and glancing at the page beside my coffee, I drag up the *thank you* that I still haven't said to her since she took me back as a roommate last weekend after Dr. Headstrom released me—"*for your safety*," is what he'd told me.

Ha! How's that for you? *This* suicidal chick the *professionals* had labeled "delusional" is safer in the big bad world than in the psychiatric hospital. Says a lot about those so-called "therapeutic institutions," don't you think?

Maybe the big Doc ought to consider calling the police to investigate those Dusters who've taken control of the hospital's NA group *before* they chase down and torment another patient who actually may need *real* psychiatric help.

Yeah. That'll take too much work, though.

"Hey, sweetie, you don't have to thank me. We've been friends since we first learned how to stick tampons in our vajay-jays. My life would be empty without you." As she's pouring a couple shots of Sambuca into her coffee, she adds, "Plus, who would be here to protect me from balding ug-os next time I'm too drunk to see any better?" She takes a long drink of her go-go juice. "That reminds me—we need to get a new baseball bat to keep beside the door."

"Hey, thanks for the reminder. This time I'll make sure I get a metal one. There ain't no bustin' that bad boy next time you need me to come rescue you from spray-on tan baldies."

"Yeah, good call." She raises her mug in the air.

We clink cups of Joe.

"I still can't believe you nailed that cop with the bat, too. What were you *thinking*?" Another laugh and another chug from her mug.

"Hey, I had no idea the cops were even here, let alone in my swinging range." I huff. "Hell, you know I was just trying to protect you from what I *thought* was a rapist, you sick perv. Stop bringing home stray dogs. It's bad for *both* of us. My PTSD can't handle that shit…" I pause, glance at her sidelong, waiting for what we both know is coming.

"*'You couldn't handle that shit on strong acid, man.'*" She laughs at the Bonham drum solo reference from *Dazed and Confused.*

Shaking my head, I kick her foot under the table, though I can't *not* laugh too.

"Shit. I still can't believe they let you out of the court-ordered Blue Papered status at that shithole nuthouse. Took 'em long enough to finally believe you were in real danger there, don't ya' think?"

I top-off my coffee to warm it up. "Sure as shit—Got the scars to prove it." I rub my shoulder. The shiv wound in my shoulder blade is slowly healing from when Toodles sliced me open after that last NA group meeting—meetings I never should've been sent to in the first place. I wonder if they've found that sketchy Nurse Hatchet or not. After all, she's the one who kept escorting me there. "Damn." I shake my head, remembering the nightmarish events.

The shiv wound—partially my fault, since the makeshift blade had been hidden in my sock. But, shit, I didn't make it. I just needed if for protection. I wasn't expecting that dude in group to get Git Girl all riled up and nutty. Had she and Toodles never snuck into my room to try to dust me, the shiv never would've come into play.

I crack my neck, pop my knuckles just thinking about those

psychos. "Thankfully, early release helped get me away from those crazy fuckers trying to dust me to death."

"Yeah, you're lucky about that one for sure."

"Huh, lucky." I shrug. "Yeah, two mandatory Anger Management meetings each week are *much* better than that psycho-filled ward and all the fucking meds they forced on me. Good thing Tim at The Drum Shop understands." I push my coffee mug aside, remembering that my first drum student scheduled for today had texted me yesterday that they can't make it for their lesson this week. Looks like I might be able to get another hour of sleep before going into work.

"I wish *my* boss at my day gig was so easy-going and understanding." She looks up at the ceiling and shouts, "Fuck! I need a new job! One that actually pays what my brain full of higher education is worth." She pretend-cries. Then she goes back to chugging the rest of her Sambuca-spiked coffee and immediately fills it up for seconds—including the spike.

"Easy does it there, lush. What gives? No lay in long time got wittle Jill-Jill down?" I try lightening the mood, get my mind off those horrific memories of mine.

Behind a pouty-playful expression, Jill huffs. "Damn, girl, two weeks is a goddamn lifetime for this pussycat. She's feeling out of shape and in need of a good workout." She takes another drink and her expression quickly morphs to frustrated, curled-down lips and down-turned eyes. "No, seriously, my student loans are in default and my boss still won't talk about my overdue raise. I'm feeling the pinch big time."

As she goes on and on, ranting about the overpriced cost of college tuition and how college should be free as "an investment in the future of this country," I'm reading about all the grave robberies happening across the state.

Before she's done with her speech, I'm on my cell phone texting Tommy and Irie. By the time I hit the arrow, I feel something warm and wet hit my cheek. And it sticks there. Without putting my phone away, I roll my eyes up and look across the table.

Jill has a fork-full of beans and rice aimed directly at my forehead. "Bitch, you're breaking your own freakin' rule—*No Cell Phones At The Table.* 'Put the fucking gadget away and be in the moment' is what I always hear. Now, take your own damn advice and put it away."

"Yeah, but..."

"Yeah but nothin'." Another splat of warm beans and rice smacks me in the forehead.

A full-fledge food fight commences.

————

Drunk as all hell before six am, Jill is slipping and sliding around the kitchen floor in her flip-flops with scouring pads affixed to the bottoms, cleaning up the beans and rice and eggs and plantains from our little food fight. *That chick really isn't right once she hits the bottle, but that's Jill.* I shrug off the thought.

Then, to top off her drunken little-girl shenanigans, she starts singing, "Dory and Tommy up in a tree," but ends the line with kissing noises.

"We're just friends, you little nympho. Grow up!"

As she passes by the doorway, I notice that signature twinkle in her eyes, a soundless laughing that she seems to have perfected. I keep glancing up from my cell periodically. I can't help it. It's quite a spectacle. I shake my head and laugh as I'm texting Tommy and Irie about the cemetery exhumations and bone theft.

ME: Yep

Not just valuables

Bones too

TOMMY: Crazy fucking dusters at it again I bet

IRIE: No bets needed.

We know it's them.

Now, how do we get them busted? This
insanity needs to stop!

TOMMY: When is your court date

ME: Oct 30th

IRIE: Then we have time to somehow get more
of them arrested.

Me: Yeah but how

IRIE: Let's get together to discuss our options.

TOMMY: Good call Sunshine

ME: Lets do it

After the screen goes black, a curiosity creeps into my brain. How the hell do Tommy and Irie tolerate working at a psych hospital where they know Dusters masquerade as patients? At least as janitors, Tommy and Irie don't need to interact with any patients. But still...

That's how Tommy and I met and became friends.

I'm thankful they work there. If they didn't, we never would've met, and I may not have ever convinced the staff that I wasn't delusional when I told them about those psycho cutters who were after my bones. Tommy almost lost his damn job to protect me. Good thing Irie had come to our rescue, or else we both probably would've ended up dead with our bone dust snorted up some low-life Dusters' noses.

CHAPTER 2
NA IN THE NUTHOUSE

A gnarly scarred up hand lands on Lou's boney shoulder as he starts hanging his metal folding chair up on the rack before heading out of Group. Lou freezes.

"Wait up, Slug Man."

The mutant-sized slug-like scar around Lou's collar bone pulses and wriggles as he turns and looks over his shoulder.

There stands Clyde, the counselor.

"We need to talk." The scars on Clyde's hand swim around like a jumble of wiggly worms when he vise-grips Slug Man's shoulder. He glances at the other patients as they all put their chairs away and begin filing out of the group counseling room. "*After* everyone leaves," he whispers as he looks back to Slug Man, who looks at him with a wide-eyed worried expression.

"Sure thing, Doc." The gravel in Slug Man's voice sounds so rough it's a surprise dirt doesn't fly out with every word. He pulls his chair back down to the floor and leans it against his long, boney leg.

Someone playfully pushes on the back of Slug Man's knee. His skeletal frame falters forward, recovers. His head whips around as quick as lighting, and he glares over his other shoulder. The slug-scar writhes around with his movements.

"Ha! Gotcha, Slug Man. Now, move on over and make some

room for me." Roxy's words trip over one another as her sly smile stretches across her sunken-in cheeks. She reaches past him, hangs up her chair. The snake-like scar running from her elbow up to her shoulder on the outside of her string bean bicep slithers and squirms along with her every move. Snake Girl.

"Sure is nice having chairs back in group rather than pillow seats on the cold floor, isn't it?" As he strikes up idle chit chat, Clyde backs away and re-seats himself.

Slug Man remains standing near the rack of chairs, not wanting to draw attention to the fact that he's staying behind for a "talk" with the counselor.

"Oh, hell yeah it is." Snake Girl spits her words out while slithering her way out into the hall. "Good thing Dory, that skinny little ball of nerves, got released, though I have no idea how the hell *that* happened." She hisses out a breathy laugh and yells, "Hallelujah! No more Chair Chucker!" and then shuts the door behind her. Her voice is so slow and droney, part of her last words trail behind her like the tail end of a snake.

Clyde jumps to his feet as soon as the doorknob clicks shut. He rushes over to the window, makes sure the blind is completely closed, and then he locks the door. When he gets back to his seat, Slug Man already has his ass in a chair waiting for him, slug scar pulsing along with every beat of his racing heart.

Slug Man croaks out with his gravelly voice, "What's up, Doc?" He slaps Clyde on the shoulder. Strained laughter leaks from him as he tries to lighten the mood and relieve the tension of wondering what he's done wrong—why Clyde wants to talk with him *privately*.

"Hey, all joking aside, I got word they arrested Toodles for aggravated assault with a deadly weapon against that Chair Chucker chick, *and* they also arrested no-self-control-Sheila for going after that skinny bitch, too. They're trying to nab *her* for attempted murder." Clyde says under his breath, "I *told* that idiot not to try, that the skinny ball of nerves was a tough nut to crack. Anyway, we need to be on our best behavior." He leans in close and continues. "By that I mean, keep everything on the down-down-*extra-down*-low, if you get my drift." Knee bouncing, scarred mess of a hand rubbing his thigh, he glances around the room then back to Slug Man. "Staff have been watching our group with hawk-eyes ever since that skinny bitch made all her psycho complaints and Toodles and Git Girl went all bat-shit on her. And that's not all..."

Clyde's eyes gaze from one side to the other then over Slug Man's shoulder toward the door. He takes one last wily look, this time over his own shoulder—though the only thing behind him is a windowless wall—before he sits up straight and gets down to business.

"Another time for that. Anyway, I found out in the morning meeting today that out of the five new patients admitted over the weekend four of them are suicidal, with wounds from their attempts, and three of them are heroin addicts. I want you to make sure their paperwork sends the four all into our group. Got it?"

Slug Man's pinched lips twist sideways. "Mmm...That doesn't add up."

"What do you mean 'that doesn't add up'? If I *say* it—*you* do it." Clyde's pinched bushy eyebrows scream anger.

"No, I mean four and three is seven, but you said there were *five* new patients admitted."

"Oh, yeah, well out of the four suicidals three of *them* are also junkies. The other one of the five newbies, I really don't give a fuck. They can't come to this group without drawing attention. Only go after the four with wounds—the suicidals. The three junkies should be the easiest of the bunch to lure to our side, but I *need* all four." Again, he glances over his shoulder, then quickly looks back to Slug Man.

"Oh, how thankful I am for our country's oh-so-fucked up society *and* its fallout." Slug Man's rubbing his palms together, eager for fresh dust. "So many suicidals and addicts for the taking."

"Yeah, yeah, thankful, yadda yadda. Now go get to work. I have some other business I need to tend to."

"Wait a minute. This paperwork tampering is going to be a Hell of a lot tougher without Nurse Hatchet around. What's the word on her? Is she coming back?" Eyebrows raised, Slug Man eagerly awaits a hopeful response.

Clyde looks over his shoulder, mumbles something.

"What was that?" Slug Man turns an ear toward Clyde.

Clyde's eyes remain riveted on the windowless wall for a moment longer, mumbling more of what sounds like gibberish.

"Yeah, yeah. Don't worry," quietly slips out of his mouth as he turns back toward Slug Man's general direction.

Stone-still, Slug Man's face appears contorted with confusion.

Clyde suddenly looks straight into his eyes and says in a low, stern voice, "What's wrong? Didn't I tell you to get to work?"

Slug Man leans forward, elbows on his knees, eyes squinted. "Yeah, I'm going. I guess I'll figure something out, but...I can't help wondering—why do you keep talking to that wall? Are there cameras in here or something?"

Clyde jumps up out of his chair and heads toward the door. "No. No *way*! Not in *this* hospital. Some do, many actually, but...It's difficult to get away with that surveillance shit in a nuthouse. HIPAA is a bitch—a bitch I love for that little *helpful* detail. If they did have surveillance in here, we couldn't do what we're doing. That's for sure. Oh, and the paperwork issue —don't worry. I got word that we might get some help with that very soon."

Slug Man dons another confused look but doesn't ask any more questions. He just nods.

Clyde peeks out the side of the blind before opening the door.

When he does finally open the door he holds it, waiting for Slug Man to leave. Then he speaks loud enough so anyone who happens along the hallway can hear him. "You're doing a great job, Lou. I'm proud of all your hard work. Now you can go reward yourself with a little time in the common room with the TV *all* to yourself." As Slug Man walks past him, Clyde pats him on his boney back.

Slug Man looks over his shoulder. "Thank you, Mr. C. Thank you very much!" His eyes don't look at Clyde while he speaks. They stare past him at that wall in the back of the room. But they see nothing. Just a wall.

As soon as Slug Man walks away and the door *clicks* shut, Clyde goes over to the back wall and starts rambling. "More are on the way. Now to assure they get sent to *my* group. I'm not so sure if Lou can get that done. We need an in. Someone to get them here and keep them here. Maybe a new meat suit? Can you do that? We *need* you."

He pauses, then starts pacing as he rambles on. "Yes, yes, I know we lost one, but we'll be fine. She was troublesome anyway. More are coming. I promise. I *will* get more for us. I just need to keep my job. I need to be allowed to stay here. This is the best spot to get fresh dust. I don't want to go back to the cemeteries. *Please* don't make me go back. I'll do better this time. I promise, I'll do better."

He pauses.

"No. Please don't replace me. I told you, I *need* this job. I just put money down on a house. I'm finally getting my family out of the projects. *Please.* I'll do whatever you need. Anything. Remember—We made a *deal.*"

He pauses again.

His eyes widen as he takes in a long, deep breath.

His head starts shaking in a *No, no, no* gesture. Now he's pacing again, and *still* holding in that breath like it's a hit of weed.

"I can't. I can't. I just *can't!*"

A heavy sigh escapes him.

Still pacing, he starts frantic-fussing with his hair, as he says, "I'm in here *all* the time. I'm working. I'm luring victims more hours of the day than I'm on the outside. How am I supposed to do *that*? That would involve a lot of vetting. Stalking. Studying patterns—at least if the person doesn't want to get caught. The only sort of person with that kind of time..." His hands freeze mid-hairfuss. One thick, bushy eyebrow arches. Speed-snapping his fingers with every beat of his words he spits out, "Wait. I got it. I got it. I fucking got it! I know just the right..."

A *slide-clink* sounds out.

Pacing halts.

Clyde straightens the collar of his shirt, finger-combs his hair, and marionettes a welcoming grin.

The door swings open.

With a huge beaming smile, an unfamiliar nurse leans into the room. "Clyde, is the room ready for the Anger Management group?"

"Yes, I was just going to the closet to get the pillows out and set up the circle. Give me two minutes, then send 'em all in." As he realizes she's a new face on staff, he also notes her breathtaking beauty: high cheekbones, come-hither eyes, luminous hair, alluring smile. He wants to ask her name, but with his nerves so frazzled he can't form the words. Or is that because he's so smitten?

She nods and gives him a wink. "Perfect." The word comes out almost like a purr from a kitten. Her smile grows bigger and her eyes widen, giving her a Cheshire Cat mystique. "I think you and I are going to work well together," she says in a breathy voice. Another wink and a hair flip later, she pops back out of the room and shuts the door.

Clyde stands frozen, mouth dropped open. A blink later comes a devious twinkle in his eyes and a wicked smirk.

CHAPTER 3
NO FUCKING, NO DUSTING

"What's got your rox rollin', Mr. C? Nurse Freyja said you wanted to see me." Roxy saunters into Clyde's office. Slow motion hips swinging in Snake Girl dramatic fashion, she sways over to his desk. In her droney voice she says, "Did I do somethin' wrong in group this mornin'? Did you call me in here for a spanking?" She hops up and plants her ass on his desk, staring him down with a playful smirk.

Sitting behind his desk with his feet propped up on the top, Clyde's eyes roll up from his paperwork. His head remains tilted down. He hesitates to respond. Yes, he wanted to see Roxy, but he never told anyone, nor did he ask anyone to send her to his office. He isn't quite prepared for this conversation yet. His brow furrows as he tries gathering his thoughts about what exactly he wants to say and how to say it.

Snake Girl's smirk grows wider as she smacks his feet off from the desk. "Chill, Mr. C. Just razzin' ya'. What's up?" She twirls a strand of her frizzy hair and starts swinging her legs like a giddy schoolgirl. She drag-drones, "You know I'm out at the end of the week, so don't you go puttin' in a bad word about me now, will ya'?"

"That's exactly why I'm asking *you* this favor...well, part of the reason anyway." He sits up and sets aside his paperwork, as well as his wonder about her showing up at his office uninvited.

"Favor? I'm your gal. Whatcha need?" She slips off the desk, strolls around to the other side, and sits at attention in the chair opposite from him.

"Well, as you may have heard, Sheila and Toodles are facing charges because of what went down here with that Chair Chucker. Sheila, she's up for big time—attempted murder."

"Yeah, I heard some rumors. Wasn't sure what was true. What's all that got to do with me and this favor?" She leans in closer, placing her elbows on the desktop, as Clyde continues talking.

Voice now lowered to almost a whisper, Clyde says, "Well, you see, there's one person who can seal Sheila's fate, and we need to stop that problem. Ya' dig?" Now Clyde's leaning forward, elbows on the desktop.

Snake Girl's deep-set eyes light up as she peers through her long curls hanging down, covering most of her skeletal face. A sinister chuckle sounds out, blowing strands of her hair around. She starts singing in a low, monotone voice,

> *"A dusting I will go. A dusting I will go. High-ho the nuthouse ho, a dusting I will go."*

She claps her hands and rubs her palms together in excitement. Then she jumps up out of her seat and begins pacing back and forth in front of the desk, speaking like a maniac eager for some sadistic, gory fun. "Who am I going after? Who is it? Hmm...Let me guess. That beer bellied psych tech, Mullet-Master Rick? Or maybe that tall redskin janitor, what's his name, uh...Tommy?"

"Oh, I wasn't talking about dusting. No. Scare tactics don't seem to work with this person. We need to *stop* the problem. See what I'm gettin' at?" He leans further across the desk and arches one bushy eyebrow. "And the person I speak of is no longer at the hospital, which is why I need *you* to get this job done on the *outside.*"

Frustrated, Snake Girl plops back down in her seat and kicks her feet up on his desk. "Look, Mr. C, stop hinting at what you want. Just spit it all out. Who and what? Go."

"Seriously? What the fuck don't you understand?" Frantically fussing with his hair, Clyde jumps out of his seat. Now *he* starts pacing. He walks back and forth behind his desk as his hands talk along with his irate voice. "It's that Itchabald Crane chick. The scratcher with the bald spots. I need *you* to prevent her from making it to those court dates. You know, slice her tires, dump sugar in her gas tank, drive her off the road into a ditch or something. Whatever it takes. Just *don't* let her get to court. Are you in? Can we count on you?" He stops and glances over his shoulder for a moment. He nods, then he spins back around, facing Snake Girl again. Placing his hands on the desk, he leans across the top and whisper-yells through gritted teeth, *"Is that clear enough for you?"*

"Oh, you mean *Dory*? That skinny little ball of nerves Sheila and Toodles wanted to dust but could never get the job done?"

Clyde nods and sits back down. "Yeah, idiot Sheila—I fucking told her to leave that chick alone, that she wasn't recruitable. Shit. She may *look* like a sketched-out junkie, but we all saw how freaked out she was when we filled her in on what we all do. That little outburst made it obvious she isn't any sort of addict. Now I'm left needing to clean up Sheila's freakin' mess before it all leads back to us or..." He glances over his shoulder again, then jump-turns back around. "...anyone *else.*"

"Oh, oh, oh...Well, won't this be fun." Snake Girl jumps to her feet again and starts twisting her hands together. "You know...dirty little rat that she is, she does have a *real* pretty face." She's now skip-pacing like a junkie ready to snort some rails as she's gazing off into Fantasyland. "And she got that kind o' ass I just wanna smack real hard." She mimes an ass-slapping as she continues skip-pacing back and forth, looking like the last person who should get released from the nuthouse *any* time soon.

"I said *stop* her. Not *fuck* her. Got it?"

"How about stop *and* fuck, a two-for-one deal, ya' know?"

Clyde slowly clenches his hands into fists and glares at her through his long bangs.

"I said No. Fucking. And no dusting her either. Your DNA will show up all over her and it will somehow lead back to, uh…" Another glance over his shoulder, like a nervous tic in the middle of speaking. "…our group. We need that rat bitch stopped. Easy-peasy. And leave *no* trace. Got it!" His fist pounds the desktop. "I've got orders to prevent her appearance in court. If Sheila and Toodles get busted, we could *all* get busted for dusting. You're ballsier than *all* the balls put together in our group. *And you're* getting out of here. I'm counting on you. Do you think you can handle this, or do I need to…" He clears his throat, hinting for her to read between the lines. "… assign someone else to the job?" Hands splayed on the desktop, he leans forward and stares her down, waiting for her to stop pacing and face him.

She doesn't stop. But he knows how to get her attention.

"How about I sweeten the deal and throw in a bag of fresh toddler dust, the best high available, but…"

Yeah. That's it. She halts mid-step, foot hovering dramatically in the air, hungry-eager expression on her crazed face.

Clyde smirks and arches an eyebrow. "You've gotta get the job done and done *right* if you want the payout. Leave no trace. Understood?" He pauses, cocks his head. "So, are you my girl or what?"

Looking about ready to hop right out of her skin, Snake Girl jump-spins to face him. Then, she steps up to the desk and leans in so close they're almost touching foreheads. Their eyes fiercely focus on one another, a staring contest.

"Ooooh yeah, I'm your girl, Doc." With extra added drone in her voice, she emphasizes, "I'm. Your. Girl. That skinny bitch won't know I'm comin'! No one need worry, not you, or..." Standing upright, she rolls her eyes all around as though she's dizzy or confused—or just fucking crazy. "...whoever else it is you keep referring to." She taps her finger against her temple and laughs.

"That's my girl." Finger-combing his long bangs out of his face, Clyde smiles and sits back down to his paperwork. Folder in his hands, he leans back in his chair, kicks his feet up on the desktop again.

When Snake Girl opens the door to leave she almost runs right into Nurse Freyja, who's standing with her knocking-fist outstretched toward the now open doorway.

"Whoa. Didn't hear you out here. Excuse me." A quick jump-sidestep gets Snake Girl around an unmoving yet smiley Nurse Freyja. That Cheshire grin of hers is immense and so white it almost glows. She nods, says nothing.

Clyde glances up from his folder of papers to see who Snake Girl is talking to. As soon as he makes eye contact, Freyja's blue eyes appear to glow—almost as bright as her smile. She steps into his office, closes the door behind her.

"I hope your meeting was productive." She winks, struts up to his desk, leans in closer with one hand on the top. "Now, I've got some paperwork I need to discuss with you, if you've got a moment."

He sits up so quickly he fumbles with the folder in his hands. Papers slip out and scatter across the floor. When he leans down to pick up the mess, he bangs his forehead on the desktop. Biting back a yelp, he just leaves them there to save himself more embarrassment. Sitting back upright, he pulls his chair in closer. "Uh, paperwork? With me?"

Her smile widens and her eyes twinkle as she nods. "Yes, you."

CHAPTER 4

NEW FRIENDS FROM THE NUTHOUSE

Looking over my shoulder one last time, my right fist hovers in front of the closed door. At the last second, I remember our signature knock.

Knock-knock-knock Kno-knock.

Toe-tapping while waiting for someone to answer, I feel sweat all over my forehead. It's almost Halloween—*in Maine.* Why the hell am I sweating?

Clink-thud.

Jingle-clink.

Slide-clink.

The doorknob turns.

I shove my way in just as the door begins easing open.

"Whoa...hello and nice to see you, too, Dabbler," Tommy says while holding the door open for me. I duck under his outstretched arm and rush into Irie's apartment.

Tommy leans his long, lanky body out into the hallway. He looks right, then left, then right again, before stepping back inside and closing the door. All three locks immediately get relatched.

A wisp of Nag Champa incense and the sound of Nina Simone's bluesy velvet voice wrap around me like a warm hug as I move further into the living room.

"Welcome," Irie says as she's walking out of the kitchen, drying her hands on a dishtowel. "Here, I think *you* need this more than me." She approaches, reaching out toward me with the towel in her hand. "No offense, but you *really* need to get a handle on that tic of yours."

She's standing so close her calming scent of sandalwood engulfs me. For just that moment the whole world washes away. Then she makes contact, wipes my forehead.

I flinch.

"Ouch! Fuck! That stings." The words burst through my gritted teeth.

When she pulls the towel away from my forehead, I notice the blood.

She's not bleeding.

To my left I see a frameless mirror hanging on the living room wall. At first, I thought it was a window into another room. I step over to it and peer at my reflection.

I may feel overheated but I'm *not* drenched in sweat.

My reflection shows blood smears streaked across my forehead. A drop rolls down my left temple. With the dish towel now in my hand, I wipe it away. "What the...Dammit! Why don't *I* realize I'm scratching *before* all the blood and the bald spot appear?"

So much for letting my wound heal. I've gone and scratched the almost-healed scabs from my recovering bald spot and ripped open the skin again. The hairs that have started growing back are sticking together, making my hair look greasy. This nervous scratching tic really needs to find its end somehow. With a few gentle swipes with the towel, I clean up most of the mess. Then I reach in my pocket for my emergency bandana, tie it around my oh-so-beautiful blood-sticky hair, then I plop down on the couch. Irritated with myself, now I'm even more overheated. I remove my zip-up hoodie and drape it over the arm of the couch. Leaning against the back of the sofa, I take a deep breath and try to chill out, but my hands reflexively start drumming on my thighs.

"I really would like to at least *appear* sane." A nervous laugh escapes me. I wish I was joking. "A full head of hair would be nice, too. I'm so sick of wearing hats and bandannas to hide the bald spot."

Tommy steps closer and nods down at me. "Well, if it makes you feel any better—your veil looks like it's healing nicely."

What is he talking about?

My drumming hands freeze as I look up at him. "My veil?"

He reaches out his left arm, fist clenched, displaying the L-I-V-E tatted in black block letters across his knuckles. Then he rolls his arm over, forearm facing up. "Your veil between worlds."

His arm tattoo stares me in the face. A red scar–*his* "veil"–runs up the middle of the design from his wrist almost to the crook of his elbow. One side of the forever-reminder depicts a black and gray image of a torturous and wicked world for the dead, and the other depicts a colorful image of a lush and wondrous world for the living.

How could I forget about his veil?

That scar-tat and his story behind it had assured me, back when I was trapped in Silver Springs Psychiatric Hospital, that he was genuine and not another Bone Cutter. When I had first seen the scar on his cheek, I suspected he might've been one of them. I was afraid of him. Then he showed me his veil, the scar in the center of his tat that was *his* work—his suicide attempt after Bone Cutters had killed his wife Kaya and left his face scarred.

His words from that day etched themselves onto my brain the moment they hit my eager ears. I can still sense their every nuance, feel his every vocal inflection.

Where you are now, I once was...The veil. There's a very thin line between life and death...I've crossed that line and live to tell about it.

Don't let those crazy junkie-cutters push you over that line. Not everyone makes it back across.

After I'd heard his tale, we just sort of connected. I knew he understood.

Seeing his veil-tat again now...I look down at my left arm resting on top of my leg. *My* scar.

"Yeah, I finally had the stitches removed the other day," I tell him as I pull my arm in close, forearm against my stomach. The reminder sucks. "I may need to get mine worked into a tat to help hide the broken."

He pats my shoulder. "Don't think of yourself as 'broken.' Negative self-talk is what pushed us both to cause these scars. Do what I do—think of yourself as a work-in-progress...At the end of that day, that's really all any of us are."

Yes, that does sound much better. I look up at him and smile.

"Always be kind to yourself, Dabbler." He winks. "You deserve it." He steps away and sits in the wingback chair beside the sofa.

Compression on the cushion next to me tugs at my attention. Irie folds her long, lean legs up under herself in the middle of the sofa. Feeling her eyes on me, I turn toward her. Her curious and concerned expression exudes warmth. Those big, round, caramel-colored eyes of hers threaten to pull it all out of me.

Man, she's just like her dad.

"There are so many things in this world that could push a person over that edge, wanting to end it all. My dad came back *stronger* and so can you." She tucks a long dread behind her ear. Her eyes feel like they're peering into my soul. Like father like daughter.

I look away, building up courage to spill my skeletons, then look back again, as I tell her, "I understand your pain...sort of." Talking about my past makes it hard for me to hold eye contact. As I glance away again, it all spills out of me.

"My mom was murdered, too. I didn't witness it, like you did, but I was the one who found her."

I will never forget that traumatic day.

After rushing home from class, running late to take mom to her doctor's appointment, I couldn't figure out what her front door was stuck on, why it wouldn't open all the way.

A whiff of cigarette smoke assaulted my nose. I sneezed.

Where was it coming from?

No one else was there. No other cars in the driveway except mine and Mom's pickup truck.

Figuring the door was just stuck on the front hall rug, I turned from the door toward the smell, searching for its origin.

On the small round table beside the door on the farmer's porch sat an ashtray. Half of a partially stubbed out cigarette. Smoke still trailing up.

How strange.

Confusion set in, since I thought Mom had quit months ago after the doctor told her she was killing herself with that bad habit.

I leaned down and saw that it wasn't a Winston but a Marlboro Red—my sister's brand.

Maybe she came and took Mom to her doctor's since I was running a little late. Then a nauseating curiosity hit me.

Was she back trying to con Mom out of more money? Mom's hard-earned money that good 'ol sis would spend on more drugs.

Furious at the thought, I turned back to the door and forced it open. That's when I noticed what had been blocking my entrance.

Mom.

She lay prone on the front hall floor, neck turned at an unnatural angle, left lower leg bent frontward at the knee rather than backward.

A gasp rushed out of me. I leaned down to check her pulse,

though I already knew. A light touch to the inside of her wrist confirmed what I didn't want to accept.

Another detail grabbed hold of my heart and squeezed—

She still felt warm.

I had only just missed it.

The cigarette burned on as my heart withered.

All I wanted to do was hug her and tell her how sorry I was for getting there too late, but—

I couldn't touch the evidence.

Like a rag doll, I crumbled and collapsed down beside her. I reflexively grabbed her hand and held tight. She couldn't hold back. Curling her fingers over my hand with my free hand, I imagined she was still there with me, holding on. A part of me swore I could still feel her presence, like she was watching me.

Two months later I testified against my sister, who is still serving time for Mom's murder.

Justice prevailed.

My sanity did not.

Doped up on drugs, my *former* sister ripped mom off and shoved her down the stairs to keep her from blocking the exit. Flying higher than a cirrus cloud, the idiot had forgotten that I had convinced Mom to install security cameras inside and outside her house after *someone* had stolen twenty-five of her medicinal marijuana plants two months earlier.

The numbskull addict also had no idea I'd saved those fifteen answering machine messages she'd left a week prior— the ones harassing Mom, calling her every name in the book and telling her what a terrible mother she was. She had also left threats to put *me* ten feet under.

Yeah, such a gem, that one.

Good 'ol born-again-Christian-sis, self-declared "recovering" addict, ran off with a handful of Mom's best jewelry and the fur coat my great Aunt Josie had passed down to me.

The cops never did recover the stolen items. They'd already been traded or sold for more pills.

A handful of death threats and three stalkers later, along with a diagnosis of PTSD, and—

Hello darkness, my old friend.

———

Not allowing my emotions to take over, I distract myself by tapping rhythms out with my feet and looking around Irie's place.

Irie rests her hand on my shoulder and lightly rubs. I flinch.

"Sorry," she says as she pulls her hand away.

"No worries. Just another one of my quirks…touch."

Irie nods.

Tommy leans over, places his hand on my bouncing knee, and squeezes gently. My unsettled feet relax. Then he pats my leg and sits back.

It's strange how his touch doesn't make me flinch.

He smiles his signature crooked smile, dimple-scar crinkling on his cheek.

Every time my attention gets drawn to that, I'm thankful those dusters who killed his wife weren't able to kill him, too. An ache of sympathy rises up within me.

Except for the low volume of Nina Simone singing "House of the Rising Sun," silence surrounds us.

Yeah, I'm used to that reaction.

Silence.

Maybe I should suggest we switch to Miss Simone singing "Sounds of Silence."

I actually prefer the silence. Better than rote sympathy comments. Those I can't handle.

A few moments pass.

"You have a beautiful voice." Irie's words startle me out of a mind-wander.

What was I even thinking? And what is she talking about?

My last thought-question must show on my face, or she's a mind reader.

"You were just singing along with Nina. It reminded me of..." She glances over at her dad.

"Your Mom...my Kaya." Tommy finishes the sentence for her.

Irie smiles, nods, and looks back at me.

"What? I was *singing*?" Heat rises to my cheeks.

"Sure were. I guess instead of sleepwalking, you're a space-out-singer." Tommy chuckles.

"Lame one, Dad." Now Irie's laughing, too, as she tosses a throw pillow at Tommy. He's now sitting on the floor in front of a small bookshelf, flipping through vinyl albums.

Lovely. My space-case-self lightened the mood for them.

I rub my non-bloody hand across the soft, plush fabric of the antique burgundy sofa, trying to distract my mind from embarrassment. The dark wooden frame has an intricately carved design, though superficial chips speckle the surface. The living room is tastefully sparse, with a touch of bohemian flare: colorful, silk patchwork curtains drape down over tall windows; a beaded curtain made from dark wood sways in front of an over-stuffed floor-to-ceiling bookshelf; a wrought iron lantern with rainbow-colored stained-glass panels hangs from a black chain hooked in the far corner of the ceiling.

"Hey," I say, still looking around, distracting myself, "you've got a really nice place here, Irie." A huff comes out as I admit, "And here I was expecting a dorm room sort of vibe. But you've got *style*."

A flash before Irie responds, Tommy stands up and throws me his signature crooked smile again, with a hint of a smirk mixed in—his obvious response to my deflection. Somehow, I can read that look of his. I'll always remember it from when we met in the hospital. Laughter hadn't passed through my lips in a long time, but Tommy had somehow boosted me out of my funk for a bit—even as I sat locked in the padded room.

Huh...the padded room. Not the best location to first meet someone, but that's *exactly* where Tommy and I first met, as he mopped up my vomit. Ugh...*that* was embarrassing. But he still hung out a bit longer than he needed to—and he still talks to me, so I guess it's all good. *And* he got me to laugh, which is *not* an easy feat.

Tommy's got a mysterious way about him. I can't quite put my finger on it, but he's got this sort of...What do you call it?... The "it factor." His presence is electric, contagious, and addictive. He somehow lights up a room just with his presence, which is quite the feat when my darkness hovers heavy and massive wherever I go.

I shoot him a smirk back, letting him know—*yes, I see you, and yes, I'm done talking about uncomfortable shit, and no more compliments, please.* Yes, I know he can read all that from my reaction because...he's Tommy.

"Awe, thanks." Irie trills, voice like a songbird. She takes a quick look around as she gets up and walks to the kitchen then quickly comes back out. In her hands is what looks like a take-out menu. A warm smile spreads across her face. "It's my cozy little corner of the world." Over at one of the windows she pulls the curtains apart, glances outside, then pulls the curtains back together. "I couldn't tolerate the dorms anymore. Too noisy. No privacy."

"Yeah, not very conducive to studying, I'm sure." Thinking about why we planned this get-together to begin with, I reach for the article I brought with me. The rolled-up newspaper scrapes against the skin on my back as I pull it out of the back pocket of my jeans and out from under my shirt. I unfurl it and toss it on the glass-top coffee table.

"Well, here it is. That article I texted you two about. Those Duster-fucks are at it again. I *know* it's them."

Tommy pulls the wingback chair closer to the coffee table. He leans over the paper and reads the article.

"At least these ones are preying on the dead rather than the living," Irie says as she sits down beside me again. "But that's still just not right. Not right AT ALL."

Tommy slides the paper across the dark wood-framed table to Irie. She flips a couple of her long loose dreads behind her shoulder as she reads the brief article.

"We need a plan. How can we get these psychos busted?" With his elbows on his knees, Tommy's leaning forward and drumming his thumbs together. An instant later he's sitting back up, readjusting his ponytail, tucking loose strands of hair back into the hair elastic.

After she hands the paper back to me, Irie places her hand on my bouncing knee. Only a small flinch happens this time. The bouncing stops as she says, "How are *you* doing? I mean..." She glances away as though uncertain how to word what comes next. "I would imagine this might bring up unwanted memories. Nightmares even. Has any of that been happening since last we texted?"

It had been a couple days since I texted Tommy and Irie about the cemetery incidents. It was tough finding a time for all of us to get together, since father and daughter work opposite shifts at the psychiatric hospital. That's where I had been attacked—more than once—by *two* Dusters. Now Git Girl and Renfield, I mean Sheila and Toodles (I can't remember what Sheila's minion's real name is, and I don't really give a fuck), are up on some serious charges: attempted murder and assault with a deadly weapon. I need to appear in court *twice* to seal the deal.

Yeah, how pleasant for me to have to face my attackers again. If I show up in court with bald patches and crusty scabs all over my head, no one is going to believe a fucking word from this "delusional" psycho.

With that thought, I start scratching again. The bandana has slid to the side and my middle finger scrapes across a loose scab. I flinch. Grit my teeth. The scab sticks to my finger.

At least this time I *realized* I was scratching. Maybe I can stop this tic after all.

Irie eases the towel out from between my clenched fingers and wipes away the blood on my head again. She then pulls the bandana gently over my open wound. When she notices the scab in my hand, she passes me a tissue from the Kleenex box sitting on the shelf under the coffee table. Her mannerisms remind me of a nurse, one of the good ones.

Unable to stop thinking about my upcoming court appearances, I remain silent.

I need to get my shit together.

I need to get this nervous tic under control.

I need to at least *look* normal again.

Then maybe I can...

How's that saying go?

Fake it 'til you...

Tommy starts snapping his fingers in front of my face. "Dory...Earth to Dory. Are you in there, Dabbler?"

I turn toward Tommy, then glance, eyes only, at Irie. "I think you got your answer." An uncomfortable laugh slips out under my breath.

A couple more minutes of silence.

That's when I realize—

"Hey, I never really said *thank you* to both of you for saving my ass at the hospital." My eyes remain aimed down, staring at my fingers fidgeting and fumbling with the tassels of my belt. "So...uh...thanks, to *both* of you. Thank you *so* much. I don't know what I would've done if none of the staff ever believed me about those crazy junkie-cutters trying to carve me open." Embarrassment colors my cheeks, again. I can feel the heat.

Gruff laughter erupts from Tommy. "Yeah, don't thank me. I almost made it worse. Sunshine here is the one who *really* saved the day—for you *and* me." He shakes his head before he adds, "Damn. If Irie hadn't told Dr. Headstrom and the others all about my dear Kaya and those Bone Cutters, I probably would've lost my job." He looks at his daughter and smiles. "Thank you, Sunshine, for speaking up for us *and* for your mamma."

"Hey, no worries. Of *course* I spoke up. But it wasn't just me. Rick, the psych tech, corroborated my story *and* what I told them about that sketchy Nurse Hatchet, who, by the way, did a mysterious disappearing act. No one has seen or heard from her since…"

Uneasy looks exchange between the three of us.

"The camera…" Lost in the memory, I take in a long, deep breath, unable to form more words.

"That's something I will *never* forget. That flickering image…wings, skull-face, flaming eyes..Damn! That is some horror movie shit right there." Tommy shimmies in his seat, like heebie-jeebies are running through him.

"I don't think Dr. Headstrom will ever forget that either. Something he can't explain away with his psycho-babble-mumbo-jumbo, peer reviewed *whatever*." Irie's shaking her head when she adds, "I don't think he'll write an essay about *that* one for the psychology journals. Oh, and Rick, he's been quite shaken up about that night you guys got Sheila busted."

Tommy laughs. "I didn't think he'd have the balls to come back to work after he got out of the hospital. But, sure as shit, he's back. And that dude is ogling over a new nurse again. Can't get his head out of the gutter, that one."

With the mention of Rick, that time capsule of a David Coverdale wannabe, I wonder about the other two Dusters, the two guys who helped me get out of that last scary uproar of a group counseling session. What were their names? I feel bad I don't remember.

"Hey, what about those other two Dusters? Damned if I can remember their names, but you must know, Tommy—Medusa Man, with that cool Medusa tat on his calf masking his scar, and Fake Brit Boy. What happened to them? Are they still there?"

He shakes his head. "Nope. Released. Not sure how or why,

but they're gone. My janitor position doesn't allow me to know much about the patients." He sits back, kicks his feet up onto the coffee table and stretches his legs out. "But I do remember—Shawn and Davey are their names."

I nod. "Yes! Shawn and Davey. Wish I knew where they were so I could also thank them too. A couple of life-savers those two."

Tommy nods along with me. "Sure as shit right about that one, Dabbler. A couple of good eggs with bad reps. Those fucking Dusters, man—always luring in the weak and vulnerable and then sinking their addiction claws in."

———

An hour later...

Packets of duck sauce fall out of the paper take-out bag. I grab five, tear them open, and squirt a puddle onto my plate.

"Would you like some veggie Lo Mein with that duck sauce, Miss?" Irie, dreads swaying near her copper butterfly belt buckle, stands beside me, holding a plastic container of Chinese take-out.

"Seriously," Tommy says as he shovels another spoonful of fried rice into his mouth, "Stakeout is the only answer. A different cemetery every time." More rice shoveling. "I mean, we may not get 'em *all* busted, but we can get a bunch of 'em." He shrugs. Takes a haul off his Coke.

A moment later he kicks my foot under the table. "Hey, Dabbler. Say something. *Anything*. You with me? What do you think of my plan?"

"Uh, yeah, and you can tell me 'when' any time now. The container is almost empty."

With a shake of my head, I look down at my meal. Irie hesitantly drops another forkful of Lo Mein onto my already-piled-high dish.

"Whoa. Too much. Too much." Confused laughter leaks out of me. Where did my mind wander off to a moment ago? Swaying dreads. A shiny butterfly. Tommy's voice. A stakeout or something. Then poof. I got lost somewhere.

"Sorry. Don't mind me." I nod toward the container in Irie's hand. She passes it to me. I scoop half of what's on my plate back into the container. "I get lost sometimes. You know?"

"Um, yeah, I've realized that. Anyway, cemetery stakeout—what do you say?" Another forkful of fried rice fills Tommy's mouth as he nods, eyebrows raised, and looks back and forth from me to Irie and back to me again. The scar on his cheek crinkles from that signature crooked smile of his that emerges.

Irie and I share a knowing glance. Then we both look over at Tommy.

In stereo, we say—

"Let's do it."

As soon as the words fly out of my mouth, a sinking feeling of dread fills me. I stuff it down deep with a forkful of Lo Mein.

Grave Robberies Continue Across the State

With over two hundred and seventy-five grave robberies already reported throughout the state, the trend of unusual criminal activity continues. This past weekend police discovered that the small Friends Cemetery in Fifield, Evergreen Cemetery in Lakeland, South Buckstown Cemetery, as well as the large Calvary Cemetery in Havensport have all been added to the list. Authorities have strong suspicions of drug activity taking place. Drug paraphernalia, similar to heroin use, has been discovered at every location, though no heroin residue has been found through laboratory testing. Vandalism also appears to be part of this ongoing trend. Police have discovered similar images spray painted around many of the exhumed gravesites: a winged figure, similar to that of an angel, though some are gravely different, with a skeleton-like face, flaming red eyes, and black wings. Authorities are trying to determine if this activity is somehow gang related or not. Police are asking for anyone who may have any information that can lead to the violators, or anyone who witnesses cemetery activity after dark to please call the State Police tip line at 1-800-555-7686. All calls can be made anonymously.

CHAPTER 5
SNAKE GIRL SLITHERS

Behind the basement door, Snake Girl hides in wait like a python ready to pounce and coil around its prey.

She's coming. I can smell her. Nice. A fresh bleeding wound makes this much easier for me.

The small window with its mirrored outside surface gives her optimum coverage and a great lookout for observing, vetting, stalking.

Mmm...that sweet aroma...

But if she keeps her cheek pressed to the glass, lured by the scent of blood, she's likely to draw some attention her way.

Before Dory makes it halfway up the front porch steps, she stops, looks over her shoulder, hesitates before continuing up. By the time she does finally make it to the front door and grasps the doorknob, she has stopped three times to look behind her.

That skinny little ball of nerves. How does she even make it through life, the paranoid freak that she is?

Dory has a black and white bandana peppered with mini skull and crossbones tied around her head. It covers her hair like a hat.

Who the hell do you think you're kidding with that bandana around your head? No matter how you try to hide your wound, my kind can still smell you bleed.

A set of drumsticks stick out of the back pocket of Dory's jeans, reaching up high to her lower back, scrunching up the bottom of her zip-up hoodie as she moves. A small cooler dangles from one of her hands.

Drumsticks in your back pocket? How do you, of all people, dare keep a potential weapon in such an easy place for someone to snatch and beat you with?

No. No. No! Stop thinking that. Too visible. Someone could walk in during the beating. Plus…too messy. I don't want her blood all over the place, all over me. And a beating allows her too much time to scream for help.

Shit. That's right, "Leave no trace," he told me. I just need to keep her from getting to court. Fuck. This ain't gonna be easy. I just want to dust her to death already. Getting a piece of that sweet ass would be mighty fine too.

Dammit!

Over the past week and a half Snake Girl has watched Dory come and go. To and from work—pretty much the only places she's been, with one stop at the grocery store midweek. The first day of stalking had Snake Girl worrying about how to stop her from getting to court when Dory didn't appear to own a car. And even on foot, it was still a bitch trying to keep up with her on her way home that day.

Dory's a runner.

That first day of Snake Girl's stalking, Dory had changed into stretch pants before heading home, and she wore a mini backpack. Drumsticks in hand like a relay race baton, she jogged home. With all the paranoia she carries around with her, she kept looking over her shoulder so much she'd never noticed the trash receptacles in plain sight. It must have been the collision and tumble over that line of trash cans she had in the final stretch that made her stop jogging.

Now she drives to work. And now Snake Girl has a target, another way to stop Dory from getting to court—her little orange car. *But what if she just calls an Uber or gets a ride from someone else, though I doubt that paranoid freak has many friends. I'll probably have to mess up more than just her car. Oh well, more fun for me.*

The stairs groan and creak with each slow and cautious step Dory takes up toward the second floor. Stopping to look behind her after every third or fourth step makes this climb take much longer than Snake Girl anticipated.

Holy shit! Can you just get up those stairs already? Turn back around. Nothing to see here.

Damn! What is she looking for anyway? I know she can't see me here. This spot is too perfect.

With only five more steps to get to the second-floor hallway, Dory climbs up three, stops, turns back around. Not only does she turn completely around this time, but she also leans over the railing and peers into the extended part of the hallway stretching past the bottom of the stairway.

Oh, no you didn't, bitch! Seriously?!

Girl, you're never gonna grow old with anxiety like that. Your heart will explode before you hit fifty. I should just dust you now, turn you into one of us, help you live a much longer and more satisfying life.

No. I've got a job to do and a clan to protect. She's too...I can't remember the word Dr. C used, but I just don't think she's...turnable. She's not the junkie-type. Even as anxious as that bitch is, she sure does seem to have one strong-ass will.

Now at the top of the stairs, Dory turns left, away from the stairwell to the third floor. A moment of hesitation, a fumble around in her jeans pocket, another glance down the stairs, then she steps out of sight and scurries down the second-floor hallway.

Bingo! Second floor apartment it is.

As she eases open the cellar door, Snake Girl peeks around the edge in both directions, making sure no one else is present. At the bottom of the stairs, she listens for Dory's movement above, trying to discern how far down her apartment is from the top of the stairs. Keys jingling, sneakers scraping and clomping.

A little quieter.

A little quieter.

Feet stop.

The sound of jingling keys shifts, grows more jumbled. Less consistency. Less rhythm. More random, messy.

Then comes the distinct *slide-clink*. Then again. And again.

A doorknob turns. A change in acoustics follows.

The door softly shuts. *Slide-clink. Slide-clink. Slide-clink.*

The vacuum-quiet of the hallway tunnels returns.

Bingo! Shouldn't be too hard to figure this one out, especially with all those fucking locks. Might as well hang a sign on your damn door: "Paranoid Dory Lives Here." Thanks for making this additional task easy for me.

Sticking to the wall side rather than the railing side of the stairway, Snake Girl keeps a steady pace up the stairs with minimal creaking. At the top of the stairs, she looks down the hall and sees only three apartment doors. Two in the straight-away stretch and one at the end like a punctuation mark. It's situated partially around a small corner.

Oh, glorious day! It's gotta be one of these first two. She didn't go far enough down the hall to make it to the one at the end. I just need to figure out which one. Just look for all the locks.

As she slowly strides up to the two apartment doors, it's now not quite so easy to figure out which apartment Dory went into. A line of locks runs up the edge of both doors. An ear to each should help.

But she doesn't talk much. What am I listening for? Music maybe?

But what does she listen to?

Maybe I can rule out one if I hear, let's say, a couple or a man or an old-fogey or kids or a family or...

Yeah, rule out one and that would make the other one her apartment.

Awe, damn, I'm so fucking smart I could kiss myself.

She leans in close to the first door, making sure to face the stairs, watching for any potential newcomers who could catch her. With her attention so focused on noises from behind the door, she can't count on hearing the creaking of stairs should someone come through. Best to use her eyes. With her ear pressed against the door, she waits, focuses, listens.

TV's on. Sounds like a soap. That rules this one out. Can't imagine she watches soap operas. That leaves only one other option. Now I know, and knowledge is power...or some shit like that.

Just to make sure...

She pulls away from the soap opera apartment, quietly steps over to the other door, eases in close. Even before she gets her ear to the wood, she hears it.

Music.

Is that Reggae?

Pressing her ear to the wood confirms it.

Yep. That's full confirmation. She sure does seem to love that shitty music. After hearing it, I now remember her little titties bouncing around in that Bob Marley tank top she wore when she was in the hospital.

Damn.

Stop. Stop. Stop!

Gotta keep my mind on task or I'll end up busted.

Ear still pressed against the door, she shifts her head ever so slightly, gets her nose closer to the wood. Draws in a deep breath.

Oh my...that sweet, sweet aroma. I can smell that coppery scent right through the door.

Another deep breath. She lingers.

"Ooooh, that smell...the smell of death..." No, no, no! Remember, he said "Leave no trace."

Well, there I have it. Reggae plus that enticing scent of fresh blood —Double Bingo!

Now's the time for Snake Girl to get the Hell out of here and come back during a better time for getting this job done. Rushing down the stairs and out the front door, she desperately hopes she can get this job done without leaving a trace. The toddler dust payout Clyde promised has her skin itching really bad for a fix.

Hey, maybe if I do a real good job, Clyde will even throw in a chunk o' change.

Yep, I'm sure he will. He's a stand up kinda guy like that.

CHAPTER 6

"JUST BECAUSE YOU'RE PARANOID
DON'T MEAN…"

Why the hell is there no peep hole in our goddamn door so I can see who the creeper is?

I really want to open the door just a crack, try to catch a glimpse of who it is, but what if there's still someone right outside the door waiting…waiting for me to do exactly that. Hopefully they'll slip up and let their guard down, make some sort of noise now that I'm inside and the music is on.

Wait. The music.

How will I ever hear if they make any sounds with the stereo so loud? Good thing I can count on Little Miss Organized Jill to always put the remote back on the coffee table.

As quickly and soundlessly as possible, I step over to the coffee table, grab the stereo clicker, and tap the volume down lower. In an instant I'm back at the front door with my ear pressed against the dark wood.

Nothing.

No sound from the hallway. Though I do hear a bit of Priscilla's *General Hospital* leaking through the walls from next door. Maybe if I shift my ear near the deadbolt more sound will somehow leak through around the edges.

Wait for it.

They're bound to make a sound.

Wait.

...

Come on, creeper, I know you're going to mess this up.

Don't they always?

Wait just a bit longer.

...

Aha! There it is.

The creaking stairs. And not creaks made by a casual walk down the steps. Only a rush job sounds like that. A quick escape. Running.

No way could Priscilla, with her prosthetic leg, move that fast, especially not down the stairs. Plus, nothing pulls her away from her soaps. And Mr. Stale Beer Stink, the lush who lives at the end of the hall—whatever his name is—always stumbles down to the ground floor. Damn drunk can't even walk across the hallway without stumbling. Plus, it's happy hour. He's definitely at a bar right now—always, every day of the workweek.

Yep, and now the downstairs front door slams shut. I push away from the door. Without looking, I aim the remote over my shoulder to turn the tunes back up. Bob Marley's singing, telling me not to worry because everything's gonna be all right.

Yeah, I don't know about that, Bob.

Punching the door, I shout, "I fucking knew it!"

"Uh, Dory, who are you talking to? Please don't tell me you're hearing voices now?"

When I turn around, there gawks Jill. She just stepped out of the bathroom, long hair wrapped in a towel, jaw dropped and looking shocked. She looks quite concerned, though somehow —in her Jilly-way—she still has that mischievous twinkle in her eyes; it's as though she's about to burst out laughing at a joke I know nothing about.

How does she do that?

"Someone followed me home from work. And before you say it again—'Oh, don't be so paranoid'—I just heard them, only maybe a minute or two after I got inside, running down the stairs and slamming through the front door down there."

By this time the sweat is pouring off me like I'm some hot-yoga freak. I know it isn't blood. It's everywhere, making my clothes stick to me.

What to do? Sit and chill out after a long day of work? Not happening. Not now.

I start pacing. Circle after circle around the living room.

In the midst of the fifth roundabout, I peek out the living room window at the street below. With a start, I jump back, realizing what I'm doing—making myself visible. I immediately pull the curtains shut, then yank the cord, closing the blind underneath.

The pacing resumes.

Jill steps in front of me, wet hair hanging in tight ringlets over her shoulders. With one hand gently pressed against my right shoulder, she stops me. With her other hand, she eases the stereo remote out of my grasp.

"Well, you know as well as I do what my Kurt always said—*Just because you're paranoid don't mean...*" With a tilt of her head in the stereo's direction, she changes the song.

And there it cranks—Nirvana's "Territorial Pissings" right on cue.

That's my Jilly. She always knows how to snap me out of it, even if only for two and a half minutes.

We both start stomping and thrashing around the living room, singing along as loud as we can. I grab my drumsticks out of my back pocket and start air-drumming along with Dave Grohl.

When the chorus kicks in, one of my sticks turns into a microphone. The remote-control morphs into Jill's mic. We throw our arms around each other's shoulders and scream the lyrics to the heavens—or the ceiling and the upstairs neighbors who will, no doubt, be the ones stomping on *their* floor as soon as the pause between songs comes.

Song over, Jill and I plop down on the couch laughing and out of breath. While leaning against one another I grab the remote from her and hit pause before "Drain You" kicks in.

"You're damn right! That man knew what he was talking about. He obviously knew all about *Catch-22*. And he *still* somehow let his guard down and let them get him." Shaking my head, I sit up and lean forward. Tense again, here comes the rant. I pound my fist on the coffee table.

"Drugs, man. What the fuck are people even thinking? He should've known they'd have an easy way to pin it on him. 'Oh, all those sad, sorry drug addict rock stars, always offing themselves.' What a fucking joke! Just like Chris Cornell's death."

Jill leans forward beside me, throws her arm around my shoulders again. "Yeah, and poor Chris had been clean for years. And just like Kurt—Chris also knew someone was out to get him. And then that icky wife of his with all her..."

"Don't go there. Don't even get me fucking started on that subject." My shoulders hike up to my years as I take in a huge breath. I squeeze my eyes shut just for a moment before—

Filled with adrenalin, I burst up off the couch. "Yeah, well, those fuckers aren't getting me. No fucking way! This shit is going to end. I can't take it anymore!"

And with that, the pacing starts again. Sweat dripping down my back, Killswitch Engage concert tee sticking to my skin.

"You can't let your guard down. Not EVER. As soon as you do—BOOM!—That's when they get you."

Jill adds in, "And even if you don't, they still sometimes find a way to get you." Just as she picks up the stereo remote from her lap and aims it at the stereo—

Now comes the stomping from upstairs. Not right on cue but predictable enough.

Yeah, I'm psychic. Really. I am.

The stereo doesn't go on, but our laughing hits epic volumes.

I plop back on the couch next to Jill. Our laughter continues for a moment longer. As soon as it dies away, it feels like the right time to fill Jill in about my plans for later that night.

"Yeah, me and Tommy and Irie have mapped out the cemeteries that have been hit already, trying to figure out which ones might get hit next. We couldn't really make out any kind of pattern, but we're gonna take our chances with a couple of small-town graveyards that would be easy targets—no local police departments."

"What makes you think *any* cemeteries will be easy to stakeout for criminal activity right now of *all* times? With Halloween zooming right up you *know* every teenager, goth, metalhead, and horror addict will be out in abundance in their favorite locales—cemeteries." A playful dunce-punch in the shoulder hits me before she continues. "Come on, D. This stakeout could end up being a total waste of time this month. Maybe you guys oughta wait until Halloween passes."

"Fuck that! I was just followed home by some psycho! I know damn fucking well it's one of those crazy cutters wanting to dust me to death. If I wait for this month to pass, I might pass away with it. No way in hell am I waiting for shit. This needs to happen *now*. We need to get those Bone Cutter freaks busted for the inhumane creatures they are. They just aren't right AT ALL." Again, I punch the table. The TV remote bounces.

Jill rests her hand on top of my fist. "Easy on the furniture, sweetie. I paid good money for this at Wayfair, and you *know* I'm low on funds. This can't be replaced right now. *Nothing* can." She punches my shoulder again, grabs the TV remote and clicks it on.

The six o' clock local news.

Perfect timing—there's a clip playing about the cemetery incidents.

I slap Jill's knee, and we immediately sit up at full attention.

———

WCSG Channel 6 News, 6 PM

"Due to numerous instances of grave robberies across the state, as well as gravesite vandalism and apparent drug use in cemeteries after dark, all Halloween cemetery events have been canceled for the rest of the month of October. We now go to Jennifer Lewis at the scene of the most recent grave robbery."

The inset image takes over the full screen image as the on-the-scene reporter fills us in on what's new. She's a quick-talking, articulate porcelain doll, with round pinchable cheeks and long, thick curls of dark hair. Her smile beams as she delivers the grim and bizarre report.

"Thank you, Bill. Yes, I am here at the South Buckstown Cemetery in the small town of Buckstown, where graves were disinterred, robbed, and vandalized last night. What's strikingly different about this case compared to the numerous others across the state is that these criminals were actually brave enough to take the huge risk of using the cemetery's own backhoe to dig up the graves."

The camera pans out to show some shirtless guy, in his thirties, standing there with Jennifer at the graveyard. Golden tan, short blond hair, six-pack abs, and wearing nothing but mid-thigh spandex bike shorts.

It's October in Maine. What's this guy trying to prove?

Plus, no one should be wearing those shorts.

It's not only the second-skin-shorts and the bare chest in chilly October, but that GQ pose of his shows he's obviously full of himself, though not full in the pants. Not that I really care, but if he's trying to show off his huge package for all the ladies and gentlemen of the viewing audience—which is why most guys wear those type of short to begin with—he's failing miserably. Those shorts are just so damned tight, this detail screams to get noticed. And *all* that man-thigh—too much.

Oh, here we go.

He is *truly* full of himself. To top off the show, the guy keeps his mirrored sunglasses on while on camera with the adorable and chipper news reporter. Hmm...trying to impress someone there, Mr. Man?

"I have here with me Mr. Kevington, neighbor of the South Buckstown Cemetery *and* the man who reported the loud backhoe operating in the graveyard during the early morning hours long before the sun had yet risen."

Jennifer turns and addresses the neighbor. "Mr. Kevington, you said that the loud disturbance of the backhoe operating after hours in the cemetery woke you up last night?"

She holds the microphone out for the no-shame half naked dude to talk. As soon as the mic gets in front of him, his abs tighten and his chest puffs out.

Sunglasses remain on.

"Yes, Jennifer, that's correct. It was around three in the morning when I heard the unmistakable sound of the backhoe. Having lived next to the cemetery my entire life, I'm quite familiar with that particular sound. I first went out onto my bedroom balcony to see what was going on. I thought I'd see the cemetery Superintendent out there partying with his buddies and showing off his heavy equipment operating skills or something. But that was *not* the case *at all*."

Jennifer pulls the mic back to speak. "Does the Superintendent *often* party in the cemetery after dark? Is that why you thought it was him and you didn't immediately call the police?"

Back to Flexing-Man showing too much guy-thigh. "Well, when he was younger, yes, he did. I haven't witnessed it in the past few years or so." He grabs the mic out of Jennifer's hand and instantly flexes his bicep. "But I've *never* heard the backhoe running after dark, though I'm not surprised the key was left in it. The Super is a metalhead-kid gone goth-grownup, with a penchant for hard liquor. It's not unusual for him to show up at work blasting his Devil's music and reeking of alco..."

Jennifer grabs the mic back and faces the camera. "As you just heard from Mr. Kevington, the police have confirmed that the key to the backhoe had been accidentally left in the ignition, which is how the grave robbers were able to facilitate its use for their criminal activity last night. Two graves were completely disinterred, and *all* remains are missing. The third grave was not completely disinterred because of this concerned citizen who took his civic duty and called in the unusual after-hours activity to the State Police, since Buckstown does not have a local Police Department of its own."

Just before Jennifer passes the story back to the newsroom anchor, Mr. No-Shirt Kevington lowers his sunglasses to the tip of his nose and gives the pretty news reporter a sleazy up-down, resting his eyes on her cleavage. Just before the camera cuts back to the newsroom anchor, he flashes her his pearly-white douchebag smile. Her eyes stay focused on the camera, as she holds that smile like a pro.

Before the image cuts back to the newsroom anchor, the viewing audience gets to hear what Jennifer obviously did not intend for us to hear.

"Ew. Nice try, asshat. No one is interested in your sad little Vienna sausage, you fucking overcooked potato."

Bill Bukowski, newsroom anchor, smirks but says nothing of the slip. "Again, if you see or hear any activity after dark in or around cemeteries, please do as Mr. Kevington did—call 911 immediately. If you have any information that could lead authorities..."

Jill hits the power button on the TV remote.

I'm speechless.

We exchange a brief look. That's all it takes. Hysterical laughter erupts from both of us.

Unable to catch my breath, my words come out choppy. "Man, I can't believe that was caught *live* on air. She shut him down for *everyone* to witness. Yeah!" A fist pump in the air follows, accompanied by more laughter.

"What the fuck *was* that creature we just saw?" Jill's stare remains on the TV in disbelief. A quick, high-pitched giggle escapes her. She turns toward me. Trying hard to hold in her laughter she adds, "'*Vienna sausage*'—so freaking perfect...Jennifer is my new favorite reporter." Battle lost, guffaws burst out of her contorted expression like helium surging out of a popped balloon. She shakes her head and covers her face, trying to stifle her uncontrollable laughter.

"That sicko is definitely more concerned with finding a piece of ass than helping the police catch these...uh...sickos."

Our laughter fades to silence.

Jill uncovers her face. With a tight-lipped expression, like she's holding something back, she looks over at me.

We both burst out laughing again and fall against the back of the couch at the same time. The laughter rushes out of us so intensely we have to wipe tears from our eyes.

———

A little later, dressed all in black, including a black bandana wrapped around my head with most of my hair—and *all* my scabs—hidden, I walk to the kitchen to grab a bite to eat. Jill is sitting at the table chowing-down a bowl of pasta. After tossing together a salad I sit across from her.

That skinny bitch. She can eat whatever she wants and never gain weight.

Not me.

"You might want more than veggies to last you through your stakeout tonight." She shovels another forkful of Farfalle noodles smothered in a creamy tomato sauce into her mouth.

"You know I really hate you and your high metabolism, right?" I shake a few almonds on top of my veggie-filled bowl. "There, more protein. Happy now?" I smirk.

"Yeah, well, you *know* I'm just going to go throw all of this up after you leave, right?"

Her slippered foot kicks me under the table. She follows it

up with her own smartass smirk. Then she suddenly turns serious.

"I *really* hope you and your new friends know what you're doing. If anything happens to you, I will hunt those newbies down and give them a serious ass-whippin'—and not the fun kind." With that, I get a wink.

"Don't worry. My 'new friends,' as you call them, are seriously careful, like me. We don't plan on going *into* any cemeteries. We're just scouting out for any after dark activity so we can call it in ASAP and get those fuckers busted." I grab the pitcher of iced green tea Jill has set in the middle of the table, and fill the empty glass she has already placed beside it for me.

Jill.

She *always* looks out for me, even sets the table in expectancy of me joining her for each meal. She's a true lifesaver for letting me still live here after I busted out the teeth of that surfer-wanna-be douche she had brought home for a fly-by-fuck. That black-out reaction of mine is what got me Blue Papered in the nuthouse. Well, nailing the cop with the baseball bat, *by accident*, might have had something to do with that little nuthouse detail, but whatever.

I may razz her about her promiscuity, but man—she owns that shit. She knows she's a whore and she wears that badge with pride. Honest and genuine. Jill's an example of what a great friend should be. She doesn't judge me. That's a hell of a lot better than most of my damn family. She's more like a sister to me than my own blood.

"Yeah, well, I put together a little care package for you and your crew for tonight." She turns around and reaches for something in the cabinet behind her. When she turns back around, she plops a little cooler in the chair between us and unzips the top flap. "Snacks and drinks for three, all ready to go." She rifles through it, showing me the various items: a bag of mixed nuts, dried apricots and cranberries, plantain chips, veggie sticks, pretzels, and six cans of Coke. "I've watched many of those cop show dramas; stakeouts are long and boring and snack-needy."

"Awe, thanks. But I must ask—What's with all the sugar-in-a-can?"

"Hey, can't let you fall asleep on the job and get yourself dusted to death for reals this time. Gotta keep my girl safe and on her toes. Never know when one of those...what do you call them?—*Duster-Fucks* may catch you by surprise."

"Coffee would suffice."

"Yeah, but this was quicker." She smacks me in the shoulder. "And *you're welcome*."

With a tight-lipped smirk, I roll my eyes. "Thanks...Really. I appreciate it."

We finish eating and chatting together, and when I'm just about ready to head out the door, cooler in hand, she grabs me by the shoulder.

"Hey," she says as she spins me around to face her. With her other hand, she's holding something out toward me. "Take this. Tuck it in your boot, clip it to the side. Strap it to your leg. Whatever. Just *take it*. You can never be too careful. *You* know." She nods and glances down at what she's offering me.

A boot knife. It's in a brown leather sheath, with a metal clip on the back and a strap attached.

I look down at my jeans and Chuck Taylors. "No boots, but —Damn! Sweet leg strap!"

"Yeah, good thing you wear flare-bottom jeans. Perfect for hiding weaponry. But, ya' know, now that I think about it, maybe you should switch to your black combat boots. The whites of those soles on your Chucks will stick out like a flame in the dark."

"No worries. No one will see my feet in the truck." I lift my pant leg and strap the knife to the side of my calf. "I never knew you made a habit of carrying a weapon. Plus, where the hell do *you* hide it when you always wear as little as possible?" I smirk.

She throws a smirk right back. "From my Topless Donut

Shop days. You know—lots of pervs at that shit-hole." She shakes her head. "I'm so glad I don't have to do *that* demeaning work anymore. But it did prepare me for my late-night bartending shifts. This bad boy helps me feel safer walking out to my car after work. Yeah, a bouncer always escorts me out, but ya' still just never know. Anyway, I started wearing it again when you were in the loony bin. Not having you around made me feel vulnerable." She closes her eyes for a moment and takes a deep breath. When she opens them up she adds, "You be careful out there. I know you don't like the term, but we're *sisters*. Family. The kind of family you *choose*…You know, I really do see myself as your '*Good* Sis'—the type of sister you *wish* you had."

She pulls me close.

We hug.

"You're the *only* one who can use that term and get away with it. Got it?" With shifty eyes and rapid blinking, I smirk and give her a playful shove. Talk of emotions…yeah, not my comfort zone. "Now enough with the mushy stuff."

A text chimes on my phone. I pull it out to check.

"Tommy and Irie are here. Gotta go. I got some Duster-Fucks to bust."

"Grr…You go get 'em, girl." She shoves me out the door. "Breakfast at ten tomorrow. Be there or be square…*sis*." I get a playful kick in the ass as I start heading down the hall.

Before I even make it down to the front door, I catch myself scratching my head.

Dammit!

My scabs *cannot* get busted open—especially not tonight. The smell of fresh blood doesn't get past those bone dust addicts. They can smell it like vampires. Creepy fuckers!

I readjust the bandana wrapped around my head. The sheathed knife rubs against the side of my leg as I walk.

Man, if I had *half* as much confidence as Jill, imagine the things I could do. I'd definitely be able to grow my hair longer again and *not* have a hideous bald spot and scabs. And that's just the least of what I could accomplish.

Shit. I don't know what I'd do without Jill. Such a great friend.

I had no idea that having me around makes her feel safer. She never told me that before.

Well, she can count on me to stay safe at the cemetery. I won't even get out of the truck. After all, I may need to protect her from other stray dogs she's bound to bring home again.

CHAPTER 7
GRAVEYARD SHIFT

In the shadow of a dugout in the Little League field, we sit in Tommy's pickup truck facing the hopeful site of one of the next gravesite desecrations. The flicker of fireflies and the glow of low-lying solar lights glitter throughout Hillcrest Cemetery across the street. If we weren't here for the sole purpose of catching psycho Dusters, I'd say it's quite beautiful.

Tommy clicks his cell phone with his skull-tatted hand and shows us the time. One a.m.

"Need some caffeine, anyone?" Cooler in hand, I reach in for the Cokes.

A hand reaches out from the extended-cab backseat. "Yes, please. Not that I need help staying awake; I just sure do love a fizzy Coke once in a while."

"Yeah, graveyard shifts are nothing new to my Sunshine." A throaty laugh follows Tommy's words.

"Ha. Ha. You're *so* funny." Irie smacks him in the shoulder.

"What? It's true."

"Yeah, yeah...So, not sure why you insisted I sit in the back, Dad, but it sure is comfier back here than I thought it would be." She pops the top of her can, takes a gulp, then leans over the back of the front seat. "Tonight, of all nights, I sure am happy you have an extended cab. Three in the front would have been a tight squeeze." I feel a light tap on my shoulder. "Thanks for the Coke, Dory. It sure is tasty."

"You can thank Jill, my roomie. She packed the cooler for us." I nudge Tommy with my elbow. "Yeah, can you believe it—the untrusting nervous-wreck that I am, and I *do* actually have a close friend—a *roommate* even?" I huff and take a sip of my fizzy cola.

"I'm not surprised at all, Dabbler. You're a good egg. Like I already told you, many people deal with anxiety like you; theirs just might not be as visible as yours." He hesitates before he adds, "That tic of yours, we need to help you figure out how to kick that." The light emanating from his cell on his lap spotlights the crooked smile that emerges, crinkling the scar on his cheekbone. And there's that dimple.

Shaking my head, I smile, too. "I need to kick that tic, huh?"

He laughs.

"Dad, you're *such* a dork." Irie smacks him in the shoulder again.

"Hey, I didn't even realize it until I said it. Cut me some slack, Sunshine." He reaches for the can of Coke I'm holding out for him. "Oh, and why the backseat—No offense, but this is sort of mine and Dabbler's fight. And you only have one year left to graduate. If anything were to happen to you, I'd never be able to..."

"Hey, this is *my* fight *too*, Mr. Overprotective." Still leaning over the seat, Irie puts her hand on Tommy's shoulder. "They *killed* Mom. Maybe not the ones digging up graves—who knows —but it's their kind that did it. Eventually the diggers will give in to their urges when the cemeteries are no longer safe to steal from. I'm here for *Mom*—I need to help stop them from doing that to someone else—someone else's mom, dad, sister, brother..." She places her other hand, cold and wet from the can of Coke, on my shoulder. She gives it a gentle squeeze as she adds, "or someone's friend."

A chill runs through me. A brief hesitation, then I glance over my shoulder.

She looks me straight in the eyes and smiles. Such a genuine smile.

It gives me even more shivers.

Such caring and honest people like Irie and Tommy are not what I'm used to. This is all new for me. Besides Jill, not many people stay in my world for long. So many hypocrites and haters and backstabbers and judgmental fuckers.

Tommy looks over at the Sunshine of his life. She gives his shoulder a squeeze.

He smiles, a full smile. "Yes, you're absolutely right, sweetie. I'm sorry. You know—*Dad*. Protecting my baby girl is like a reflexive action. You're my world. You *know* that."

"Whoa! There it is." I lean forward and grab the dash with my free hand. "Sorry to break up the love-fest here, but I swear I just saw someone, or some*thing*, moving in there. More than one, I think."

We all shut up and stare across the street at the cemetery.

A minute or two passes as we all look with unblinking eyes at what's stirring in the dark.

A couple flashlights. Small beams side by side.

Then another set.

And another.

The second and third sets are lower to the ground than the first.

I whisper, "The first set must be the Supervisor and probably the lookout. The others, the diggers inside the hole. Gotta bring some worker bees to get the job done quicker."

A couple more minutes slither past.

As our eyes are glued to the graveyard, waiting for confirmation those are Dusters, an adult fox and two kits creep out between the rungs of the old black metal fence. Then they dart across the street into the baseball field next to where we're parked.

"Shit!" Tommy has his cell in his hand, screen lit up. "I was just about to dial the second one to nab those..." a titter accompanies his last words, "wily foxes."

"Ha, ha. So funny, Dad. You really are full of it tonight." Irie huffs and falls against the back of the rear seat. "Phew...my muscles are all tensed up from that one."

"Yeah, I hear that." Nerves taut, I lean back and take a long swig off my Coke. The carbonation hurts my throat. I set the can in the cup holder on the door. "After that, I don't think I need the caffeine anymore."

"It's early. Didn't you say the latest grave robbery happened around three?" Tommy sets his phone on his lap and grabs the can of mixed nuts sitting on the recessed part of the dash.

"Yeah, that's what the neighbor who reported it said."

Tommy sits back and relaxes—for a brief moment.

"Shit. Can't believe I didn't mention this to you guys already, but someone was outside my apartment door tonight right after I got home."

"What?!" They say in stereo, both wide-eyed and sitting up again at full attention.

"Yep. You heard correctly. Not sure if they followed me home from work or were somewhere outside watching for me to get home, but I sensed them. Then I heard them run down the stairs and slam the door on their way out." Shaking my head, I add. "Neither of my neighbors are capable of moving at the speed I heard that psycho stalker run out of the building."

"Could it have possibly been someone upstairs from you?" Tommy asks.

"Nope. Never heard footsteps come down those stairs. The sound started *right* near the door to my place."

"Damn, Dabbler. Think it could've been one of those Dusters?"

I shrug. "Last I knew, both Sheila and Toodles were still in jail. Unless someone posted bail until their trials." Another shrug. "No idea."

"Maybe someone else from that crazy NA group?" Irie chimes in.

"If any of them have been released, maybe. I don't know, but I am *definitely* not jogging to or from work anymore. Not that I have in a while, but still...Easier to stay ahead of the psychos when I've got my wheels."

They both nod.

"Maybe you ought to think about carrying some pepper spray or a whistle or something," says Irie. "Gotta stay safe when psychos like that have your scent."

I nod. "Good idea."

She leans into the front seat again. Her dreads are so long they touch and tickle my hand that's resting on the middle console. She reaches into the can of nuts her Dad's holding, and she asks, "Hey, I've been meaning to ask—What's up with this Dabbler nickname anyway?"

Tommy looks over at me. "Dory here dabbles on drums." He laughs. "After we first met in the padded room at the hospital, it took me a few days before I ever found out her real name, and that discovery happened only by chance." He tosses more nuts into his mouth and goes on. "She was so stressed and furious about finding out about those bone cutters *and* that no one believed her about them, those feet of hers were tapping out some sick double-bass-drum rhythms when I walked in. I asked if she played. Her answer—'I'm a dabbler.'" He nudges my arm with his elbow, winks. "It just sort of stuck."

"Aha! Now I get it." She grabs another handful of nuts. "Did you tell her you used to play?"

I sit up bolt straight and turn toward Tommy. "*You* play and you didn't tell me?"

"Sunshine, that was the past. You know I haven't touched a drum in years." Glancing at me sidelong he adds, "Hand percussion. Not a whole kit. No pedals and cymbals and shit." He laughs before adding, "Yeah, yeah, I know I fit the stereotype, a Native American who plays hand drums. What can I say? I've got rhythm." He shrugs, laughs. A blink later, his laughing stops, and his smile fades. "Me and Kaya used to play and sing together. Ever since she was itty-bitty, Irie used to sing with her Mamma and me." He looks back out the windshield toward the graveyard. "Enough about that. We have a stakeout at hand. Let's stay vigilant. We don't want to miss anything."

Irie and I share a look. She shrugs. Donning a crooked smirk, I cock a curious eyebrow.

Then we both look out the windshield and watch for, well, anything unusual.

Time ticks by so slowly it feels as though it's going in reverse. I crack a cold Coke. Force down the throat-tearing fizz.

A nudge to my leg makes me jump.

"Don't chug too much. Don't want the need for a wiz break to hit ya."

"Just making sure I don't doze—miss somethin'. Ya' know?"

"Right. I'm wide awake, man. I'm willing to wait here all night to catch these sick-fucks." Tommy shakes his head. "My Kaya...she needs justice. Sleep won't take me, that's for sure. Not tonight."

"We won't be here *that* long. Look." Irie reaches her arm out toward the windshield, pointing into the dark of the cemetery beyond.

Two beams of light flicker and bounce from out of the woods at the far end of the cemetery. These lights are not level with one another, like the eyes of the foxes.

Silent, we watch.

A third and fourth light emerges a couple minutes later. This time from the back of the cemetery.

Still, we watch.

We wait.

It's now almost 2:30 A.M.

With cell in hand, Tommy whispers, "What do you think? Give them maybe ten minutes or so to get to digging, then call it in?"

"Maybe twenty?" Irie chimes in. "Give them time to get down deep."

I remain silent, still just watching, waiting.

My heart is pounding so hard it feels as though it's in my head, ready to bust out of my skull. Remembrance of the nuthouse fills my mind—running from those junkie-cutters, waking to find them in my room ready to carve me open like a fucking jack o' lantern.

The memories sicken me. I'm sweating. My stomach is twisted like a Celtic knot, tightening more and more with every moment longer that I wait and watch.

Shit! What the fuck am I doing here?

Someone hits me in the shoulder.

"Earth to Dory. Are you in there, Dabbler?" Tommy. "When do you think we should call it in?"

I shake my head. "Not just yet. Let those sick fuckers put in a lot of backbreaking, sweaty labor first. Ha! Then the cops can rain down on them, and those duster-fucks will come away with nothing but jail time for all their hard work." I can't even force a smile.

Torment for those sickos is what I want, worse than Git Girl and Renfield did to me in the hospital.

Shit.

Tommy and Irie—I can't imagine how much they want to hurt those Duster-fucks. If they had killed my wife or mother, the cops would *never* get called.

Those sickos would die by my bare hands. I'd strangle every last one of them, and, when they look at me with their eyes bugging out and pleading for mercy, I'd curb stomp them repeatedly until I hear their skull crush under my Dr. Marten combat boot.

The exact same thing I wish I'd done to my former sister for killing my mother. But good 'ol Dory went the legal route instead.

I can still dream, can't I?

CHAPTER 8
CLOSING A DOOR

All is quiet at Silver Springs Psychiatric Hospital.

Hushed conversations among staff float through the air like the flapping of a bird's wings. The night shift nurses chat quietly together inside the medication station. All the psychological technicians hang around the large counter at the T-intersection of the corridors, gossiping with whispering voices. Dim lights hang over the hallways. All the patients are assumed asleep. Two empty chairs sit, one on either side of the hallway, outside the bedrooms of the four suicidal patients' rooms. This is where the two psych techs assigned to twenty-four-hour watch should sit vigilant until their turn is up. Not even bathroom breaks are allowed without finding someone to fill-in for them.

The newest nurse on the team flutters out of the half door of the nurse's station, led by her beaming smile, as she heads out into the hall to perform room checks. Her long, golden, ombré hair is clipped back with a blue and black feathered clasp. A few loose strands of hair hang over the front of her shoulders. Those strands of two-tone hair blow like the feathers of the clip as she saunters along. Her footfalls make no sound. Multi-colored images of cats cover her lavender scrubs. The name on her swaying lanyard reads Nurse Freyja.

Rick, the psych tech with the shoulder length 80's hair-metal mullet, sits up and watches every hip-sway as she appears to float past the counter. Since her first shift last week, he has not been able to keep his eyes off her whenever she's near.

As soon as Rick sees her pick up the clipboard with the Room Check Checklist attached, he calls after her.

"Hey, Freyja. If you want someone to walk you through room checks, I'm your man."

She pauses a few feet in front of the counter. With a flip of her long ponytail over her shoulder, she turns toward Rick and flashes her beaming Cheshire smile. "Thank you. That's very kind of you to offer, but I'm pretty sure I can handle this alone." She turns away, about to walk off, but she halts and looks back at Rick. "If I do find that I need *any* assistance, I'll be sure to call on you, Rick." She winks before she turns back toward the hallway of patient bedrooms.

Eyes wide, Rick just nods and smiles. The spell her beauty—her mere presence—casts over him completely blocks out any question as to why she's doing *his* job right now. Extra time to kick back and relax works for him. After all, that's why he was fine with filling in and working a couple doubles this week while the new nurse gets her feet wet. Well, that's part of the reason.

The eye candy is quite enjoyable, too. The wink—an extra bonus.

Normally night checks get completed by a psych tech. But it's Nurse Freyja's second week at the hospital, and she says she wants to familiarize herself with everything pertaining to her assigned unit. That's what she's told Nurse Taylor, the head nurse she's working the graveyard shift with.

To start the check, Freyja first peeks into the two rooms at the head of the hall, the ones closest to the staff counter, the ones designated for high-risk patients. These doors always remain open for suicide watch. Each patient, both new arrivals, appear sound asleep. Clipboard in her hand, she checks off the box beside each patient's name, documenting that they're well and accounted for. Moving on, she smirks when glancing at the empty chairs between each of the first two rooms on either side of the hallway. A quick glance over her shoulder reveals the two techs on twenty-four-hour watch are engrossed in conversations at the counter with their co-workers. She shakes her head as she turns back toward the patients' rooms.

She glides on to the next two rooms, whose doors are also opened. Two more new arrivals. Two more on suicide watch.

Again, both patients appear asleep.

Looking as though her pearly white smile is leading her on, the newest nurse on staff turns from that fourth room check and quietly eases the door shut. Again, she checks the boxes on her clipboard next to two more patient names. Floating down the hall as though the feathers in her hair are wings carrying her, she eases open each successive door in turn. The hallway is so dim and her teeth are so white, her ear-to-ear smile appears disembodied, sailing along on its own as it finishes the 2:30 A.M. room checks. Next patient check should occur in thirty minutes.

All boxes checked. All patients accounted for. Nurse Freyja strolls back toward the Nurse's Station. As she moves past the counter where the psych techs are gathered, Rick sits back up at attention, practically drooling over her beauty. His eyes remain riveted on her as she hands the clipboard to Nurse Taylor.

"All are well and sound asleep." Nurse Freyja's smile never wavers.

Nurse Taylor blinks an excessive amount of times and backs a step away. "Great. Thank you, Freyja." She glances away, then turns back to the new nurse. "I hope you don't mind me asking, but *how* do you get your teeth so white?"

"Oh, I don't know. Nothing special. Just a good healthy diet, I suppose." Still beaming, she turns to the iPhone in the speaker jack, clicks on SiriusXM radio and chooses the classic rock station.

INXS is playing "The Devil Inside."

As Michael Hutchence's breathy voice rolls out of the small speaker, Nurse Freyja sways her hips over to the counter at the T-intersection of the hallways where the psych techs are still gathered. She strikes up an eye-batting conversation with Rick. She has his undivided attention, along with the other four psych techs, men and women. All of them are so mesmerized by her spellbinding Goddess-like presence they've pushed aside their paperwork and other nightly assignments, forgetting everything else but her.

———

Behind door number four—

The shimmer of the waning gibbous moon shines through the bars on the closed bedroom window. As soon as the door *clicks* shut, out from behind the bathroom door skulks a skeletal-thin image. A long, lanky shadow stretches across the floor, moving slowly toward the bed. Something cloth-like dangles and sways from their right hand.

The shadow approaches the bed ever so quietly. The sleeping patient is turned, facing the wall, snoring, long red undercut mohawk fanned-out across his pillow. Just as the shadow figure makes it to the edge of the bed, it reaches down and places a bandana, folded long and narrow corner-to-corner, into the patient's open mouth and then slides it between bed and face and ties it behind the patient's head. There is no pillow.

Now the patient starts waking. Groggy from whatever meds they were given at 9:00 P.M. but waking.

Out from under the desk behind The Shadow Skeleton crawls another image. The short, husky shadow jumps up and over to the bedside and quickly ties both the patient's wrists and ankles together with tall tube socks to restrain them as much as possible. Then the new shadow reaches into its own pocket and pulls out a small baggy. They blow some sort of white powder into the bound and gagged patient's face. Soon, it's as though the patient never started to wake at all.

This particular patient is a young man in his twenties. His attackers can't even remember his name, but they know he's on suicide-watch and he's a junkie.

The perfect victim.

The perfect recruit.

The attackers now look at one another. Slug Man, with the mutant scar around his neck glistening with sweat, grabs hold of the patient's arm and nods to his clan member, Big G.

Wide-eyed, Big G hands over the shiv—a toothbrush with its handle shaved down so thin it's as sharp as a blade. Eager, he takes in a deep breath and rubs his palms together. The springy black curls of his shoulder length hair bounce with his hyper head nods.

"Calm down already. All that bouncing might make the shiv slip. Shit. We need to get in and get out ASAP. Got it?" Shiv at the ready, Slug Man sits on the edge of the bed.

"Yeah, yeah. Sorry. It's just been so freakin' long."

"I get it. I get it. Now chill."

Shaking his head in frustration, Slug Man now unties the young man's wrists. Noticing the multiple track marks in the crook of the victim's elbow, he smiles and turns the arm over, eager to get to work. With his sleeves already rolled up to prevent blood stains, he places shiv to skin, slices deep, all the way down to the ulna bone on the outside of the victim's left arm. Starting near the wrist, he carves upward, on the opposite side from the freshly unstitched suicide wound. The shiv opens the skin as easily as slicing a piece of bread. The end of the slice makes it almost all the way up to the elbow.

After carefully peeling the flesh from the bone to reveal more of the goods, his least favorite part of this bloody job, Slug Man works quickly to chisel the bone. Using the tinfoil he snatched from his baked potato at dinner and snuck out of the cafeteria, Gary—AKA Big G—collects as much bone shavings as he can. But they're not *too* greedy. They need to get out of there fast before any staff notice the closed door.

Plus, they don't want the guy to bleed to death. This one's a recruit, like most.

Before they leave the patient's room, they force small bits of the product, caked in blood, into the patient's mouth. A pinch of his nose helps force him to open up. Blowing in his face makes him swallow.

He never wakes.

Tinfoil folded up tight, Slug Man wipes his bloody hands off on the patient's blanket and pockets the goods. Big G wipes off his bloody hands the same way, then unties the new recruit's ankles. After wiping the blood and his prints off the shiv, Slug Man wraps a piece of the blanket around his own hand then slips the nuthouse knife into the victim's hand, wraps the patient's fingers around it, and gives it a good squeeze. With the corner of the sheet, he grabs the tip of the makeshift blade, careful not to wipe the victim's prints off or get his own prints back onto it, then drops it on the floor beside the bed. Easy to find.

Slug Man and Big G slip out of the room just as quietly as they'd slipped in just before Nurse Freyja's check-in, making sure no one is in the hallway. Sure enough—both chairs for the techs assigned for the twenty-four-hour watch still sit empty. Looking toward the counter at the head of the hallway, they notice Nurse Freyja. All the psych techs are facing her as she has them engrossed in an animated conversation.

Perfect.

The guys slither back to their own rooms well before the next room-check starts. Since Big G's room is next to the victim's, he waits for Slug Man to slip into his own room. Once his partner's door eases shut, Big G peeks back toward the staff counter, then he makes sure to slam his door before diving into bed.

The new recruit needs medical attention right away. He can't die.

When the techs come to check on the noise, these two guys will be in their beds as though they'd been sleeping all along.

It's only seconds later when it comes.

———

Mary's scream fills the halls, the rooms, and all the offices of the adult unit. "Help! Room four. I need assistance. *Now!*" As the only psych tech who responded to the echoing slam of that door, rage blooms red on her face. This shouldn't have happened.

Lead psych tech Rick, with his hair-metal mullet bouncing in time with his rotund belly, skids around the corner of the counter, followed by three other psych techs. Left standing in shock, it appears as though Nurse Freyja's feet are frozen to the floor. All the attention no longer focuses on her. No one is hanging on her every word anymore. They all left her there alone, and she looks like she has no idea what to do now.

At the head of the hallway of patient rooms, one of the psych techs stops short. She looks back over her shoulder at the new nurse. "Looks like it's in a high-risk patient's room. I guess an open door and a twenty-four-hour watch doesn't keep the patients safe after all." With a shrug, she turns around and beelines it toward the emergency.

Still unmoving, Nurse Freyja's eyes glow like high beam HID headlights. With a shake of her hair, she marionettes a bright white smile and moves out from behind the counter. As hesitant steps lead her forward, she follows the path to where the others have gone. Twitching at the corners of her lips, that Cheshire grin shudders along with the sway of her hips.

This new nurse doesn't appear as eager as everyone else to arrive at the scene of this emergency. Whether nervous or scared or shocked, it's hard to say.

Is it her newly hired status that keeps her at a turtle's pace? Does she realize she made a mistake when she closed the door to the room of a suicidal patient? Or is there something else holding her back? Could it be that she's simply upset to have lost her audience?

How new to this profession is she? Whatever the answer, she best get used to this sort of call if she expects to keep working at Silver Springs Psychiatric Hospital.

CHAPTER 9
CEMETERY SKULKING

Silence surrounds us as we continue waiting. Unsure how long is long enough, I break the silence.

"Maybe we should sneak in and see if they've dug down far enough yet?"

"Shit. Do you really *want* to be bald?" A chuckle slips out of Tommy. "That's quite a risky step to take. Where you diggin' up all this bravery, Dabbler?"

An image of Jill handing me her knife flickers across my mind. She's always so brave.

Her courage must be contagious.

"I just want to be certain they get busted on big charges." Squinting my eyes, I lean toward the windshield. "I can't see what they're doing. Dammit! I can't really see much of anything but the vague flickering of their flashlights. How 'bout you guys?"

"Yeah, same here. Not much." Now Tommy leans toward the windshield.

Irie suddenly leans into the front seat again. "I'm in. Let's go. I can't see a damn thing sitting back here." She's drumming on each of our shoulders, waiting for a response. "Let's go. Let's go. Let's go. Before these sickos get away with more depravity."

With his veil-between-worlds scarred and tatted forearm

resting on the steering wheel, Tommy shifts in his seat, looks at Irie and me. "Ho-ly...Slow down, ladies." He shakes his head. "You women sure do have more balls than me. What if *we* get busted for what *they're* doing? Let's not fuck this up with our eagerness to bust some Dusters."

"Dad, don't forget what they did to mom." She squeezes his shoulder. Then she leans closer and kisses him on his scarred cheek, the constant reminder of the Duster attack seven years back. "Let's do it for her."

He rests his hand on top of hers, takes a deep breath and closes his eyes for a moment.

As soon as his eyes open, he pulls the key out of the ignition and pockets it. Then he turns toward Irie and gives her hand a squeeze. His eyes, those dark doorways to other dimensions, glance toward me, then back to Irie. "Well, what are we waiting for? Ladies, let's *do* this already."

We both respond with a smile.

———

Feet in the grass to avoid the crunching sound of the gravel road, I'm thankful the cemetery workers have done such a great job with leaf cleanup. We'd never make it through here without getting noticed if they hadn't done their job so well. Then I look down and see the neon signs that are the bright white toes and soles of my Chucks.

Shit! Jill was right. I should've worn my black combat boots. But on second thought—

What if I have to run?

I shake that thought from my mind and focus on the task at hand.

The three of us move slow and steady, sticking to where we see the tallest headstones looming in the dark. Easier for hiding. With so many solar lights lit up at various gravesites, along with the clear sky and half full moon overhead, we're able to vaguely see our way through the cemetery without a flashlight. The standing stones look like shadows. The flat tablet markers look like holes that might swallow us.

We're only about six or seven family plots away from the Dusters chosen dig site. Their low, indistinct chatter sounds like *chittering* squirrels at this distance. I keep glancing over my shoulder to make sure Tommy and Irie are keeping up. No problems so far, until—

A cement border around the perimeter of a large, old family plot trips me up. Face-planting an inch away from the largest gravestone, I stay on the ground.

The thud and shuffle of my tumble must have made a loud enough noise for those sickos to hear.

Vandals' discussions cease.

To my right, Tommy and Irie have already scooted behind neighboring headstones in the same family plot.

With their eyes so wide open and the whites so bright, it looks like I'm hiding with a couple of coyotes.

Are Tommy and Irie nocturnal and they didn't tell me?

Would make sense with Irie working the graveyard shift at the loony bin.

Shaking the silly, intrusive thought from my mind, I listen more intently on what lies ahead.

Are the junkie-cutters privy to others skulking in the cemetery? Maybe they just think it was the scuttling of an animal. A dear. A raccoon. A fox.

As soon as that thought hits me, so does something else.

Bat guano. On the upper arm of my sweatshirt.

Well, it could be regular old bird shit, but there's no white. Just a long, thin pellet of black stench.

Lovely.

If the cutter-vandals didn't hear my graceful tumble or see my neon-sign feet, they'll probably smell me coming, no bloody wound needed.

Should I take this as some sort of divine sign?

Is the bat shit screaming for us to abort this bat-shit-crazy mission?

Up in the open stretch of sky between the surrounding treetops I see a handful of bats swooping and darting about, feasting on the night's insects.

If I get shit on one more time, *then* I'll take it as a sign to get the fuck out of here ASAP. I'm not letting this slight inconvenience ruin our chance to bust some Bone Cutters.

We remain hidden, listening for a cue we can safely progress closer.

Another minute or so passes.

Whispers spill forth from further ahead.

We wait a bit longer.

The whispering gets a little louder. Still only indistinct words.

I glance around the edge of the tombstone I'm lying behind. Beyond the stretch of graves between the Dusters and us, two heads bob up and down while shovelfuls of dirt fly in two different directions. To the right of them I see two other Dusters, out of focus, backs facing us, with their flashlight beams aimed down at the grave the other two are disinterring. Three plots before and to the left of the digging sits a large sarcophagus.

I duck my head back into hiding and look toward Tommy and Irie. It takes a moment for them to see me looking at them, but when they do I mime the shape of the sarcophagus and point to it, then to us, and then toward the large tomb again.

They both glance around the headstones they're behind. After they tuck their heads back into their hiding spots, they both look at me and nod.

Tommy points to himself then to me and shrugs his shoulders.

I jab my thumb toward my chest.

Peeking around my headstone hiding spot, I see that the Dusters appear engrossed in their dirty work.

Up on my feet now and in a runner's starting crouch, I creep toward the sarcophagus. I stay crouched down, trying to stay level with the standing stones I pass so as not to draw attention my way.

For a town so small that it doesn't even have its own police department, they sure do have a larger than expected cemetery.

Ducking behind various stones on the way to my destination, I begin to realize we're in the old part of the cemetery. Crumbling foundations. Broken grave markers. Headstones that split in two epoxy-sealed back together.

I guess it doesn't matter how old the bones are? Fresh bones of live people. Bones of people that died long ago. Bones of newly deceased people.

No.

Wait.

Formaldehyde is a carcinogen. Embalming has been going on for quite a long time. Fresher dead *won't* work. Unless they've not yet been prepared for viewing and burial, or unless it's a green burial. But green or not green, how would these psychos know? Maybe the cemeteries list the information on their websites and these sickos actually do their research.

Ick! Whatever. Old bones. New bones. It's all disgusting.

I wonder what would happen if they ingested bone dust from an embalmed person?

Nothing good, I imagine.

So, dead or alive—it must all scratch their jonesing-itch, or they wouldn't do all this back-breaking grave digging just to get a fix.

Digging graves is tough fucking work. Jill's aunt was a grave digger. Now she's on disability with a fucked up back. Last I heard she couldn't stand or sit for long periods of time without experiencing excruciating pain, and she was going to physical therapy three times a week to try to get some relief.

I duck behind two more old stones, then I make it to the sarcophagus. As I lie in wait for my stakeout partners, the sound of the fluttering wings of bats swooping overhead pulls my attention to the bat shit still on my sleeve. I grab a half dead leaf from the ground, wipe it away, toss the leaf aside. With a little silent shimmy, I peek around the stone coffin.

Now the two that had been off to the side supervising are also in the hole with the first two diggers.

Shit. They might crash right through the damned casket with all four of them in there. Those old coffins are simple pine boxes, nothing like the thick and sturdy airtight luxury caskets made of steel today. Plus, I doubt they used cement burial vaults back then. How the hell is a grave robber supposed to get through one of those bad boys? I guess that's the point, or at least part of it.

Shovelfuls of dirt fly in all directions. Beams of light shine down into the hole from their flashlight's they've placed on the ground all around the perimeter of the grave. But I still can't see what any of the Dusters look like. It doesn't help that I'm only getting quick blips of them as their heads keep bobbing in and out of the grave with each shoveling heave.

How are they all in there shoveling together without whacking each other? That is some serious skill. Makes me wonder how many times they've done this before.

That's too disturbing to think about.

Wait.

Why aren't Tommy and Irie here yet? Back in my hiding position, I glance back to where I had left them. I don't see them at all.

Maybe they're on their way to me and have ducked behind different stones.

Suddenly I hear the sound of clinking, like shovels knocking together. I face forward again and listen.

Have the diggers already reached the casket?

Listening intently, I wonder if we're too late. Are they going to grab the bones and make a run for it already?

A conversation starts. At first the words are indecipherable.

Then I hear some shuffling around. The words rise in volume a bit and grow clearer.

"Fuck! This shit is getting old. I'm so fucking sweaty the dirt on me is turning to mud." More shuffling around. "Uh...did anyone bring more water or just *this* canteen?"

A strained voice says, "Nope, just the one."

"Dammit! I don't know if I can dig anymore. Why can't we just dust someone instead of reverting to this?"

Another clink of shovels knocking together.

More shuffling sounds.

No more digging sounds.

Are they taking a break?

A strained voice, high pitched and kind of squeaky, says, "I told ya', man, I ain't carving into anyone *ever* again. That kind of shit almost hurt people I care about. No fucking way am I going that route. So stop being a wuss and grab your fucking shovel...Shit! Give me some of that water before you drink it all."

That voice...It sounds so familiar.

Before I can place where I've heard that voice before, the talking stops and the sound of shovels scraping against rocks and dirt sounds up again. Then someone slams into my side.

Irie.

One of her long dreads brushes against my cheek. I turn toward her. We both smile. Then Tommy scuttles up on the other side of her. His crooked smile emerges. Dimple-scar on his cheek crinkling.

Man, I can't imagine the pain of some crazy Bone Cutter carving into my face. Tommy sure is a tough motherfucker to withstand that type of torture, *and* after watching them Dust his wife to death. I have no idea how he can stomach working in that psych hospital knowing that Dusters are there. And Irie, too.

Well, now's our chance to get some justice—for them *and* for me.

A few minutes pass. I fiddle with the blades of grass to keep from scratching my head. I can*not* bleed with Dusters so close. No matter how quiet and out of sight we are, they will smell me.

Tommy peeks around the corner of the sarcophagus. I do the same.

All four diggers are working like mad.

I duck back into hiding, then nudge Irie with my elbow. When she turns toward me, I nod back toward the way we came and then toward her dad.

She nudges Tommy. He ducks back behind the sarcophagus and looks over at us.

I motion with my thumb for us to leave. Then I mime a phone to my ear. With the Dusters so far into their work now, it's prime time to call this in.

Tommy nods.

Irie nods.

With a finger point toward each of us, Tommy motions for Irie and me to go ahead of him.

Irie looks at me and shrugs a shoulder. Then she mouths the words *You go first*.

I shrug and nod.

With a glance back around the sarcophagus, I make sure the Dusters are all busy.

Confirmation.

I duck back behind the sarcophagus and start creeping back the way we'd come. Anxious to get back to the car and call 911, I move quickly, quicker than when we arrived.

Dumb. Dumb. Fucking dumb!

A grave marker trips me up. I hit the ground hard. Not much different than tripping over the border of the family plot on my way into the cemetery, the klutz that I am. But something is much different this time.

My fall knocks a solar lamp into the base of a headstone. The *crunch-scrape* sound freezes my breath and my body. I don't dare move.

I wait to hear...

well...

anything.

Did the Dusters hear that?

Where are Irie and Tommy?

Are they still hiding behind the sarcophagus?

Did that crash sound bring attention to them fleeing?

Stupid me.

Why do I always have to be so anxious? Why such a rush? Remember, slow and steady, steady and slow...

A few moments pass.

Now that I'm much farther away from the Dusters, I have no idea if they said anything about hearing the sound or not.

I wait another minute or so.

Still no Irie. No Tommy.

Too worried yet to raise my head all the way up off the ground, I just glance over my shoulder.

I see no one.

I hear no one.

I take a chance.

After slowly easing myself up onto my hands and knees, I start creeping back toward the road and the ballfield. No way in hell do I dare get back up on my feet. If the Dusters *did* hear my fall, they could be watching for movement.

I stay close to the ground. There's not much farther to go to get to the ditch beside the road. Maybe I'll wait there for Irie and Tommy to catch up. Then we can all dart across the road at the same time and back into the parking lot of the Little League field.

By the time I make it about ten feet from the black wrought iron fence around the perimeter of the graveyard, Tommy appears at my heels, also crawling. We both roll into the ditch one after the other. Reaching down, I touch my calf, making sure Jill's knife is still secure.

In hushed voices, we both speak at once. "Where's Irie?"

I shrug. "She *was* right behind me at first. Let's wait here for her. Cross back over together."

He nods, but a look of fear washes over him a breath later. "I *can't* wait. What if something happened to her?" Hair all messed and falling out of his ponytail, he appears quite frantic. Shoulders rise and fall with each deep anxious breath. Then he jumps to a crouch, turns back toward the cemetery, is about to stand and head back in to look for her.

Up on my knees, I reach out across his lower back, grab him, hold him there. "No. She's a smart girl. You taught her well. Trust that she's smart enough to get out. She wasn't far behind me."

Lips in a flatline of frustration, he shakes his head, staring straight into the cemetery, and starts leaning forward as though about to run back in.

"Tommy, just give her another minute or two. If she's not back by then, I'll go back in with you."

He looks over at me with a no-way-in-hell expression. His shoulders rise high with his next deep breath, staying near his ears for such an extended period of time that I wonder how he can hold it in for so long. When he finally releases that breath, shoulders lowering, he gives me a hesitant nod of agreement— though his lips stay pursed, like he's biting back an argument. But he remains in the ready-to-sprint stance. And he's higher up on the edge of the ditch where someone could potentially see him if they look this way.

I reach out with my other arm, wrap both around his waist, and tug him back. To keep him from getting spotted by the wrong person, I pull him lower into the ditch with me. He stumbles into me. "Sorry, but I was worried they'd see you. Gotta stay low."

He nods.

Side by side, unable to catch our nervous breaths, we wait.

"Be patient." To show my support and try to reassure him, I pat him on the shoulder, rest my hand there. "Give her a chance to prove herself. I don't want you to get *yourself* busted when I *know* she'll be here any mo—"

Cutting my sentence short, Irie rolls into the ditch like a giant bowling ball.

Tommy and I are the pins.

We all tumble over into a jumbled mess, hair disheveled and peppered with grass and dead leaves. My bandana has twigs and leaves sticking to it, poking out all around the edges, making my head itch even worse than normal.

With huffs and groans and quiet chuckles, we unjumble ourselves and pass around looks of relief. We all made it out.

I raise my finger to my lips, making sure we stay quiet. Raising my other hand, palm facing out, I motion for us to stop for a moment. "Make sure they didn't hear us."

All three of us wait and look back up toward the cemetery side of the deep ditch. After a few seconds, something tugs at the back of the bandana on my head. I spin around. Tommy's crooked smile greets me. He's plucking twigs and leaves off from me. "Thank you," I silently say with a smile.

Then I tap Irie on the back, nod at both of them, and whisper, "Let's cross together. On three."

They both nod in agreement.

With my fingers I visibly count—

One.

Two.

We're all up on our feet before—

Three.

We dash across the road, through the parking lot, and to the pickup truck sitting in the shadow of the dugout.

We get back down low—just in case—behind the tailgate.

Hesitant to open a door and make any sort of sound, we wait a little longer.

Hearing nothing but crickets and the fluttering of bat wings overhead, we all let out heavy sighs at almost the exact same moment.

Tommy reaches into his pocket and retrieves his key. Before going to unlock the doors, he glances around the bed of the truck.

A moment later he scoots out from behind the tailgate and unlocks the doors.

As soon as we're all back inside, Tommy dials 911 and reports, "Flashlights and suspicious activity of what appears to be multiple people in the Hillcrest Cemetery."

As soon as he hangs up, he looks over at me in the passenger seat and Irie leaning over from the backseat. "Looks like our job here is done." Nothing gets mentioned about his worry that Irie might've been caught. Nothing gets mentioned about his doubt she would make it out without his help.

I understand and say nothing about it. No father wants their grown daughter to think they doubt their ability to take care of themselves without help from good 'ol dad. Even though I don't know my own dad, I do know that much.

Just as he reaches to put the key in the ignition, Irie grabs his arm.

"No way. Not yet. I don't want to miss this."

He shoots her a curious look, no words. Just a furrowed brow and a head shake.

"Yeah, I agree. Let's *make sure* they get busted. What if the cops get here too late and those sickos are already gone?"

"That could still happen even if we wait here," Tommy says.

"Yeah, but," Irie chimes in, "wouldn't you love the satisfaction of *knowing* we got some of those psychos busted?" She glances at me.

Wide-eyed and eager, I nod.

She looks back to her dad. "Plus, they'll hear you start the truck, then they'll look toward the sound and see us pulling out. That would ruin everything."

Damn. She's very convincing, like a lawyer. Is she going to law school?

He takes his hand away from the key in the ignition and sits back. A huff of a slight laugh escapes him.

I reach into the cooler, pull out a bag of pretzels, tear it open. With a tilt of the open bag toward my new friends, I offer them both a crunchy-munchy. My sign that I know Tommy can't refuse when it's two to one. They each reach into the bag at the same time and grab a snack.

Before taking a bite, Tommy says, "You win. We'll stay right here and make sure those crazy Duster-fucks get busted!"

With a smirk and a clenched fist, Irie reaches her hand toward me. We fist bump. Then, she plops back in her seat, grabs her Coke and starts chugging.

Tommy shakes his head. "Yeah, I see you two ladies teaming up." He laughs. "Outnumbering me."

Nodding, I smile, rub it in a bit.

Irie sets her empty can in the cupholder on the inside of the backdoor. "Why does that crack-in-a-can have to taste so good?" She leans into the front between Tommy and me. "If there's no sign of anything happening over there, I really need to step outside for a moment?"

Tommy's eyes widen. "Sunshine, what if they see you wandering around out there?"

"Dad, I'm not going to be 'wandering around.' I can just step outside and go beside the truck. They won't see a thing."

"Yeah, well, what if the cops show up while your pants are around your ankles?"

"Dad, you worry too much…Would you rather I let loose in here?" She shakes her head and laughs, then turns to open the door but hesitates, looks to her dad. "Just make sure the interior light is still off."

He nods. "You're all set. Make it quick. And be *quiet*."

She eases open the door with barely a sound, then slides

outside just as quietly. Leaving the door only resting against the latch, she avoids the *clicking-thud* of a closing vehicle door.

Waiting for those sickos across the street to finally get busted, and praying no one sees or hears us parked over here, my knee keeps involuntarily bouncing. I put my hand on the top of my knee, hoping to make it stop somehow. No luck. So I just start drumming rhythms on my leg, trying to ease my mind with music, or at least distract myself.

Tommy checks his phone. Then, phone screen still lit up, he reaches over and puts his hand on mine, quiets my nervous drumming. My heart skips a beat, wondering if I did something wrong, as I look over at him.

He smiles that crooked smile, dimple winking at me. "Thank you." His eyes, filled with sincerity, look straight into mine.

"For what?" I really have no idea what the hell he's talking about. We're sitting here, hiding in the dark, staking-out sadistic Dusters thieving from the dead in a cemetery with cops headed our way. What the fuck does he have to thank *me* for? I'm pretty much the reason we're here to begin with.

Man, can my life get any more fucked up?

Tommy shifts in his seat, turns toward me, squeezes my hand. "For reminding me how strong and capable my own daughter is. For helping me allow her to be that strong, intelligent woman her mama and me raised her to be. For helping me be a better father. For thinking so highly of my Sunshine, my blood, my life…Should I go on?"

His words, his stare, both so intense, I have to look away. Hearing so many kind things spoken about me, and to my face, well, I just don't know how to take that. It feels awkward. Unwarranted. And if I'm going to be honest, really honest with myself, I don't really know how it feels. All mixed up is what it is.

I glance back at him, not knowing what to say. His smile grows. Then, he leans closer to me and whispers, "And thank you for not saying anything to her about dear ol' dad thinking I needed to go in and rescue her. You know, you'll make a great mother one day." He winks, releases my hand, and sits back in his seat as the back door starts easing open.

"You're welcome." The words squeeze through my lips as I sit in shock. I try to smile, but my nerves are so taut it probably looks like I'm constipated.

A good mother? Me? Doubt it.

"'You're welcome' for what? What'd I miss?" Irie plops into the backseat, leans into the front and reaches for more pretzels. As she glances back and forth from Tommy to me, Tommy just laughs and looks back across the street.

I shrug and stuff a bunch of pretzels in my mouth.

CHAPTER 10
GET THE JOB DONE

All's silent inside. At three in the morning, it makes sense. Why would she, or anyone—except people like me—be awake at this hour?

With her ear still to the door, Snake Girl fishes around in her coat pocket for her supplies. She pulls away from the door, looks at the multiple locks, glances at the tools on her palm: a bump key, a small screwdriver, a rubber band, a few paper clips. The elastic and the paper clips go back in her pocket, for now.

Why are there so many damned locks on the freakin' door anyway? It definitely advertises the freak's insane paranoia. Doesn't she realize multiple locks are a neon sign leading thieves to places with stuff to protect? At least she didn't splurge for a pricey Medeco deadbolt—the billboard of door locks, flashing dollar signs of pricey possessions inside.

People are so fucking stupid, trying to keep out the bad guys but luring them instead.

Sure, maybe it will take a few extra seconds or so to pick more locks, but...

Bump key in one hand and screwdriver in the other, she goes for the top deadbolt first. She carefully inserts the key, hardly a sound. Using the screwdriver handle, she gives the edge of the key grip two quiet taps, turns the key.

So fucking easy a five-year-old kid could do this shit. Thank you, ignorant scaredy-cat! This isn't my first rodeo, motherfucker.

If she wasn't such an antisocial freak, she could easily just get a roommate. That's a good way to feel safer living in a city filled with people like me and my clan. Lucky for me, I've never noticed anyone else coming and going from here except Itchabald Crane herself. And I've never heard or seen a dog. All perfect signs for gettin' this job done.

Down to the next lock, she does the same as with the first. For the lock on the doorknob, she pockets the bump key, opting for something a bit quieter, though just as simple. The tap of the screwdriver against the key could cause a lot of clanking and jangling on a doorknob, since it's not flush against the wood like the deadbolts. With a couple of bobby pins, she stretches and bends and reshapes them just right. Then, she inserts them into the keyhole, knowingly maneuvers them around. She quickly finds the locks pins and...

Open sesame.

Though filled with excitement at getting through all the visible locks, Snake Girl, drenched in the Jonesing sweats, anticipates another. For this reason, she only eases the door open slightly, after using her sleeve to cover her hand, eliminating the chance of leaving fingerprints on the doorknob.

Yep. There it is.

A chain lock.

Easy to get through with a thick and trustworthy rubber band.

Snake Girl pockets both the bump key and screwdriver, but she doesn't pull out the elastic. That step's not necessary tonight. For some reason the chain lock hangs loose, disengaged.

That's odd. Home alone, she locks both the deadbolts, the doorknob, but leaves the chain lock unlatched. Is she a toker or what? She does seem to love that pothead reggae music an awful lot. She must've just got high and forgot.

Snake Girl pushes the door open wider, enters on feather feet, begins her search. Nose held high, like a wolf's snout to the wind, she hopes the scent of blood will lead the way to her prey.

"Slash her tires…dump sugar in her gas tank…" Ha! *Clyde never gave me the impression of being a sissy, not until* that *ridiculous suggestion. There's only one way to* guarantee *the snitch can't testify in court. And I ain't no sissy.*

The tall windows and thin curtains allow enough of a glow from street lamps to light the place. Even if dim, it's enough. Floating through the living room, hand in her other pocket, she grips the case of carving tools, pops the latch open. A couple steps away from the doorway to the kitchen, she stops, turns right, notices the open bathroom door. She nods to herself. Confirms she's got to keep looking to find the bedroom.

Looks like a small enough place. Shouldn't be too hard.

From her pants pocket she pulls out a couple latex gloves, slips them on. Wearing them to pick locks makes the getting in part take longer. Not a good enough grip or maneuverability, too much fumbling. A sleeve over the hand when turning the doorknob has always worked best for her.

Wandering into the kitchen she notices two doors off to the right. One open. One closed. And it's a lot darker in here without tall windows like the ones in the living room. No way does she dare risk flashing a light into the open doorway. With her silenced cell phone from her inside jacket pocket, she shines the flashlight on the floor a short distance away from the open door.

Wondering why one person would have two bedrooms, she notices the collapsed cymbal stand on the floor leaning against the doorframe of the open doorway.

Yep. There it is. That metal thingy looks like it goes to a drum set. That room must be a music room or some shit like that. That's why two rooms for one person. The closed door—that's where she sleeps. I just know it. My gut tells me so.

Shit. I really am a fucking genius!

She moves in stealth mode to the closed door, places her ear to the surface, hoping to hear snoring or something to signify occupancy.

As she waits, a ton of *whys* fly through her mind.

I still don't understand why Clyde didn't trust me to dust her without leaving a trace. I'm no fucking newbie at this shit. And converting her—that's the best way to keep her from testifying against Sheila and Toodles.

Toodles...such a stupid nickname, and damned if I can't remember what the fuck her real name is.

Forget that lackey. I don't really give a shit what her name is.

Back to the task at hand.

The Chair Chucker.

If I just dust her then she'll be one of us. Just think of the sweet satisfaction of turning her into a creature she despises. Plus, she wouldn't testify against one of her own. And I'm jonesing for a fucking fix. Nothing beats fresh dust.

Yeah, so what if Clyde's heard of a few who didn't turn after a dusting. That was a very long time ago, and only very few. So why just tamper with her car and take the huge risk of her finding someone to drive her to court. Uber. A taxi. The city bus. So many other options. Why not a dusting?

I may never know. But what I do know—

She definitely won't be making it to her court dates.

Time to get this job done.

With a slow turn of the knob that takes at least ten seconds to assure little-to-no noise, Snake Girl, stiletto switchblade in hand, enters the bedroom.

CHAPTER 11

FAMILIARITY AT THE CEMETERY

Twenty minutes and a whole bag of pretzels later, the Staties finally show up. And it looks like they came prepared to catch a whole crew.

Two cruisers and a paddy wagon pull up and park across the street.

Nice.

Hopefully they don't notice Tommy's truck parked here. The sign at the entrance of the Little League parking lot says the park is only open from dawn 'til dusk.

"It's about damned time! Hopefully the psychos are still in there to *get* busted...What if they snuck out the other side where we wouldn't be able to see them leaving?" I reach into the empty bag for more munchies, realizing, "Maybe we should've just called it in right away, like you said, Tommy."

He shrugs but says nothing.

We're all staring across the street intently to see if anyone gets hauled out in cuffs.

"Nah." Tommy finally says as he shakes his head. "Looks like they nabbed 'em. I see a couple gettin' led out now." He nods toward the front of the cemetery. "See?"

Silent, I nod. I hadn't noticed that until he pointed them out.

More silence as we watch those two, hands cuffed behind their backs, get escorted to the paddy wagon.

Through the crow-black night with the clouds now covering the half moon, I can't tell what either one of the Dusters look like, much less if they're men or women. When we were spying on them, I overheard a couple of male voices talking. But we had seen four flashlights and four figures near that grave.

Did the other two get away?

I get an elbow nudge to the shoulder.

Irie.

Still leaning over the front seat, she reaches out and points her finger across the street. But not directly at the police vehicles.

One hundred or so feet ahead of the police cruisers I see the dark image of someone running toward the back border of the cemetery. Up over the low metal fence they climb, only to get tackled by an officer just before the figure gets up out of the ditch at the back corner. A beam of light bounces around from the flashlight that falls from the officer's hand during the scuffle. Cuffed and on their feet, the vandal gets escorted back to the first cruiser.

"Yes!" Tommy whisper-yells. "Another one down. Only one more to go."

The headlights of the cruiser in the front flick on, blazing bright. As soon as the officer gets the attempted-escapee into the beams, I notice something.

Something familiar.

Leaning forward, closer to the windshield, I try to figure out if I really see what I think I see.

I rub my eyes, making sure it's not the late hour and my tired mind playing tricks with my vision.

Unfortunately, I don't think it is.

"Do you see what *I* see?" When I turn toward Tommy, I see his eyes riveted on the scene across the street. Then I immediately look back to the busted Bone Cutter, light beams emphasizing what my brain is already screaming at me.

The Duster—a stocky dude—is wearing cargo shorts, a flannel shirt, and combat boots. Running down the length of his right shin is a dark image. A tattoo. Every time that leg steps forward, the beam of light emphasizes this detail. Or maybe it's just all in my mind because I know...

Back in the cemetery...watching them dig...that squeaky voice I heard. It was so familiar. I just couldn't place it then.

But now I can.

"Shit!" Tommy grabs the steering wheel and pulls himself closer to the windshield. "Is that who it looks like?"

"What are you two talking about?" Irie asks from the backseat.

All our eyes remain riveted on the husky young man getting led to the back of the paddy wagon.

Unable to look away, unable to say the name, I nod, answering Tommy's question. Then I realize it's probably not easy to see my gesture in the dark of the truck's cab.

I force myself to say it.

"Yep. That's Shawn...From the hospital." I shake my head, frustrated and pissed off and—dare I think it—feeling a bit of regret. "One of the guys that helped save my life."

CHAPTER 12

EVERY LITTLE THING IS NOT GONNA
BE ALL RIGHT

Uneasy quiet surrounds us on the ride home. Seeing Shawn get busted felt like a massive punch to the gut.

My head pounds. Muscles are tight. My jaw aches from clenching my teeth. Thoughts keep racing so fast I can't grab hold of anything.

I have no idea what to say.

I feel like a horrible person.

Shawn saved me. He was working so hard to get clean. He didn't want to hurt anyone. That must be why...

"He's obviously fallen off the wagon." Tommy breaks the silence. "Turned to grave exhumations to satisfy his cravings and keep from *physically* hurting anyone."

Damn. Is Tommy in my head?

I nod. Then I realize, again, that no one can see my gesture in the dark.

My mouth and throat feel so dry from not talking for so long I can barely croak out a weak, "Yeah. That's what I was just thinking." Clearing my throat, I reach for my Coke. It's empty.

Irie remains silent.

I had imagined getting some Dusters busted would feel great.

Man, I could *not* have been more wrong.

What if the other three with Shawn were also like him, refusing to hurt others while struggling to kick their habit?

Yes, desecrating the dead is quite horrific, but considering the alternative...and the fact that many dust users get turned —never given a choice. I wonder if the other people with Shawn are users like that—turned against their will, now stuck with an addiction they can't control, afraid of hurting the living, while seeing no other choice than to defile the dead.

I shake the reverie from my head. I can't dwell on that. I can't...

No. Dammit!

They are still devouring the bones of the dead!

But Shawn...

Fuck! This sucks.

About twenty minutes of silence passes before I see the end of my street in the distance. Funny thing is—I hadn't even noticed we were back in the city yet.

We stop at a red light about a block away. The signature swirl of blue lights up ahead catches my attention.

The stoplight turns green.

Reflections of the spinning emergency lights bounce off the buildings we're slowly approaching. Nothing new in the city. But they're too close to my neighborhood, which sets me even more on edge.

As Tommy slowly turns onto my street, I realize it *is* in my neighborhood.

It's on my fucking street!

This can't be good.

Easing up over the crest of the hill about halfway up my street, I'm suddenly blinded by the blues. I cover my tired eyes, shielding them from the unpleasant intrusion. I want to see what's going on, but the lights are so bright and I'm just so damned exhausted I'm unable to see exactly which building has the trouble.

Irie leans over the front seat and grabs my shoulder just as Tommy says, "Shit! Isn't that *your* building, Dabbler?"

I move my hand away from my face and look more closely.

Sure thing—that's my building with the crime scene tape surrounding the front porch.

For fuck's sake! Can this night get any worse?

We park three houses away on the same side of the street as my building. Two cops are standing at the top of my front steps. At least three cruisers are parked out front, maybe more. My heart is pounding so hard and so fast it feels as though my head might burst. It's so crazy seeing this going on at *my* building, I don't know how to make sense of this situation.

As far as I know, there are no drug dealers living in my building, and I've never heard any sort of domestic violence type noises, well—

Except for that time I flipped out with the baseball bat on who I thought was Jill's rapist.

Now more swirling lights speed around the corner and zoom toward us from the other end of the street. Though I'm now fully awake, my eyes still feel so dry and my vision is so blurry that I can't quite make out what type of emergency vehicle it is until—

An ambulance pulls up directly in front of my building.

Shit! Did my neighbor Pricilla have an accident? Or maybe she...died?

No. That wouldn't explain all the police.

"What do you wanna do, Dabbler? I don't know if you can get in right now."

"But she *lives* there, Dad. Don't they *have* to let her in?" Irie is still leaning over the seat with her head between us.

"Yeah, what she said. They *have* to let me in. Maybe if I show them my ID with my address on it they'll let me through."

I grab the cooler off the floor, unzip the top compartment, and take out my small purse with my wallet inside. *Before* getting out of the truck, I take out my ID and get it ready to show the police standing guard at the front door of my building. I don't need any cops spazzing out on me when I go reaching inside my purse to pull something out right in front of them. No need to go and get myself shot up for doing something as basic as reaching for my license.

For all they know, I'm some psycho all hopped up on drugs ready to freak out and shoot up some coppers who get in my way and piss me off.

Plus, if they see me getting out of a vehicle at three-thirty AM with a scar-faced long- haired hippy donned with ink sitting behind the wheel, and a skinny dreadhead chick they could mistakenly stereotype as a junkie, they might just shoot me for the association. Not to mention—all the cops within sight are white, and my friends are not.

Yeah, can you tell I don't trust the police?

Trust is *not* something I come by easily, no special case here for the po-po.

Let's hope these officers are some of the good cops.

With my hand on the door handle, I turn to Tommy. "Will you wait here just in case? What if they don't let me in for some odd reason? I don't have any place else to go."

Irie nods her head, dreads swaying, as Tommy pats my knee, gives it a gentle squeeze.

"You *know* it," he says at the same time Irie says, "Of course we'll wait."

Just as I pop the door open I remember, *Shit, the boot knife.* I pull up my pant leg, unsnap the strap, and pull off the sheathed blade.

Brow scrunched and jaw dropped open, Tommy stares at me as I set the knife on the center console. "When did you plan on telling us you were packin'?" A low, tense laugh escapes him.

"Jill's suggestion. She wanted to protect me. And I don't dare have this on me when," I nod toward my front porch, "cops are all around my building. Do you mind holding onto it for me?"

He nods. "No prob. Slide it under your seat. Tuck it under that stack of reusable shopping bags under there. I'll take it in when I get back home."

"Thanks." I slip it under the passenger seat, hiding it beneath the bags, then I ease myself out onto the sidewalk.

Before I shut the door, Tommy says, "Hey, if they let you in, text us to let us know what's up and that you're alright. Okay?"

I nod. "Sure thing. Goodnight...hopefully." After a smirk and a wave, I glance up the sidewalk toward my building, uneasy about how this is going to go, though I don't know why.

Not wanting to make any loud or sudden noises, I shut the door gently and quietly. With my license in my hand, I hesitantly head for my front steps.

Before I get to the stairs, the EMTs wheel a stretcher out of the back of the ambulance and up onto the sidewalk. From the porch of my building, the shorter of the two police officers, a woman, holds her hand up, palm facing out, telling them to wait. A second later the front door of my building swings open behind her and her partner.

A very tall, thin woman in a black suit jacket and black jeans steps out through the open doorway over to the two officers and says something to them. They both nod in response.

Who the hell is that? No one that professional-looking lives in my building, not that *I've* ever seen. And looking as she does at this early hour of the morning can only mean one thing.

Her next move confirms my thought.

Striding down the front steps, the right side of her suit jacket gets pushed aside as she reaches into her pocket and retrieves her cell. That's when I see two telltale signs.

A shiny star-shaped badge strapped to the belt around her jeans, and a shoulder holster with a handgun strapped in hanging at her side.

What the fuck is going on that warrants a detective's services?

Maybe there *are* some badass drug dealers living in my building. It's not like I'm the oh-so-social neighbor that gets to know everyone around me. I'm actually quite the opposite.

Or...maybe something gang related went down.

Though I've never noticed anyone around here that looks the part. Not that looks determine character, but still...

What the fuck!?

Looking over my shoulder and down the street toward Tommy's truck, I open my eyes exaggeratedly wide and shrug my shoulders. I can't quite see them, but I'm sure with all the lights nearby they must see me and my attempted expression of worry and curiosity. At least I *hope* that's what it looks like.

I turn back toward the building just as another suit steps out of the front door behind the two officers. This one's a short and stocky dude with a puffy afro, and he's wearing an actual suit, not a Debra Morgan jean-suit like his mile-high partner. (The idea of *Dexter* flashes in my mind, as well as a whole mess of crazy images of what type of crime scene might be in my building to investigate. A chill runs through me.) This detective's frantically writing on a small notepad, barely giving himself enough time to glance up and acknowledge the cops guarding the front door as he passes by. They all nod at one another, then he scurries down the steps to catch up with the other detective. She's at the crime scene tape talking to the EMTs waiting on the other side. When he catches up, she holds the tape up for him to walk under. She lets it drop back down so she can step over it. Still talking to the EMTs, she turns and points up to the officers on the porch of my building.

I slow my stride even more, not wanting to interrupt.

Then the front door swings open again. Two men in white lab coats, carrying what look like bulky briefcases, step out onto the porch next to the two officers.

Okay, now this situation has gone from curious to holy-fuck-curiouser.

Not good. Not good *at all*. Like the presence of the ambulance wasn't bad enough.

Detectives and lab techs...Am I *really* in an episode of *Dexter*?

Shit! Jill, home all alone, must be freaking the fuck out right now, wondering where I am. But there's no way in hell I'm going to reach into my pocket for my cell to text her right now. That shit will get me shot for sure, though I don't even know if I've been spotted by anyone of authority yet.

The lab techs trot down the steps and then hold up the crime scene tape at the bottom. They both nod for the EMTs to move on through to do their work.

Weird...I never even noticed the lab guys' vehicles. No van...or whatever the fuck lab techs drive to crime scenes. And no signature unmarked dark sedan for detectives. (What do I know? I've only seen this sort of thing on TV, in movies. You know, like *Dexter*.)

Well, parking in this neighborhood does suck, which is part of the reason why I walk when I can. They must have had to park further up the street.

Stop thinking about parking, space cadet. It doesn't matter what anyone drives. All that matters is they're here and this shit is serious.

Once the EMTs make it up the stairs, I pick up my pace just a bit. When I get to the crime scene tape, the officers are still holding the front door open for the EMTs to get the stretcher through. Their backs face me.

"Excuse me, officers." My voice sounds weak and squeaky.

They halt and spin around to face me.

The tall male officer with the blond goatee takes a couple steps down the stairs and says, "Please move along. It's late. You should get off the streets. Go on home. We've got a lot of work to do here, Miss." The female officer stands just two steps above him, watching my every move. Tufts of short black hair poke out from under the sides of her hat, and her eyes appear so dark they look like black holes peering straight through me.

I raise up my hand with my ID held across my palm. "But

this *is* my home. I live *here*. Is there any way I can get up to my apartment?"

"Bad timing, I'm afraid." The female cop steps down the stairs and stands beside her partner. She glances up at him, shrugs, then looks back at me. Leaning closer, she squints and points her flashlight at my ID. " You see, Dorian, we…

"It's Dory."

"OK, *Dory*, we can't let you through until after the EMTs do what they need to do."

Her partner waves his hand toward the driveway beside my building, the one for the tenants in the neighboring apartment building. "Wait over there, Miss, and we'll let you know when we can allow you through."

"Sure thing." I nod. Then I go over to the driveway.

Good thing I have the cooler in one hand and my ID glued to my other, or I might end up scratching myself bald by the end of this fucked-up night.

Feet fidgeting, I look toward Tommy's truck again. Irie's arm is hanging out the small back window, and I notice her raise her arm up, palm facing the sky—like she's asking what they should do.

I shrug and hold up my index finger, trying not to drop my license.

She gives me a thumbs-up.

Staying still proves impossible as I stand here waiting. My feet won't stop fidgeting. I keep rolling my shoulders, cracking my neck, trying to calm myself down. I want to scratch my head so badly that I just might jump out of my damn skin.

What the hell is going on in there?

Maybe ten minutes or so pass before the front door of my building flings open, and I see an EMT and the end of the stretcher coming through. The first EMT holds and carries the stretcher from the front end, with her hands behind her back and facing forward, while the other comes through the door carrying from the back. The person getting wheeled out is completely covered with a white sheet, even their head.

Not a good sign.

The two officers step to either side of the stairs, out of the pathway to the ambulance.

The first EMT makes it almost all the way to the bottom when her foot slips off the second to last step, sending the stretcher bouncing down the final two steps and tipping slightly to the side. The EMT up the stairs tries holding on tight, tries correcting it, but the patient slips to the side of the stretcher, partially out from under the sheet.

The sight makes me freeze.

My heart revs up and I lose my breath.

My mouth drops open as soon as I notice—

Long blonde tufts of spiraled hair spill out from under the sheet and dangle over the edge of the stretcher.

It can't be. It just *can't* be.

The cooler drops from my hand. I rub my eyes.

Turns out I'm not hallucinating.

The long blonde spirals of hair remain, swaying like pendulums as the EMTs roll the stretcher over the brick sidewalk toward the flung open back doors of the ambulance.

Holy batshit fucked-up night!

I run toward the ambulance.

As soon as I get a few feet away, that's when I see the face, still not covered back up. I can only see the profile, with a blood trail from the corner of her mouth, but it's now undeniable—

That's Jill!

There's a scream inside of me trying to get out, but all I can do is cry and repeat, "No. No. No." over and over and over again, as I leap toward the stretcher to give Jill one last hug.

CHAPTER 13
OPENING A DOOR

"Call 911! We need an ambulance!" Sitting on the edge of the bed with the patient's sliced-open arm on her lap, Mary yells over her shoulder to anyone within earshot.

"What happened?" Rick skids around the corner, the first of Mary's co-workers to reach the open doorway.

"Not sure. Darren's arm is sliced open and he's out cold. It looks *really* bad. I'm afraid he might lose too much blood." The gloves hanging out of her pants pocket fall on the floor as she frantically fumbles to grab them. Sniffling, she leans down to pick them up. That's when she sees the shank lying on the floor beside them.

"Go call 911. We've got this," Nurse Taylor says to one of the psych techs in the hall behind her as she steps around Rick and into the patient's room. The instant she sees all the blood, she rushes closer, tears the blanket off the patient's legs and uses it to try to slow the bleeding. "What happened here? And why is there so much blood *already* all over the blanket?"

Mary's anxious words rush out of her mouth like an avalanche, information boulders hitting hard and piling high. "Not sure about *anything*. He won't wake up but he's got a pulse. For some reason his mouth is all smeared in blood. Maybe he wiped his mouth with a bloody hand? I don't know.

When I came to see why I heard a door slam, I found his shut and *no one* on twenty-four-hour watch. I was immediately worried. He must've passed out after slamming the door, I guess. The blanket was only covering his legs—not sure about the blood all over it. I didn't move the blanket *at all*. And there's *that*." With watery eyes, Mary points with a shaky hand at the shiv lying on the floor bedside the bed as she struggles to slip her gloves on.

With her gloved hand, Nurse Tylor leans down and picks up the shiv. "Why would he wait until after cutting himself to slam the door?" Her brow furrows as she inspects the shiv. "It would make more sense to shut the door before doing something risky like that. And why is there no blood on this thing?" With pursed lips, Nurse Taylor rolls the shiv around in her palm while shaking her head, then immediately looks back to the wounded arm. "And why slice the *back* of the forearm? Why not just re-open the old wound? I've never seen this sort of suicide attempt in all my years as a psych nurse."

Mary lifts Darren's arm slightly and slides aside, allowing the head nurse closer access to care for the wound. There's blood all over the tech's baby blue cloud-covered scrubs. She remains close and helps slow the bleeding with a portion of the patient's blanket.

"This is deep," the nurse says with widened eyes. "He needs stitches and I need supplies." She turns and looks over her shoulder. "Rick, grab me any and all towels from the bathroom."

"Sure thing."

She looks back to Mary. "Thank you for helping. The slice is so long I wouldn't be able to hold this tight enough on my own. We're definitely going to need a tourniquet to slow the bleeding while we wait for the ambulance to get here."

The other two psych techs are standing in the doorway awaiting instructions.

"I'm going to need more towels and a first aid kit. You two,"

Nurse Taylor says over her shoulder to the techs at the door, "go grab a bunch of clean towels from the janitor's closet."

They both nod. Just as they turn to go, they bump into the new nurse approaching behind them. "Excuse us," is all one of them says as they rush off down the hallway to fulfill their task.

Strolling around the corner into the doorway, Nurse Freyja finally arrives on the scene. "Oh my. How can I help?" Wearing a shocked expression, she remains in the doorway away from the blood.

"You can bring me the first aid kit. Go! Before Darren bleeds to death." Only a quick glance comes from Nurse Taylor as her and Mary continue trying to slow the bleeding with the thin blanket.

"Oh, of course. You can count on me. I'll be back in two shakes of a Persian kitten's whiskers." She marionettes a smile then turns and disappears down the hall.

Rick steps out of the patient's bathroom and hands Nurse Taylor one small hand towel. "Sorry. This was the biggest and only one. Suicide watch and all."

With gritted teeth and a grimace, Nurse Taylor shakes her head when she sees the towel. "This will have to do for now." With an outstretched arm she holds the shiv out on the palm of her hand toward Rick. "Go put this in a Ziplock baggie, please." With her eyes focused on his, she sternly says, "Make sure it's in a spot where *no one* can touch it. We'll need that for the police."

As his gloved hand plucks the nuthouse knife from her palm, his face crinkles with confusion. "Police?"

As she's now holding the towel tightly over the gushing wound, she throws a quick glance at Mary, then looks back to Rick. "Just in case. We can't be certain this is Darren's handiwork." She looks back to Mary. "He's out cold. And you said you came here *immediately*, right?"

A wide-eyed Mary nods, sniffles, wipes her nose on her sleeve.

Rick still stands close by, leaning in and listening intently to what comes next.

With eyebrows raised, Nurse Taylor says, "I have a strong suspicion this young man couldn't have been the one who slammed that door."

"Then who could've done it?" Mary and Rick ask at the same time.

"That's a damn good question. And take a look at his other hand there." With a nod toward the other side of the bed, she adds, "No blood. How could he make this slice without getting blood all over the hand that did the carving and all over this makeshift knife. Yeah, he could've wiped them off on the blanket, but if you're going to commit a messy suicide, you're not going to try to wash the blood off your hands and the weapon. No bloody hand brings up another question—how did the blood get smeared across his mouth? With the hand attached to *this* arm?" She smirks and glances down at the blood-soaked blanket covering the gushing wound. "I highly doubt it. And, as I already said, I've never seen a suicide-slice on this part of the arm where a bleed-out would take longer. People who commit suicide want it over and done with as soon as possible—unless it's a cry for help rather than a desire to die."

She throws a look to Rick again. "After you tuck that there shank away where others won't see it, go ahead and do room checks *now*. Doing them a little early—maybe you'll catch someone off guard."

A sly smile spreads across Rick's face. "You got it." He turns to go, but before he leaves the room, he looks over his shoulder and says with a wink, "I like the way you think."

"Yeah, yeah. Go. Now! Or the room checks won't be early." A quiet and nervous laugh comes from the unsmiling nurse whose uniform is now covered in blood.

———

He peeks into the first three rooms, the only others with their doors opened, to see if the other three high-risk patients are awake. This room check is going to be tougher than most. Mary's screams and the commotion of finding Darren may have woken many patients. The ones that did wake could also appear nervous, wondering what's going on that warranted a scream for 911. So, what exactly should he be looking for?

Blood.

He hopes that if anyone else is guilty of what happened to Darren, they'll show some kind of obvious signs, but what those signs may look like is a mystery. The only one certainty is if he finds blood.

Just as he'd thought, the three suicide-watch patients all lie awake in their beds. With their doors open and their rooms so close to Darren's, it's no wonder why they woke. Who wouldn't wake after that screaming? All three wide-eyed patients have their blanket pulled up to their necks, like it could block out everything going on around them.

This room check may not do anything to help.

Rick assures each of the three patients, "Just want you to know everything is under control. You can go back to sleep now." He walks away with an ache of sympathy in his chest.

At each of the remaining patients' rooms, Rick gives a soft knock on the closed doors before opening them to check on everyone. Just as he'd worried—everyone lies awake.

"Just coming by to tell you that everything is under control. You can go back to sleep." He gives the same reassurance to every patient when they see him open the door and peek into their room. As he'd expected, with everyone awake and looking worried, noticing signs of a potentially guilty person proves difficult. But one thing does help.

On the inside edge of the door to Gary's room Rick notices a smudge of what looks like blood. He can't miss it. It's at face-level to Rick when he peeks in. Intentionally avoiding any visible reaction to it, he just makes a mental note. He gives Gary the same reassurance he gave to everyone else. After nodding, Gary rolls over and faces the wall.

As soon as he gets back to Darren's room, Rick sees the two towel-fetching psych techs standing at the door. He squeezes past them into the room. Nurse Taylor and Mary now use fresh towels to tend to the patient's wound.

Still no first aid kit and no sign of Nurse Freyja in sight. Maybe she's on the phone with 911. If so, why not send the first aid kit back with a psych tech?

"You guys," Nurse Taylor nods at the two psych techs at the door, "one of you go find out where Nurse Freyja is with that first aid kit, and one of you wait for the EMTs to arrive. When they do, bring 'em here." Her ability to stay so calm during such a drastic situation certainly shows her many years of psychiatric nursing experience.

Both psych techs nod. "You got it," says the taller one.

As soon as the techs make it down the hall and out of earshot, Rick eases the door closed and quietly tells Nurse Taylor about the potential blood on the door to Gary's room.

She looks at Mary. "That's probably why it sounded like Darren's door slammed. Gary's right next door. And being in the next room makes for a very quick escape." She spins back to face Rick. "Does he know you saw it?"

"I don't think so. And I never said a word about it."

With a nod, she says, "Good. Go call the police. Do it from the bathroom or somewhere no one will hear you. I don't want anyone else knowing we suspect foul play. Got it?"

He gives her a salute. "Yes, Ma'am. Hide the shiv. Call the fuzz. I'm on it."

CHAPTER 14
LETTING GO

Warmth still emanates from her body. Not much. But enough to make this all feel unreal.

Just like when I found Mom.

My sobbing intensifies.

It's so hard to believe that she's not here. It's just a body. Jill's body—with no Jill. How can that even be? How can she be gone? She was in there before I left and now she's not.

Where is she?

Grasping her hand, I squeeze tightly. She doesn't squeeze back.

Just like when I found Mom.

Jill's fingers have not yet stiffened. They dangle limp, pointing down...like a head hung low from disappointment.

Dammit!

If I hadn't run off to play detective, she would still be alive.

I don't want to let her go. After lifting my head from her silent chest, I brush her hair out of her face and kiss her on the cheek.

Her mouth hangs slightly open. Lips have turned pale. Emptiness stares back at me from her once laughing eyes. No more twinkle. No more private jokes.

Just as I rest my head back on her motionless chest, someone tugs on me from behind. I resist, holding onto Jill tighter.

"Miss, move away from the body *now*." A man's deep, stern voice comes from behind me.

"It's not a-a-a *body*," I stutter through sobs. "Her name is Jill and she's my best *fucking* f-f-friend." Anger boils up from inside of me but I'm unable to yell.

I just don't want to let go. Ever.

Now I feel Jill's hand getting cold. My grip tightens, as though I can somehow squeeze the life and warmth back into her.

Yeah, it doesn't make sense. Clear thinking eludes me right now.

"Miss, the lab still needs to collect evidence from the body, and right now, you're potentially messing with that. Move away *now*."

The guy behind me lets go of my shoulder. Then he immediately reaches around me with both his hands, grabs my arms, and pries me off from Jill's dead body.

"Get your fucking hands off from me! That's my best friend. Let me go!" Screaming and frantic, I wriggle and twist to get free. I'm ready to spit daggers, until the man spins me around to face him, and I see...

He's in uniform.

A damn cop.

"Miss, I suggest you get a grip on yourself before I cuff you, take you to the station, and charge you with assaulting a police officer."

Before he finishes his threat, I've already stopped resisting. With him holding my arms tight to the sides of my body, I can't wipe my eyes. Blurry vision, runny nose, I can't see Tommy's truck down the street. Where did they go? Did they leave already? Shit.

"You say the victim here is your friend?" He releases his

hold on my arms and pulls a notepad and a pen out of his jacket pocket, aims, ready to write.

Stuttering and having a hard time catching my breath, I manage to say, "Yes, and she's my roommate." Finally able to wipe my eyes, I now see Tommy and Irie still sit parked and waiting right where I'd left them.

"Your roommate, huh? Well, miss, what's your name and where were you this evening? And what brings you home at such a late hour, conveniently missing the brutal murder of your best friend?"

I freeze. Breath hitches. *Brutal murder?* "What? Brutal? Holy shit! What happened to her?"

"*You* tell me. What's your name and where were you?"

What the fuck?! Mind frantic, I blurt out, "Dory. I'm Dory. I was just out with a couple friends. They're still parked right down there. See?" Pointing to Tommy's truck, I add, "If you don't believe me, you can go ask them yourself."

With a head nod, he signals me to lead the way. "Good idea. Let's go see these other *friends* of yours, Dory."

This motherfucker better not start thinking *I'm* a suspect, though I've got a sinking feeling that's exactly what's going on here.

Dammit! I can't go getting in trouble with the law again. Not with those court dates coming up. Fuck me running! How do I manage to fuck shit up all the time?

As we step up to Tommy's truck, the passenger side window rolls down. The passenger seat still sits empty, probably still warm from my stupid ass. Irie's confused expression appears between the front seats where she's leaning in from the back. Tommy twists to face us, leans on the armrest console and says, "What's going on? Is everything okay, Dory?"

Seeing their concerned faces side-by-side looking out at me gives me a flicker of hope. A feeling that quickly vanishes.

When I open my mouth the speak, the cop holds his hand up, palm toward me, basically telling me to keep my fucking mouth shut. The officer—I don't even know his name yet—then rests his forearm on the door, leans down to look inside, and laughs. "So, this riff-raff's your alibi? Huh...Dory?" He glances back at me over his shoulder. "You were hanging out with *these* two and that's supposed to make me feel better, convince me you weren't up to something...unsavory?"

"What are you talking about? This is Tommy and Irie. I've been with them all night. They just drove me..."

There's his hand again, palm in my face.

Biting my tongue is proving really difficult right now. What the hell is this guy's problem?

He stands back upright and hauls open the back passenger side door. "Both of you...out...Now! We're *all* going to take a little trip down to the station, find out what you were *really* up to tonight, while your pretty young *friend* was brutally slaughtered."

Both Tommy and Irie's eyes widen and mouths drop open as they look at me in shock.

———

Uncomfortable silence surrounds us on the ride to the station. Nothing but my stuttered breathing fills the void of unspoken words, as I try not to turn into a complete blubbering mess again. Rhythmic tapping on my thighs and my feet on the floorboards helps distract me from crying for the duration of the short drive.

Officer Davenport, the dickhead cop who disrespected us all, insisted Tommy and Irie ride to the station with him, and he told me to ride with Officer Blaine. He obviously thinks we'll try to *get our stories straight* if we spend any time together before they question us. Not sure how the hell that could've happened while in the back of a cruiser. But whatever.

Officer Blaine hasn't said one word to me. Thankfully, it's a short drive. As we pull into the parking lot of the police station, he finally says, "We're here."

Like I couldn't figure that one out myself, genius.

Blaine steps out of the cruiser, opens the back door for me, and escorts me inside.

Walking behind the Officer through the busy police station, it seems like it's the middle of the day rather than four in the morning. I had no idea they were this busy at such an early hour. Several desks are occupied with officers tapping away at their computers. Inside an office with its door flung open, a meeting of about five or six suited men sit gathered around an oblong table.

"Have a seat." Officer Blaine motions toward a plastic chair with a cushioned seat outside of a closed office door.

I sit.

He knocks on the door beside me. The brass plaque above the shaded window says *Detective Landry*. A few seconds of silence pass before he reaches his fist out to knock again. A female voice halts his hand, saying, "Come on in."

As he opens the door and steps inside, I see Officer Davenport manhandling Tommy and Irie into the station.

Why the hell are they cuffed?

"Stop dragging your feet and get in there already!" That bullheaded deep voice of the officer travels far. He shoves Tommy through the door. His other hand has ahold of Irie's upper arm, tugging her along.

The officer—Officer Dickhead is his new name—pushes Tommy toward a line of five plastic chairs sitting flush against a window-wall lined with offices just inside the door to the station. Tommy sits in the last chair in the line. Irie tries to sit in the seat next to her dad, but Officer Dickhead yanks on her arm and forces her to sit in the chair furthest away from him.

"Yeah, no sitting next to each other trying to get your stories straight. I know how you shifty people work." He turns around, looks across the station, and his eyes immediately land on me.

Maybe he felt my infuriated stare boring holes into the back of his head, as I imagine my combat boot landing real hard against his skull as I curb stomp him.

What the hell is up with them getting cuffed and shoved around and yelled at while this other officer has barely said anything to me and hasn't laid one hand on me at all? Not that I want to get treated like that. Shit. No one wants to get treated like that. That guy has no fucking right! What were Tommy and Irie doing except waiting to make sure I got home safely?

Maybe he's just the asshole officer on the force, giving the rest of them a bad name. Wouldn't be the first time. There's usually at least one prick in every different group of people.

Why did I have to go dragging Tommy and Irie into my mess again? I could've easily gone to stakeout a cemetery by myself.

Or, Dory-with-revenge-on-the-brain, you could've not gone to stakeout a cemetery at all. Then Jill would still be alive, and Tommy and Irie wouldn't be getting treated like criminals just for existing.

Tommy catches eye contact with me, smiles that crooked smile and winks. Irie raises her chin toward me, saying *Hi* with the movement. Then she shrugs, shifts her cuffed arms a bit to the side to show me she also has no idea why they're cuffed.

Huh…Looks like now I know *exactly* why Officer Dickhead cuffed them. No way Irie would've done that if something had happened on the way to the station that caused the cuffing. That is, nothing but the color of their skin.

Officer Dickhead starts talking to a cop sitting at a desk nearby. I can't hear his words, but I see him nod his head towards Tommy and Irie. In response the officer nods, shuts his laptop, rests his hands on top of the computer, and sits staring at them. With his eyes now riveted on me, Officer Dickhead starts walking across the station in my direction.

Officer Blaine steps back out from Detective Landry's office and ushers me to follow him down the hallway to my left, saving me from needing to interact with the racist motherfucker headed my way.

———

With Detective Landry following a few steps behind us, Officer Blaine leads us down the hallway, almost to the end. On the right at the far end of the hall, he opens a door to an interrogation room. He flicks on an overhead fluorescent light so bright I squint to adjust my eyes. One small, rectangular table sits in the center with one chair placed on either side. A large mirror faces me when I step inside, obviously the one-way window for others to observe from behind. I've watched enough cop show dramas to know there's a real good chance at least one person is on the other side of that mirror watching and listening. I make it a point to look away, not wanting to see how shitty I must look.

Detective Landry steps out from behind me and circles around to the table. As she pulls out the chair that faces the door on the opposite side, she looks over at me. "Hello, Dorian, I'm…"

"It's Dory. Just Dory."

"Well, hello Dory, I'm Detective Landry. Please, have a seat." She motions to the empty chair a few feet in front of me.

I remain silent, pull out the chair.

"Officer Blaine, if you'll excuse us, I can take it from here. And please tell Detective Morris which room we're in. Thank you."

"Sure thing."

I hear the door click shut behind me as I sit down.

And with that, I now sit alone with the detective on the case of my murdered best friend and roommate. I don't think I'm ready for this.

"Just so you know, it'll only be the two of us in here. Detective Morris, my partner, he won't be joining us. He's conferring with the lab and crime scene photographer, though he may pop in before we're done here."

My hand reflexively moves to my head, wanting so desperately to scratch. The bandana tied around my head reminds me to stop the anxious tic. Knee bouncing so fast it feels like the room is rumbling, or maybe that's just my nerves, I try tapping out rhythms on my leg to relax myself.

It doesn't work.

On the table in front of the detective sits a pad of paper and a pen. I feel her staring at me, but my eyes seem to want to look everywhere except at her. I know she's about to start grilling me with a ton of questions any moment, but the lump in my throat is so big, I don't know if I'll be able to push any words out. If I look her in the eye and start talking about…Fuck! I can't even *think* her name let alone speak it…the dam is sure to burst open.

"So, Dory, Officer Blaine tells me the victim was your room-mate and best friend. Is that correct?"

Victim? Doesn't get much more impersonal than that.

I nod.

"But you weren't at home tonight. Where were you and what were you doing that kept you out so late?" Picking up her pen, she flips the notepad open and prepares to write.

Hesitating, I wonder how much to tell her about what we were doing tonight. Will she think I'm crazy? Will she think *we're* some of the graverobbers trying to get others busted to take the cops' eyes off us? Worried my words will come out all wrong, not to mention the fear of drowning in my own tears if I start talking, I take a stuttering deep breath and remain silent.

"Why can't you look at me, Dory? Feeling guilty about something? Maybe you're afraid you'll say the wrong thing, get yourself busted?" She pauses. After setting her pen down, she leans forward, elbows on the table. "If you're not going to talk, I'm sure Officer Davenport can bring your friends down here and I can get it all out of them. Is that what you want? You want to get more of your friends in trouble?"

What the hell is this bitch's problem? I just saw my best friend's dead body. Just found out she was murdered while I wasn't home. Does she not realize why I can't and don't want to talk right now? It's not like I've had any time to process this shit yet. Man, I just want to fucking scream right now.

Forcing another stuttered deep breath, I realize I've got to say something, even if just to help keep Tommy and Irie out of my bullshit.

What the fuck should I tell her? I can't say we were at that cemetery. She'll think we were in on it and just took off quicker than the ones who got busted. But if I don't say anything she'll think I had something to do with what happened to…Shit! I can't fucking think straight. I don't want to be here right now. Can I just hit the rewind button, go back to singing Nirvana in my living room with…

"Okay, looks like you don't want to help us find Jill's killer, which must mean…"

There it is and here they come. Tears. Well, not really. More like rushing rapids gushing down my cheeks as I turn into a blubbering mess.

"I never should've left. She told me not to go. She said it wasn't safe. *She* was worried for *me*. I should've been there for her. Maybe I could've stopped it. Maybe I could've saved her. Maybe I could've…"

"*Why* was Jill worried for you, Dory? *Where* didn't she want you to go?"

"I shouldn't've left her alone."

While wiping my nose on the sleeve of my hoodie, Detective Landry catches eye contact with me. Her deep stare freezes me. "Where were you tonight, Dory? Why was Jill worried about *you*, but *she* ended up dead? Stop keeping secrets. What did you do tonight, Dory? I can see the guilt all over your face. I suggest you spill now, or you and your friends will have a long twenty-four hours in holding cells while you think about what you've done."

Uh, yeah, I'm pretty sure what's all over my face are tears, you fucking genius. My friend just got fucking killed, and this bitch sees my tears as evidence of guilt? And she wants to lock me up right after I just came home to find my best friend murdered? This chick's got a heart of god damn nails. Rusty nails.

Shit. I can't let Tommy and Irie get locked up because of me. Fuck!

This stare down needs to end. I can't take those eyes boring holes into my skull, watching my every twitch and tear.

"My friends out there, Tommy and Irie," I point a thumb over my shoulder toward the door and the station outside it. Then, I need to take another deep, stuttering breath before continuing. "We were staking out a cemetery, watching for graverobbers so we could get them busted." I sit up straighter, lean on the table to emphasize my point. "And we did. We got four graverobbers busted up in…"

"Whoa, whoa, whoa. Slow down. So, you're telling me you and those other two out there were out all hours of the night playing amateur detectives? Looking for graverobbers? Really?"

"Yes. That's exactly what we were doing. Call and check for yourself. Tommy, check his cell. He called 911 and reported it. We were sitting in his truck across the street from Hillcrest Cemetery in the Little League field parking lot. We saw the Staties come and arrest all four of them. There's a trail. You can check for yourself." She doesn't look convinced. "Seriously. Check. Tommy's. Phone. He made the call anonymously, but it should still be in his call log with a time stamp. You can check the time stamp. You can check when dispatch received the call. You know…evidence and shit…you're the detective. I'm *not* lying."

"Okay, I hear what you're saying. I do." Detective Landry sets her pen down, leans back against her chair, folds her arms across her chest. "But if what you say is true, what I don't understand is why the hell do you guys care? Why risk your own safety to watch for graverobbers? It's not like you're bored teenagers looking for a rush. Were you protecting your own family's plot or something? Help me understand this, because right now, from where I'm sitting, it all smells like a desperate crock of shit."

Man, she's right. It does sound like a lie. Story of my fucking life! Usually when people hear about the shit I've been through and the shit I've seen, they always look shocked, in disbelief, like I'm some drama queen or delusional or just someone looking for an exciting story to tell. Shit. I *wish* it was all make-believe.

How do I tell her more without her thinking the same thing? What if she wants to lock me back up in the psych hospital? No way in hell will I let that shit happen again! Nope, not getting a bunch of unneeded head-meds shoved down my throat everyday again. Nope. No more getting locked up in the padded room for telling the truth about those Duster psychos trying to carve me open.

Man, my life sucks!

"Well, holding cells it is." She stands up so abruptly her chair scrapes and squeals across the linoleum floor.

"No, wait." I reach across the table, slap my palm against the surface. "We know who's digging up all the graves."

Notebook in hand, she freezes as she's reaching for her pen. "You do?" Brow furrowed, eyes squinty, the mile-high detective with legs as long as half of my entire self, stares down at me, watching my every breath and blink.

"We call them Dusters, or Bone Cutters. And the first time I ever found out about them was just a few weeks ago when I was in Silver Springs Psychiatric Hospital. The same hospital where Tommy and Irie work as janitors." All the details spill out of me. Everything. Well, at least everything from tonight.

She immediately sits back down. Her pen flies across her notepad at an incredible speed as I'm speaking.

Does that mean she believes me?

Though her hand keeps writing after I stop speaking, she somehow manages to pull a packet of tissues out of her suit jacket pocket and tosses them to me. I catch them in the air like a pitcher on the mound. While wiping my tear-soaked face, I wonder just how shitty I must look. No doubt, my mascara and eyeliner must be smeared all over my face by now. And at this time of the morning, and having not slept at all, the dark circles must look quite evident under my eyes. But I don't even know why I care about that right now.

She shuts her notebook and sets the pen down as she says, "I've taken down your story so I can check up on a few things, but I will need you to fill out an official statement in your own words. Do you understand?"

I nod while blowing my nose.

"I'll be right back."

All alone now, all I keep wondering is why.

Why would anyone want to kill Jill? She's always so happy and friendly. I can't imagine she could've pissed anyone off enough to make them want to kill her.

And though I don't want to think about it, I can't help but wonder how. How did they kill her? Why do I even want to know? I don't know, but...

About ten or so minutes later, Detective Landry comes back into the room with a couple sheets of paper for me to write up my statement. As she pulls a pen out of her jacket pocket, I blurt out, "What really happened to Jill?" I have to pause a second, catch my breath. "I mean, how did they do it? And *why*? Why her? She was always the life of the party. The happy smiley one of the bunch, the light up a room kinda gal. Why the hell would anyone want to..."

Rather than handing the pen and blank papers to me, Detective Landry pulls out the chair and sits down again. Looking down at the papers she just sat on the table in front of her, she pauses a moment, adjusts her suit jacket, shifts in her seat, obviously trying to figure out how to say whatever she's about to say.

"Look, Dory. I pulled up your record, and…I'm not so sure it's a good idea for me to…"

"Please, I need to know what happened to her. I need to know why. You've gotta understand, Jill was my best friend. You pulled up my record, so you know—I got blue-papered in the fucking psych hospital trying to save her from what I *thought* was a rapist. And I wasn't home this time to try to save her. *Please*, tell me."

She folds her arms on the table and leans forward towards me. Just before the words come out of her mouth, she cocks her head to the side as though they're difficult for her to say. "Actual cause of death is yet to be determined, but my assumption is that she bled to death. What I *can* tell you for *certain*—Jill was carved open on both of her shoulder blades, and for whatever twisted reason, the killer chiseled away at her bones." She pauses but very briefly. When she starts talking again, it sounds like thoughts she'd say to her partner rather than me. "What I want to know is, why are there no signs of a struggle? How did the killer manage to do that to her without Jill fighting back?" The instant her eyes meet my intense stare of curiosity and shock, she bites her lip as though biting back any more words that may fly out at me. It's obvious she doesn't want to tell me anymore and that she may have divulged more information than she'd intended.

Maybe because she now notices my face contorted with sorrow, disbelief…and guilt.

Now I understand *why* Jill was killed.

Her stare intensifies as she says, "Well, all that might make more sense if Jill *knew* her attacker."

Oh, no she didn't! Dammit. I'm still a suspect?

Before I realize what I'm doing, the words slip past my lips. "The killer was after me."

Eyebrows raised, she turns her head to the side and leans her left ear toward me. "What was that?"

Before her last word comes out, more waterworks pour down my face. The idiot label is definitely a perfect fit for me. I'm the one that's supposed to be dead right now—not Jill. If I hadn't run off to play *Catch a Criminal*, Jill would still be alive. Or, better yet, if Jill hadn't been the oh-so-accepting-friend and welcomed psycho-me back into the apartment, she'd still be alive.

Any way I look at it, that baseball bat fiasco was basically me smashing my life to pieces.

That's what got me blue-papered in the psych hospital.

That's what put me in the Bone Cutters crosshairs.

That's what made me blinded by revenge.

That's what got Jill killed.

"I am the one to blame. The killer was after me."

Detective Landry pulls out her notepad from her inside jacket pocket. With her pen at the ready she asks, "What makes you think that?"

It all pours out of me. As I tell her everything that happened at the hospital with the Bone Cutters that were after me and about the murder of Tommy's wife Kaya seven years ago, her pen fills three more pages in her notepad. That doesn't surprise me at all. I'm actually a bit shocked she didn't fill up more pages.

There's no expression of shock or skepticism on her face as I give her all the details. Not the slightest hint of amazement at my story about getting chased by a bunch of Bone Cutters who wanted to carve me open, scrape my bones, and get high off my bone dust. No surprise about Kaya's murder—Dusters chiseling her bones in front of her restrained husband until she finally bled out and died, all while their daughter, Irie, hid in a closet and saw the whole thing. Rather than any sign of disbelief, Landry just nods along with everything I tell her, as her hand races to keep up with me.

My talking ends.

Landry's writing ends a moment after.

She flips back to the first page of notes she's written. Then she sets the notes aside and looks at me with an *aha* sort of expression.

Her reaction surprises me. Maybe she already heard word about all this around the precinct after we'd baited Sheila and got her arrested for attacking me in the hospital. I don't know, but that is definitely not the reaction I expected.

"Well, from the sounds of it, you sure have been through a hell of a time, Dory, and it also sounds like you really *were* surprised by what happened tonight. Thank you for telling all of this to me. Believe me when I tell you—it's a *huge* help. Now I know *why* the bones were chiseled *and* why remains are getting stolen from the cemeteries." A slight laugh slips out. "And here we thought they stuck to the old graves because the cement vaults the caskets are in for newer graves are near *impossible* to break into. Wait until Morris hears it's the formaldehyde they're avoiding." A grimace of disgust appears on her face as she mumbles, "Fucking sickos are everywhere."

My bouncing knee halts. I love hearing people of authority breakdown and curse. It shows they're just like us.

"It's called 'dusting,'" I tell her. "Those 'sickos' want the bone dust. They crave it just like any hard drug. It reminds me of cocaine, but I hear it's like heroin. I've also heard it has a *very* high street value."

"Well, that's strange, because there was also a strange white powdery residue on Jill's pillow. We had assumed the killer was all hopped up on drugs already. But now you tell me they're after drugs when they do this?"

I nod.

"Hmm..." She turns away for a moment, as though in deep thought.

Waiting for her to tell me more or ask me more or both, I wipe my tear-soaked cheeks on the sleeve of my hoodie in an attempt to appear more well put together, in control. A minute or so passes, though it feels much longer.

Detective Landry's shoulders hike up toward her ears as she takes in a long, deep breath. She glances over my head toward the door, then she looks back at me and says, "There was another case a couple weeks ago, one somewhat like Jill's. It was another bone chiseling incident. But the perpetrator actually took the time to stitch the victim back up. And the victim *didn't* die, which shows that the intention in that particular case *wasn't* murder. And it was staged to look as though it was self-inflicted."

"Staged?"

"The knife was found in the victim's hand with only *his* fingerprints, but the thread and needle used to stitch up the wound...nowhere to be found." A tight-lipped laugh escapes her.

She shakes her head. Under her breath, she mumbles, "Idiot." Then she adds, "The victim also had ligature marks on his wrists and ankles—another detail different from Jill's case."

Pausing, she leans back in her chair and turns away again in deep thought, but only for a moment.

Her head whips toward me, then she sits up bolt-straight. "There was also none of that powdery residue found at the scene of the other attack." Her eyes roll up toward the ceiling as she adds, "Why the differences, I wonder?"

As soon as the words come out, she looks at me with surprise. "I only share this with you because you might have some answers to my questions, since you've had more experience dealing with these types than me or any of my colleagues have." Another pause, like she's wondering if she should tell me anymore.

She does.

"If you think *that* case is strange, it only gets stranger," Landry continues. "The victim in that case was busted at one of the graveyards that was hit by vandals; he was caught running away with a bag of bones. He still refuses to answer the question of why he stole them. But now, thanks to you, I *know* why. Hearing what happened to you in the hospital with these 'Bone Cutters' and what they did to your friend's wife, I finally have more of an understanding about these crazy crimes. I still don't know the *whole why*, but with this very crucial information you've provided me with, maybe now my partner and I can finally bust the perps once and for all."

She starts sliding the blank papers across the table. "I will still need you to write up a…"

The door of the interrogation room flies open and slams into the wall. Landry instantly jumps to her feet. I duck and spin around at the same time, unsure what the hell is going on.

What the fuck?!

My alcoholic neighbor stumbles toward the table, holding out his cell phone. He's yelling something, but I can't understand one single word of his gibberish.

Right behind him comes Detective Morris. "Clayton, stop." He rushes in and grabs the guy by his shoulders, then he yanks his arms behind his back, but not before the guy drops his cell on top of the blank forms Landry was handing to me to write up my statement.

I jump out of my seat and move aside as Detective Morris slams my neighbor down onto the table. He leans down near Clayton's ears. "Do I need to cuff you, or are you going to calm down and present what you have to show us in a calm and civilized manner?"

"Morris, what's this all about? I'm in the middle of an interrogation! Why is this man in here?" Irritation and rage appear on Landry's face. With a pinched brow, multiple frown lines stretch across her forehead, and the flush of her cheeks grows redder and redder.

"Sorry. This is Clayton. He lives in the same building where the murder…"

"Ask *her*! She knows me!" The belligerent drunk starts wiggling all around, trying to look at Landry and me.

Morris yanks on Clayton's arms. "That's enough. Calm down. I'll tell you when it's your turn to talk." He looks up at Detective Landry. "Sorry. I was just bringing him down here to show you something. Something I didn't want to show *anyone* else before you see it." He yanks on Clayton's arms again. "Settle down, Clayton…He stormed into the station claiming to have seen the killer. Told me he's her neighbor." Morris looks to me. "You know this guy?"

I shake my head. That drunk may live in my building, but I don't know him. I didn't even know his name until he barged in here acting all crazy.

Morris yanks on Clayton's arms again, starts hauling him up off the table. "You lied to me? Why'd you…"

"No, wait!" I hold up my hand in a stop gesture and step toward them. "He *does* live in my building, right down the hall from me. But I don't know him. We've never actually met before."

The expression on Morris's face softens. "Okay, so he didn't lie about *that*. Good." He looks back down at Clayton. "Now, Clayton, if you can remain calm, I will release your arms, and then we can show Detective Landry what you showed me. Can you do that, Clayton? Can you remain calm?"

Clayton just nods his head. His long greasy bangs flop in his face and sway with the frantic movements.

"I need to hear it, Clayton. I need to hear you say it. If I release your arms, will you remain calm?" Morris looks up at Landry, rolls his eyes and shakes his head.

"Yes, I'll stay calm."

Slowly and carefully, Detective Morris releases Clayton's arms and takes a couple steps back.

Straightening up, Clayton adjusts his wrinkled t-shirt, making sure his beer gut stays covered. He runs his twitchy hand through his bangs, slicks them back out of his face, then he snatches his phone from the table. After wiping his veiny purple-tinged nose with the back of his forearm, his words start flying out from between his sweaty lips in rapid fire succession. "I saw them. The killah. I was on the roof. I saw. Ovah the edge of the building. The killah went out the window. On the fi'e escape. I heard a scream. But an outside scream."

Clayton's cheeks have moved through three shades of red during his short tirade, finally settling on drunken-rage-red. The beer stink burns my nostrils. I can't take this drunk's bullshit right now. How can he have any idea what the fuck he saw, when I know damn well he's been drunk since happy hour *yesterday*?

For some reason, he continues waving his phone around while he's talking, trying to emphasize his point somehow. "I neva' heard anything befo'e that scream. It was so loud. I couldn't igno'e it. But then…when I looked ovah the edge, it wasn't just the killah…There was something else…Some giant *bird* or some shit swooped right down. Giant clawed feet grabbed her. More screaming. Then it flew away…*with* the killah. And I caught it all on my phone."

"A giant fucking *bird*?!" Irritated laughter leaks out of me as I step forward and hold my hand up for him to shut his inebriated fucking mouth. "Okay there, Clayton. Is that your name? We don't have time to hear about your drunken hallucinations. What were you even doing on the roof at three in the fucking morning anyway? Trying to capture UFO footage? Ha! Maybe it wasn't really a giant bird, Clayton. Maybe it was an alien and it beamed them up into its spaceship." More sarcastic laughter. It's all I can do to keep from backhanding this fucker for wasting our time.

"How'd you know?" His hazy, bloodshot eyes widen. "Yeah, I was trying to capture a UFO sighting. They've been all ovah the news. All ovah Maine. But no, it wasn't an alien. It looked *kinda* like a bird. But it looked mo'e like…When you look closah, it looks like…" He holds out his phone toward Detective Landry. "It looks like a huge gahgoyle."

"A fucking *gargoyle*?! Really? Dude…what the fuck?!" I practically choke on my words. A surge of anger rushes through me so fast I worry what I might do to this idiot. I have to look away. My hands move to my bandana-covered head, wanting so desperately to scratch, to do something, anything but pound my fists into this drunk fucker's face repeatedly. But Landry steps up to take control of this scene.

"Clayton, whatever it is you *saw*…" Detective Landry steps between the drunk and me. Hearing her now closer to me, I feel safe to turn back around, knowing she'll stop me should I not be able to resist the urge to pummel this fucker for wasting the detectives' investigation time. Reaching her arm out slowly toward Clayton, she grasps his hand holding his cell. "You say you captured it all on your phone. Correct?"

Clayton nods eagerly, looks at his hand and Landry holding it, and slowly releases his grip on his phone. He lets her take the cell. "It's all on there. See fo'ya'self. Pass code's 1-2-3-4-5-9."

Out of my peripheral, I see Morris shake his head and smirk. "Clayton, I suggest you replace that passcode with one more difficult for hackers to figure out."

With a creased brow and pinched nose, Clayton says, "That's what the nine is for. Throws people off. Makes it toughah." He shrugs as though to say, *You couldn't figure that out?*

No response from Morris. He just shakes his head again, moves closer to Landry to get a closer look at the phone in her hand.

I hear the scream come from the cell. Is that Jill? I move closer to watch the footage with the detectives, but Landry stops the video and drops her phone-wielding hand to her side. She turns to Morris. "Could you grab my laptop? This will be easier to see on a bigger screen."

With a nod, Morris turns away. "Sure thing. Be right back."

About three uncomfortable minutes later, Morris comes back in with a laptop. While he was gone, Landry prepared the video to be sent to her email, while trying to explain to Clayton why he should change is passcode. He still doesn't get it.

"It's almost finished sending to my email. Hopefully once I log on and sign in, it will be there."

Morris sets her laptop on the table, and Landry sits back down in her chair to bring up the video. We gather around behind her to watch over her shoulder.

For the first few seconds the screen remains black with only a few speckles and streams of faint light. Then I hear that scream again. Definitely a woman. The camera angle quickly shifts, sending trippy streams of light streaking across the screen. A bouncy blur of the brick building next to my apartment building zooms past, then the driveway, and then I see the fire escape. The images are shaky, bouncing with Clayton's movements. Then the camera angle moves up, showing the entire length of the fire escape. The shakiness stops. That's when I notice that the image of the woman screaming appears right outside my kitchen window. But what's even more noticeable—slightly above and beside the fire escape hovers a huge *creature*, massive wings flapping over the length of the driveway. It reaches out toward the woman with what looks like a large taloned foot, or maybe a clawed-hand. I can't tell which. Neither the woman nor the creature appears clear enough to identify, and the flapping wings keep covering the screaming woman as the bird-thing keeps shifting around. While the creature is obscured, one detail stands out—red glowing eyes, flickering like flames. Then that scream intensifies as soon as the creature grabs her and flies up and out from between the buildings. It disappears out into the night sky.

My urge to laugh in Clayton's face ceases. I can barely breathe.

"What the fuck *was* that?!" Those eyes. The wings. It reminds me of the image from Dr. Headstrom's camera at the hospital that night I helped set Sheila up, except this creature has black wings, not red. Plus, this one is a hell of a lot bigger.

No one answers me.

The video is so dark and at such a distance, it's difficult to see exactly what the hell that thing could be. And the woman, being so much smaller than the creature and often blocked by its positioning above her, I also can't see what she looks like.

Landry seems to have similar thoughts because she rewinds the video and tries zooming in at various key moments. Nothing appears clearer no matter what Landry does.

When she finally stops and closes the video, Landry laughs an uncomfortable titter. A laugh that never reaches her eyes. "It's like something straight out of the god damn *X-Files*." She looks up at Detective Morris standing to her right. "I see why you brought this straight to me. Thank you."

Tight-lipped and eyebrows arched, Morris nods.

Landry's reaction seems a bit off. Yeah, she seems a little unsettled, even a little shocked, but not as shocked as someone should be after seeing that. And what about Morris? And why is she thankful he brought the video to her first?

What is up with these two? What we just saw…that shit's not normal, not natural, not…Damn! I don't even know what to think right now.

Landry saves the video from her email to her laptop and closes the screen. We all back away when she stands up. Turning around to face Clayton, she says, "Thank you very much for this, Clayton. And thank you for rushing right down here to make sure we have this footage." She glances at Morris and then me, then back to Clayton. "Sorry about not believing you at first. But with the claims you were making, I'm sure you understand."

Hands twitching at his sides, Clayton says, "Oh, yeah, I *know* I sounded crazy, but I just had to make sure you would listen, make sure you'd believe me." He steps toward the table and reaches for his phone. With his hand just above his cell, he halts and looks over at Landry. "Can I have my phone back now?"

"Sure. Go ahead. I have a copy of the video now. Thank you so much." She reaches out her hand toward Clayton.

Looking a little surprised, he hesitates, as though wondering what she's doing. Then a timid smile slowly spreads on his bloated red face, and he reaches out and shakes her hand. "Sure thing, Detective. Anything I can do to help."

I really need a copy of that video.

Morris escorts Clayton out of the interrogation room, and it's back to just Landry and me alone again.

Landry motions for me to sit down at the table. She sits back down, folds her arms on the tabletop, and looks across toward me. "Well, that was certainly something interesting to see. Definitely throws a big twist into this case. And, needless to say, it adds even more evidence to clear you. So, Dory, please accept my apology for treating you like a suspect in all this. But, as I'm sure you already know, I was just doing my job, trying to catch your friend's killer."

"Of course." I nod. "Thank you."

Yeah, yeah, I know the deal. But that doesn't instantly make me feel less pissed off. And even though I still feel irritated by the accusations, I certainly don't want any bad blood between me and the detective on Jill's murder case. Maybe I'm a bit messed up in the head sometimes, but I still know better than to piss off people who I need help from. Does that sound selfish? Oh well, fuck it if it does. It's the truth.

Detective Landry glances over my shoulder toward the door, then leans across the table, getting closer to me. She looks me straight in the eyes when she says in a hushed voice, "I think this is as good a time as any to tell you..." She pauses, looks down at her hands then back up at me. "This is not the first time I've heard of this bizarre...*creature*. There was a similar citing a couple weeks ago, revolving around that other bone chiseling case I mentioned. Two of the victim's neighbors had reported seeing a similar creature flying above their neighborhood around the time of the attack."

All of this sounds freaking crazy. "If I hadn't just seen that thing myself, I'd think the report came from over on Sherman, you know, Crack Town." I try to laugh, but it sounds forced. Why do I try to joke at the worst times? "But...damn...I can't even..." Not knowing what the hell to say, I just shake my head, try to take it all in. This shit is even *more* messed up than before.

"Well, as you already saw, there's no way to identify the killer without a little assist, what with the odd angles and the dark and the distance. So, I'm going to send this video to the tech department, see if they can work their magic, clear up that image, get an ID on Jill's killer. Hopefully they can also get a better view of that creature too." She pauses, and then what looks like a surprised expression appears on her face. "Oh, and now that you're no longer a suspect, I can share with you that our lab crew found traces of blood on the fire escape. After what we just witnessed on that video, there's a very good chance it came from the killer rather than from Jill. But we won't know for sure until the lab finishes running their tests. With that video *and* the blood, hopefully we'll get a hit on who did this."

Landry shakes her head, and then she actually smiles. I don't know how anyone can do this kind of work. Makes me wonder how long she's been at it. Has it numbed her to the horror of it all?

What she says next helps her smile make a bit more sense.

"Now that I have video evidence of that creature, maybe my colleagues will stop laughing at me behind my back for taking the statements from that other case so seriously." A sardonic laugh escapes her. "Yeah, my colleagues thought I was insane for holding onto the statements from the other victim's neighbors, but now with this..." She leans back in her chair, laces her fingers together and rests her hands on her rib cage. "It's like I'm Fox Mulder and my partner is Scully."

She must notice my look of confusion because she follows

up by telling me, "My partner, Morris, he's *still* quite skeptical about this sort of 'uncanny phenomena.'" She air-quotes that phrase. She shakes her head. "It might be time to call in the cryptozoologists, get 'em to stop chasing Bigfoot and start searching the skies for *this* beast." She laughs again, though her words are serious.

She goes on, reminding me about the graffiti found at many of the grave exhumations—images of black winged creatures similar to what Clayton captured on his camera, and similar to what those witnesses reported seeing near that other bone chiseling case. Though some of the images look sort of like angels, she tells me many others look similar to that creature.

Whatever the fuck those images are, and whatever the hell that thing in the video is, they look nothing like any creatures of this Earth. None that we know of anyway.

"Now, about the cemeteries and the grave robberies...I'm sure I don't need to tell you how dangerous that was for you and your friends to go out on that stakeout. Though I *do* appreciate you and your friends' concern and interest in helping us catch these graverobbers, you must *promise* me you won't do anything like that again."

She pauses, waiting for my response.

Heat fills my cheeks. Thinking about what we did, I feel like a fucking idiot. I can't even make eye contact with her. Glancing down at my hands in my lap, I notice one of my knees bouncing again. I wrap my foot around the leg of the chair to stop the involuntary movement and then start picking at my fingernails. Anything to try to distract my mind from the embarrassment.

"I don't want to answer another call like tonight and end up finding *your* dead body at the scene. Promise me you'll leave the detective work for the actual detectives. I don't want you to end up like your friend."

Still unable to look at her, I force out some basic words. "Yes, I promise." The words come out as I keep picking at my fingernails.

"Please look at me when you say that. I need to know that your response is sincere." Her voice sounds stern but not angry.

Red face and feeling awkward, I stop picking. I slowly look up at her. "I promise. I really do."

She reaches into a pocket on the inside of her jacket, pulls out her business card and hands it to me. "I'll be sure to notify you once the blood analysis comes back and once the cause of death is determined. Please, call me if you find out anything, *anything at all*, that could help us with this case."

I nod as I take the card.

"Is there anything else you haven't told me that might help us find Jill's killer?"

I shake my head. I'm still trying to process what I just saw on that video.

She stands up and pulls keys out of the side pocket of her jacket. "Well then...Dory, thank you very much for talking with me. You've been extremely helpful. Now, do you have someplace I can drop you off? You can't stay at your place until we're done with the crime scene."

Shit. Where the fuck am I supposed to go?

CHAPTER 15
THE AFTERMATH

Curled up in the fetal position in the corner of Irie's antique sofa, I try hard to stifle my sobs. Practically hyperventilating ever since we left the station, I haven't been able to tell Tommy and Irie everything that happened during my meeting with Detective Landry. Not that I even know what *really* happened. All I know is that freaky shit my drunk neighbor caught on video and what Detective Landry told me.

Just the anticipation of having to talk about it all brings me right back to how I felt when I first saw Jill's dead body getting rolled out on that stretcher. It's still so damn hard to breathe. My rapid heartbeat pounds inside my skull. It feels like my head might explode.

Something warm touches my shoulder. I glance up and see Tommy holding out a ceramic mug steaming with hot coffee. I smell the alluring aroma.

"Insomnia assistance in a cup." Tommy smirks. "Though I don't think sleep will be your friend right now."

That word—

Friend

My chest caves in. It feels as though my insides plummet past the floor and into the depths of fucking hell.

Jill was my *only* friend.

Well, only until...

"I know an amazing bakery that delivers. They'll bring cookies, brownies, Danish, cannoli, coffee cake—whatever your indulgence craves—right to your door." With a takeout menu in one hand and a coffee in the other, Irie sits on the other end of the couch.

A slight titter escapes Tommy. "That's my Sunshine, always ready with the takeout menu." He cocks his head. "Food does have a way of relaxing the mind."

"It's called 'comfort food' for a reason, Daddy-O." Irie throws him a wink.

Twenty minutes later I'm finally sitting up. While nibbling coffee cake crumble and sipping more hot coffee, I spill, as best I can through sobs and sniffles, what went down when Detective Landry took me into the interrogation room. I make sure to mention the red flaming eyes, like the ones we saw on that thing from Dr. Headstrom's camera.

Their wide-open eyes never turn away as they take in every word of my story. Even though I know it's true, that's exactly what it sounds like, some far-fetched story. I don't even notice them blink. But, then again, it's difficult for me to hold eye contact with them for long. If I do, I know I'll turn into a blubbering puddle of tears at their feet.

With their complete attention on me for so long, my hands start shaking, more than they already were. My knee is bouncing now, too, and I can feel my warm cheeks blushing. Feeling extremely self-conscious, I grow quieter and my voice trails off at the end as I'm trying to tell them about the blood. The urge to scratch my head is unbearable. Instead, I stuff a piece of coffee cake in my mouth and stare down into the mug of dark steaming coffee. The liquid sloshes all around in my shaky hand. For fear of it spilling, I quickly set the mug back down and pick up the small plate with my piece of coffee cake on it. I cram another piece of cinnamon-delight into my mouth, never looking at Tommy or Irie.

Man, I wish I had my kit. Banging out some seriously fast and loud fucking rhythms right now is just what I need to calm myself down. But I might as well get that thought right out of my head. I can't even go to my own damn home.

Fuck!

Thankfully my screaming thoughts get interrupted.

"Wait. Did you say they found blood? From the creature or the killer?" Sitting in the wing back chair across from the couch, Tommy's ass is so close to the edge it looks like he might slip right off onto the floor. The slice of cake Irie had given him still sits untouched on the small round table beside the chair.

I wipe my nose on the shoulder of my sweatshirt, forgetting about the box of tissues Irie sat on the coffee table when we had first arrived. She leans forward, pulls out a couple tissues and sets them on the cushion beside me.

As I thank her, I attempt a smile.

"They don't know yet. Landry said she'll call me when they find out who it came from." Still unable to look either of them in the face, my eyes dart around the room. An image of Jill slipping and sliding around the kitchen floor in her flip-flops-turned-scouring-pads, cleaning up after our food fight the other day, flashes through my mind. That glint in her bright blue eyes and her award-winning smile.

Here come the sobs again. Through stuttered breaths, I let it *all* out.

"That dickhead officer who treated you two like absolute shit had to p-practically...d-drag me off from Jill. I just didn't...w-want to let her go. She was...my b-best friend, my only friend. She was my...s-s-sister-by-choice—since we first learned to 's-s-stick tampons in our v-jay-jays' as Jill had so eloquently put it."

I've turned back into a blubbering mess again. I hate looking like a weak little girl in front of people but, dammit, that's exactly how I feel.

Holding a handful of tissues now, I hide my face, while drying my cheeks and chin. That's when I feel a warm hand gently grasp my bouncing knee. I flinch. As I pull the tissue down away from my eyes, I see Irie's hand, with its neatly manicured lavender fingernails, drumming on the side of my knee. The bouncing ceases as I see her soothing smile.

"A little pressure and a little rhythm—it always works for me when my emotions run away." She glances over at Tommy. "Isn't that right, Dad?"

"Sure is, Sunshine." He turns his attention to me, slides his chair closer to my side of the couch.

I glance away, stupidly worrying about how shitty I must look right now. Man, what is wrong with me?

Irie removes her hand from my leg as Tommy says, "Rhythm has a way of soothing the soul. Though I'm sure you already know, but sometimes—in times like these—we often need a gentle reminder about the magic of music." He reaches over and grasps my hand. I do not flinch. Rhythmically rubbing his thumb against my palm, he says, "I want you to know you *do* have friends, and we're here for you." After three more thumb-circles on my palm, he sets my hand down onto my thigh. Then, he goes over and grabs his coffee from the end table and comes back to sit beside me.

I have no idea how to respond. I can't even look him in the face right now. This is all just too much for me.

Irie sets her coffee on the table. Pulling her feet up onto the couch, she spins her body to face me and clutches her knees to her chest. "No need to hold back with us. You know, we're no strangers to losing a loved one to those psycho Bone Cutters."

She glances over to Tommy. He solemnly nods.

I take in a deep breath, then a sip of my steaming coffee. I've got to regain my composure. Wiping my eyes and nose again, I set the tissues down and finish my story.

"I had to tell her why I got home so late, or so early, so I'd have an alibi. By the way—thank you both for not only vouching for me when Officer Dickhead hauled you both to the station, but also, Tommy, thank you for letting them check your phone for that 911 call. And Irie, thank you so much for letting me come here. You're a couple of lifesavers."

Tommy and Irie both nod.

"You're welcome here *any* time. Don't forget that."

I don't know how to respond. I nod and quietly say, "Thanks."

"I still can't get over that asshole cuffing you two for no damn reason. Officer Blaine not only never cuffed me, but he barely even spoke."

"Yeah, well, they also left us both alone in separate interrogation rooms. Well, that was until Detective Landry came in to ask for me to show her the call to 911." Tommy shrugs it off. But not Irie.

"Yeah, that racist asshole treated us like criminals, and there's no way he can deny why." Irie glances at her dad, but he doesn't acknowledge it. "Dad may not want to talk about it..." Tossing a crumpled napkin at him, she throws him a glare that he also ignores. "But seeing how differently you were treated compared to us, I know damn well it has everything to do with the color of our skin."

"Yeah, I completely agree. And I'm so sorry that happened to you guys. I don't think I would be able to handle that sort of shit and stay as calm-n-cool as you two did. I don't know how you put up with it."

"Same shit different day." The words come out in a quiet yet stern tone as Tommy turns away, sipping his coffee.

"Well, if it wasn't for me draggin' you two into my mess again, that never would've happened. For that I am *truly* sorry." After giving Irie a quick side-eye while I'm speaking, I stare at Tommy, wondering what he's thinking as he's looking towards the stereo.

"Dabbler, it isn't just *your mess* that we're involved in. This is *all* of our mess." He tosses a look to Irie, who nods in agreement. "And mine and Sunshine's part of this mess has been long overdue for cleaning the fuck up. So, Dabbler..." He reaches over and grasps my knee and squeezes, "Thank *you* for giving us the courage to finally stand up to these fucking sicko Bone Cutters. Hopefully together, all three us can take these fuckers down."

Stinging in my eyes intensifies as his words make me want to cry even more but for a very different reason. A tight-lipped smile is all I can muster. We share looks, nodding.

"You're damn right we will," says Irie with an eager and determined smile.

"Well, you guys may not believe it, but Landry actually *thanked* me."

"She did?" Irie brings her knees down and crisscrosses her legs together.

"For what?" Tommy asks.

"Yep. She sure did. She thanked me for my concern over the grave robberies, but she also told me not to take *that* risk again. She doesn't want me to end up dead, too. Not only that, but she also thanked me for telling her everything we know about those psycho Dusters—about what happened in the hospital and what happened to Kaya." They each glance away for a moment. Tommy squeezes his eyes shut and Irie bites her lower lip. "I figured you guys wouldn't mind, since it might help them catch those crazy fuckers."

Both of them turn back to me, Tommy shaking his head and Irie nodding hers. They speak at the same time.

"No, of course we don't mind at all," says Tommy.

"You *had* to tell her. We understand," says Irie.

"What I want to know, just like Landry, is why the differences between the two cases?" Distracting myself with the clues from the crimes might hopefully keep me from breaking down again. "Why kill Jill but stitch the other guy back up? All that tells me is—I was meant to be killed and the other guy was just a recruit to that psycho cult of dusters." My hands start shaking again.

Speechless and wide-eyed, Irie cuts off another piece of coffee cake from inside the cake box and places it on her empty dish.

Yes, she had an entire coffee cake delivered, not just three slices. She sure does love her comfort food.

Tommy leans forward. "I wonder if that creature killed her or not?"

As I reach for my coffee, a mix of anger and fear starts boiling up inside me. Before I get the cup to my lips, coffee splashes over the edge and spills onto my lap. "Dammit!" I set the mug back down on the table and spill more coffee onto my plate. Good thing I already finished eating my piece of cake or it would be a soggy mess right now.

Irie reaches behind her and grabs the dish towel hanging over the arm of the couch and tosses it over to me. "Here. Use this."

"Thanks."

I set the towel over the wet spot on the leg of my jeans, then pick up my plate and pour the spilled coffee back into my mug. "I'm so fucking pissed right now I can't even enjoy my freakin' coffee!" As I start patting my jeans with the towel, I stop caring about how I look or what I sound like.

I toss the towel aside. "I hope that bitch *is* dead! If she's not, I'll find her and kill the stupid cunt myself!" Who the hell am I trying to kid? "Yeah, if you two haven't already realized—I'm just a wee-bit scared fucking shitless." And here I go—my hand starts involuntarily scratching my head.

Irie reaches over and gently pulls my hand away from my head. I rest my arm back on my bouncing knee.

"Oh, I forgot to mention that Landry assured me she'll have cops patrolling my neighborhood, this one, and even Tommy's.

Especially at night since that's when all these crimes happen to occur."

I look over at Tommy. He nods, taking a sip of his coffee.

"Well, that's good," Irie says through a mouthful of coffee cake.

"Yeah, it's all just so fucking lovely. Like sleep wasn't already a problem for me now I have to deal with nightmares that *aren't* all in my head. And you think I'm *already* obsessive about looking over my shoulder all the time and scratching myself bloody? I might just end up bald after all. If I don't die of a fucking heart attack first. Shit. Since getting released from that fucking loony bin I haven't even dared to get back to going for a run every morning before work. Have you ever tried running while looking over your shoulder? Yeah not a smart idea. Looks like Jill's knife may turn into my new best friend." All that comes out with barely a pause.

I finally take a breath and then turn to Tommy. "By the way, thanks for holding onto the blade for me."

He reaches down and pulls up the left leg of his jeans. Strapped to the side of his lean calf is the sheathed knife. He unsnaps the strap and hands it to me.

"After the way your night went, it's the least I could do. That is a shit load to take in for *anyone*." His dark eyes look right through me with shimmering compassion. Then, he laughs. "Good thing they never frisked me," he says, shaking his head.

"Speaking of 'the least we can do'..." Irie tosses me a colorful patchwork blanket. "You're more than welcome to crash here until your place is cleared."

Wow! That's just what I needed to hear. I wanted to ask her if I could crash here, but I hadn't yet found the nerve.

I muster a weak, "Thank you." Immediately placing the knife under the couch—within reach—I wrap the blanket around me and curl back up in the corner of the couch.

Tommy starts to say something but is cut short by Irie.

"Shh, let's let her get some rest," she says in a hushed tone. "We can discuss this more another time. And *you* need to get some sleep, too."

That's the last I hear anyone say. A moment later the front door clicks open and then softly shuts. Three locks *clink* into place. A restless sleep grabs hold and pulls me under.

CHAPTER 16
WHAT'S GOING ON?

Nurse Freyja, hair flowing as though wind-blown, strolls out of Clyde's office as Slug Man approaches. A huge beaming smile spreads across her girlish face when he walks past.

Slug Man nods. Then he reaches out his arm and stops the door before it closes. Disoriented, he shakes his head, hesitates before entering. He glances over his shoulder to watch her walk away.

She doesn't go far.

Standing behind the counter at the T-intersection of the corridors is Rick, eyes riveted on the newest addition of the team. Nurse Freyja, at the front of the counter, leans over and talks to him in a hushed flirtatious voice.

A pang of envy hits Slug Man like a smack in the face.

Oh, man, Rick must have a fucking incredible view right now, with those nice and tight scrubs of hers always squeezing those perky tits to the point of...

"Don't just stand there, Lou. Come on in and shut the door." Clyde sounds a bit manic. Overly excited or just impatient—it's difficult to tell.

Slug Man snaps back around.

It always sounds weird when he calls me Lou.

And that tone...

He wonders if Clyde's manner of greeting has anything to do with the hot new nurse who, for some reason, just left his office and is now flirting with Rick.

Before Slug Man can step all the way into the office Clyde crowds in beside him, pushing him inside. The counselor immediately shuts and locks the door behind them.

With another glance over his shoulder, Slug Man wonders what this urgency is all about.

Back at his desk as quick as a snap of the fingers, Clyde, all hyped up, looks as though he just snorted some rails.

Seems quite odd to his buddy.

Maybe he's just jonesing for the goods from the new recruit.

Slug Man has never known him to be under the influence while at work. Though Clyde is technically Slug Man's group counselor here at the hospital, they're also friends outside of the facility.

Yeah, the therapeutic boundaries are overstepped like a motherfucker with these two, but don't forget—

They're also Dusters, luring in more unsuspecting victims, many patients, to unwillingly join their clan.

Is clan the right term?

No.

Cult seems much more fitting.

Their friendship remains *hush-hush* to everyone outside of their counseling group. At least that's the type of secrecy the two men hope to keep. Some patients in their group also don't know about the dual relationship at all.

"What's Nurse Hottie doing visiting *you*?" A cough and a chuckle slip past Slug Man's gapped-tooth grin. "Throwing the bitch the bone like you did Nurse Hatchet, I assume?" He flops his bony body down in the chair in front of the desk.

"Never mind that," Clyde spits out. Then he suddenly looks down at Slug Man. "You have no *idea* what you're talking about. I never banged Nurse Hatchet." He shakes the thought away, starts pacing.

Slug Man lets another chuckle escape. No eye contact. He tips his chair back, fingers laced together across his abdomen, and glances up at the ceiling. "Sure. Why else would she help our group, sending new arrivals through the Dusters' door? Just for shits and giggles, huh? Yeah, no...Doubt it. But whatever you say, Doc." Giggles escape out of him like a tween kid hiding in his closet with porno on the screen of their gadget and a bottle of Jergens at the ready.

Now pacing behind his desk, Clyde frantic-fusses with his dark curls as he speaks. "Enough about that. I got news. The good and the bad. That's why you're here with me now." He keeps fussing with his hair, like a teenager prepping for a hot date.

Slug Man wonders if Clyde's developing some sort of nervous tic or something, like that Itcha-Bald Crane chick.

Clyde leans with one arm on the desktop, as though trying to look casual, or calm himself down. This lasts for only about five seconds.

Frantic pacing starts again.

"Yeah, well, I wanted to talk to you, too." Before he continues, Slug Man turns, looks behind him at the locked office door, then turns back to Clyde, who is still pacing and hair-fussing. He leans forward, elbow on the desk. "Where the hell did you get that magic knock-out-powder? Damn! That shit is a Godsend. Wish I'd gotten a hold of that a long time ago. Have you been holdin' out on me, man?"

"Well, I wouldn't say it's a 'Godsend', but...No matter. We have it now. Don't worry how. Anyway. . .yeah.. .back to why I wanted to see you. Looks like..." Something makes him stop short. He's staring at, well, nothing. Just the wall, from what Slug Man can see. Then Clyde cocks his head to one side, nods, then cocks his head to the other side. Nods again.

Before Slug Man can blink his curiosity aside, Clyde spins back to face him. "First, the here and now—Big G, he's out. Busted this morning. Blood on his door. Freyja's working a double shift, saw it all go down soon after they found the new recruit sliced open. That guy, the recruit—already loyal. Never breathed a word about anything. And as far as I know, Big G never ratted that you were with him. Huh...lucky for the *both* of them."

The only two things running through Slug Man's head— *Good thing I didn't let Gary hold onto the goods. And I sure as hell hope nothing leads back to me.*

"Well, at least *now* I know why I haven't seen Big G all morning. I thought he was stuck in a session with a head-shrinker or something."

"Yeah, well, there's another problem." Clyde throws a quick glance at the door behind the slack-jawed Slug Man before he delivers the next piece of bad news. "Snake Girl is gone." He laughs a sinister titter, before adding, "More like done gone and fucked up."

He freezes. Shakes his head. He laughs again and says, "Or more appropriately, she fucked up and is done and gone." Glancing up to the ceiling, he blows a kiss to, well...the ceiling.

What the fuck is that all about?

Speechless and confused, Slug Man leans back in his chair, white-knuckling the armrests. Trying to figure out how the fuck shit went wrong last night, he hopes no one finds the tinfoil filled with bloody bone shavings he hid in his room.

And what the hell is Clyde talking about with Snake Girl?

Clyde starts pacing again as he says, "That junkie-whore just couldn't help herself." More maniacal laughter. "More like—she helped herself a bit too much, which..." Clyde halts, spins toward Slug Man, and plants his fists on the desktop, hard, as he finishes with, "...didn't help her *at all.*"

"What are you gettin' at? Just spit it out in simple terms." Slug Man grins a twitchy smile. "You know me; I'm a simple kinda man."

"Let's just say, Snake Girl's flying with the...uh..." Clyde clears his throat. "Well, she's been flown from the coop, sort of speak."

"What the...She didn't get busted too, did she?'

"No, no. No jail. Remember—the goal is to keep our kind *out* of jail." Mumbling under his breath, he adds, "Big G went and fucked that part up, though. He better keep a handle on his cravings while behind bars." He huffs exaggeratedly and shakes his head.

"Then what...what the fuck happened?"

"Let's just say...the Devil's in the details. Now..." Clyde looks from one side of the office to the other, then over Slug Man's shoulder at the closed and locked door again. "We need to find another way to keep Dory from testifying against our two gals." He leans a little further across the desk, looks Slug Man straight in the eyes. "Any ideas?"

With a cock of his head and an ominous grin, Slug Man says, "Well...we do *somehow* have that magic fairy dust now."

A matching smile spreads across Clyde's sunken-in cheeks. "Well, let's hope she's recruitable. I've heard stories about some...troubling instances where victims intended as recruits wouldn't turn after a dusting."

"Yeah, well, I call horseshit!" Slug Man jumps up. "We gotta get that bitch and get her *now*. You said the court dates aren't far away?"

Clyde nods, stands tall, and claps his hands together. "Guess it's time to find the next brave souled..." He laughs before finishing his sentence. "...releasee and get this shit done and done right, once and for all." Just as he pushes his chair out of the way and turns to head toward the door, he shutters then immediately halts. His head turns slightly, with his right ear facing the back wall. A brief moment passes, then he nods vigorously.

A marionetted smile spreads unnaturally wide across Clyde's face, similar to that of Nurse Freyja's abnormally large smile. He turns back to Slug Man and cocks his head to the right as he says, "Looks like there might be a change of plans. Let me get back to you on that."

Clyde scurries out from behind his desk and over to the door. He can't seem to unlock and open it fast enough. While he holds the door open just enough for someone to slip through, he ushers Slug Man out as fast as he can with the waving of his scarred-up hand. He shuts the door so quickly it almost hits Slug Man in the ass.

Outside Clyde's closed office Slug Man stands there stunned to stone.

He's not surprised to see Nurse Freyja still hanging out with Rick at the counter. But she's looking over her shoulder at *him*, smiling that Cheshire grin. And she winks.

Damn. First Clyde, then Rick, now me. *That one's got quite the devil in her.*

She turns back toward Rick so quickly it's as though she didn't just do what Slug Man knows for certain she just did. With a hand behind her back, like she's scratching an itch, she gives a thumbs up. The only person behind her to see it is Slug Man.

Is that meant for me?

What the fuck is going on around here?

CHAPTER 17

GETTING BY WITH A LITTLE HELP
FROM MY. . .FRIEND

Pulling the covers off my head means I might have to converse with Irie before she heads to class. That sounds like more than I can bear at this moment. It must be afternoon by now, since all her classes are after lunch. How can she pull herself together to go to class after the night we all had? Maybe that's just me projecting my feelings onto her, but still—it was not only a late night, but a heavy one, too. But then again, she does work overnights at a psych hospital. She must have that type of schedule engrained in her brain, as well as crazy occurrences.

My brain is obviously not yet accustomed to clear thinking today. Lying here alone on the couch since Tommy left and Irie locked the door, I tossed and turned so much that I can't believe I got any sleep at all. It doesn't feel like I got much. The last image of Jill haunts and dominates my thoughts. Her pale lips and limp fingers, blood trail from her mouth, those empty blue eyes.

Those eyes.

The eyes I *like* to remember always had a mischievous twinkle. A look like she knew the punchline to a joke that no one else even knew existed. A look like she was ready to burst out laughing at any moment. Happy eyes. Laughing eyes. Fun-loving eyes. Eyes full of wonder and excitement.

Not the eyes I saw last night.

I want to wipe that last image of her from my memory forever. But how to do that evades my understanding.

Something warm touches my arm, knocking me out of the tormenting memories. Then I feel a gentle squeeze, and it makes me realize I'm sobbing and sniffling. Until I felt that touch, I had no idea.

And I didn't flinch.

With the sleeve of my sweatshirt, I wipe my eyes and my nose. That's when I smell the alluring aroma of hot coffee and sandalwood.

"Don't feel the need to come out of the covers if you're not ready. Just know that I'm here if you want to talk, and there's a hot cup of Java waiting for you on the coffee table."

Irie's soft, soothing voice helps calm me. And whenever her scent gets close it seems that my shoulders relax a bit, and my mind wanders to places unknown.

I'd like to talk, but I don't know if I can without turning into a blubbering mess unable to form words.

Shifting my body to an inclined position, I slowly peek out from under the patchwork blanket and see steam rising from the brown clay mug of coffee sitting on the coffee table. Beside the mug stands a can of whipped cream and a bottle of chocolate sauce.

The cushion my feet are resting on compresses with the weight of Irie's thin frame as she sits at the other end of the couch. I pull the blanket down slightly to throw her a questioning sidelong glance.

She smiles when she notices my expression.

"Yeah, I'm guilty. I absolutely *love* 'luxury coffees'—as my dad calls them. I thought you might like one." She shrugs and starts fiddling with a couple of her dangling dreads. "After last night, a little 'luxury' feels needed. Don't ya' think?"

A nod and a smirk come from me as I sit all the way up and come out of hiding. Before I reach for the coffee, Irie leans forward and spirals a generous amount of whipped cream on top and uses a spoon to drizzle chocolate sauce all around it for added indulgence.

"Enjoy." She hands me the finished product.

Sitting cross-legged and leaning against the arm of the couch, I accept the offering and indulge. And oh, what a pleasure it is.

"I've never been one for the frilly coffees, but...holy shit, this is so freakin' tasty! Thank you." With both hands wrapped around the warm mug, I hold it close to my face and take in the amazing smell. "Ahhhhh...Yeah, I see why your dad calls it a luxury." I take another sip.

Chatting about anything other than last night feels much easier than facing what I must face, talking about what I must eventually talk about.

She bunches up the colorful blanket, pushes it closer to me, and moves onto the middle cushion beside me. A soft laugh escapes her as she says, "Your enjoyment..." She reaches over and wipes her thumb across my upper lip. "...it shows as a whipped cream mustache." She holds up the thumb she just pulled away, licks the whipped cream off, and laughs a soft titter.

I freeze.

She just touched me again and, *again*, I didn't flinch.

Now I'm lost behind my idiot-smile.

I want to talk more, maybe about last night.

Instead of forming words, I take another sip of coffee to stifle whatever idiocy I might blurt out. If I try to talk about what happened to Jill, the dam holding back the waterworks might burst and release a deluge. Not sure how I got through last night but I did. Maybe the whole incident hadn't completely sunk in yet. I don't know. But now... And if I try to talk about something else, well—idiocy.

"I'd ask you how you're feeling, but that's a dumb question. After my mom was killed by those Dusters, for the first couple of days all I could do was cry uncontrollably. But then..." Irie leans over to the other side of the couch and reaches for her *luxury coffee* that's sitting on the end table. She sits back up and takes a long sip before she continues. When she turns back toward me, she looks straight into my eyes when she says, "All I wanted was revenge. I knew that the only thing that would make me feel *any* better at all was to either get back at her killers or get them *all* busted." With her free hand she reaches over and grasps my hand that's resting on my knee.

I don't pull away.

"That's part of the reason why I've wanted to help you so much. Well, that and...I really like you, Dory. There's something about you that just feels like a no-bullshit kind of vibe. Like there's a sort of aura of genuineness around you. You know?"

A long hesitation comes from me. I'm not used to compliments. Ever since meeting Tommy and Irie, it looks like I might need to learn how to take a compliment after all.

Wondering how to respond, I take another sip of my coffee.

Scenes from the hospital flash through my mind: Tommy helping me escape from those bone-hungry Dusters; Irie bringing Dr. Headstrom, the head psychiatrist, up to speed on what was going on right under his nose *and* convincing him I wasn't delusional with my accusations.

"Thank you." Not sure why *that* was hard to think of saying. "And here I had thought that nothing good came out of the crazy stay I had at the hospital, but you know...one good thing *did* come out of it." I put my hand on top of hers. "I met you and your dad."

She smiles as I gently squeeze her hand between mine.

Then it hits me.

An overwhelming need washes over me. My skin tingles under the touch and my mind is on fire.

I finally gain the courage to initiate eye contact when I say, "Ya' know, thinking of my hospital stay makes me realize— we're already in the process of getting a couple Dusters busted.

Now I think it's time we get to the bottom of *this* whole mess and..." Turning away for a moment, I take in a deep breath before building up enough bravery to say it. "...get some motherfucking revenge."

A twinkle shines in her caramel eyes as a mischievous smile spreads across her flawless face.

There's so much anger boiling inside the two of us I'm surprised we can't shoot fire out of our eyes.

We immediately start devising a plan.

CHAPTER 18

...BANG ON MY DRUMS ALL DAY

My three 'o clock student is a no show, no call.

No surprise.

Last lesson he had with me, I called him out on not practic-ing. He had a whole week to practice a simple rhythm exercise. It was only a two-drum beat. All snare and one tom. No off-beat funky shit, and he *still* couldn't get it.

Last time he was here I told him the same thing my former drum instructor had told me when I first started learning— "You can pay me to keep teaching you the same thing every week, but that's not how you get better on your instrument."

Whatever. His problem, not mine. Just need to make sure to put him to the test at his next lesson. I haven't been able to concentrate all day anyway. My boss, Tim, couldn't even believe I came to work so soon after what happened to Jill a couple nights ago.

I already took one day off. Yeah, I could use another day—or ten—but staying busy stands as my top priority. Now with a no-show, what am I supposed to do with my next forty-five minutes?

A couple questions have been bouncing around in my head since I spoke with Irie again this morning. So I guess it's a good time to dig out Detective Landry's business card in my purse, give her a call.

That's at least one thing I can think of to fill a few minutes of this unexpected free time. And right now, free time is not what I want. Free time equals more time for horrifying intrusive thoughts to plague me. No, thank you!

After I'm on hold for a minute, Landry answers.

"No, I don't have any new info. for you, but I would like to know if I'm clear to get back into my apartment yet. I don't really *want* to go back, but I really don't want to wear the same outfit to work more than one day. It just doesn't look good. You know?"

Yeah, good ol' Dory, anxious babbler that I am. Just working my nerve up to ask my burning question.

"I was meaning to call you earlier, but I was stuck in a meeting. Yes, the scene was cleared this morning. You can go back any time."

"Uh...great. Good to know."

Hesitation on my end.

A muffled phone and garbled chatter on the other end.

Stupid me, unprepared. I knew I should've planned ahead how to ask her.

"Um...Yeah, uh...that's not all I called for. I...uh... was wondering about that graffiti. You know, what you told me about and what the news reports say has been found at the grave robbery sites?"

"What would you like to know? If it's information I can release, I am *more* than willing to share it with you."

"Well, remember that cemetery in Sokokis, the one I told you my friends and I had called in about people trespassing and questionable after-dark activity going on?"

"Yes, I do. What would you like to know?"

"Well, was graffiti found there, too?"

"Yes, we did document more graffiti there as well. A similar image to the ones we found at some of the other sites. An image like that of the creature in the video was next to the plot they dug up. Why do you ask?"

"Uh, well...just something I recall from when I was attacked at the hospital. I have a hunch about something. I need to look more into it before I know if I'm just dreaming crazy stuff up."

"Well, Dory, I have to say, with careful scrutiny like that you don't sound like someone who was just recently released from a psychiatric hospital." Detective Landry muffles her end again before she adds, "If anything comes of your 'hunch', please call me with any information you have *before* you go out investigating potential crime scenes again. Okay?"

"You bet. I just need to go see a man about a thing."

Silence. More muffling.

"Dory, there was another reason why I was going to call you today.

"I found out the cause of Jill's death." A moment of silence. Then she asks, "Are you ready to hear it?"

"No better time than the present." My chest tightens, as does my grip on the phone.

"She bled to death from the...What did you call it —'dusting'?"

A quiet, "Yeah," squeezes past the lump in my throat and into the phone.

"But that powdery residue found on her pillow still remains a mystery. It isn't any sort of drug. This case still has us all quite baffled. If you find anything out about that detail, will you please give me a call?"

"Sure." The one word is all I'm able to force out at the moment.

"Great. Thank you very much, Dory. Is there anything else you need?"

"Nope. That's all. Thank you, Detective." My voice crackles with each word as it claws its way up from my vocal cords.

As soon as I hang up, I want to smash the room to pieces. Somehow, I curb that urge long enough to send Irie a text.

> Me: Confirmed
>
> It was there

Irie: Good to know. Thanks.

I'll get that address and/or phone number,
hopefully tonight.

> Me: Thanks
>
> Almost forgot—Clear to go back to my place
>
> I'll drop your key off tonight before you go
> to work

Irie: Thanks!

There's something holding me back from telling her what I found out about Jill's death. I'll have a chance for that at another time.

With back-to-back students for the rest of the day, what's left of this unexpected forty-five-minute break looks like my last chance to eat something. I pull a snack out of my purse. As I'm unwrapping the granola bar, I wonder how I'm supposed to eat with my stomach all in knots. But that's not the only thought that hits me.

How the fuck am I supposed to face the man I just helped get arrested?

Hell, how the fuck am I going to sleep in the same apartment where my best friend was just murdered—where *my* murder was supposed to happen?

The urge to scratch my head gnaws at me.

My knee starts bouncing.

My stomach cramps up.

I glance over at my kit.

I toss the granola bar in the trash.

I readjust Jill's boot knife inside my tall Dr. Marten.

Seconds later, instead of destroying everything in my sight—I'm sitting behind my kit thrashing out some heavy metal rhythms.

Without music, I'd get locked away in a padded room for life. No doubt.

CHAPTER 19
BURNING DOWN THE HOUSE

This is madness! Should I walk up backwards? With as many times as I've already looked over my shoulder, I might as well ascend the stairs facing down.

I'm always looking down.

But what if someone is already in the hall outside my apartment, waiting?

With a whiplash turn, I spin back around toward the hallway outside my apartment and trip over the top step. The jumble of keys in my hand skitters across the scuffed-up hardwood floor, stopping just outside *the door*.

Taking in a deep breath of what I hope is courage, I pull Jill's knife out of my boot. Then I scurry-scrabble up onto my feet and slowly approach what I eventually must face...

Hand on the doorknob, my breath hitches. I close my eyes for a moment in an attempt to ground myself. It doesn't work. I still can't make myself open the door. I still can't make myself go in.

4-7-8 for ten deep breaths, all my counselors have told me.

Visualization works wonders, all my counselors have told me.

Forgive yourself, all my counselors have told me.

To hell with all those rainbow-spewing everything-will-work-itself-out liars!

It's *my* fault Mom got killed.

It's *my* fault Jill got killed.

It's my fault one of the guys who saved my life got arrested.

It's all *my* fucking fault!

Forgive that?

How?

And how am I supposed to live in the same apartment where some psycho stalker followed *me* home so they'd know where to come kill *me*, then they ended up killing Jill instead?

How?

And live there *alone*?

Do you happy-pill-prescribing, sunshine-blowing counselors have an answer for that? You all seem to have an answer for everything else I've ever brought to the table. How about this one?

Silence.

Teeth clenched, fist clenched tighter around the hilt of the knife, I punch the door.

Once.

Twice.

Three times.

Sweat drenches my forehead. The skin on my knuckles has busted open, blood seeping to the surface. I hold back the tears and rest my cheek against the door.

I don't dare close my eyes again. The length of the hallway leading back to the stairwell holds my attention.

The hard thud of my rapid heartbeat pounds against my ribcage and bellows in my temples. Fuck! A heart attack will probably take me out before some psycho bone-chiseling murderer gets to me.

After managing a couple stuttered breaths, I realize I can't do this. Not alone.

Walking back toward the stairs, I have no idea what to do.

I need a place to live.

I need a place to sleep.

I need a clean, new set of clothes to wear to work tomorrow.

I plant my ass on the top step. Head in my hands, knife at my side, I search my brain for an answer. Even a hint of some potential, even if only temporary, answer.

Something.

Anything.

In the least, I need someone to talk to.

Yes, that's me, Dory. I just thought that. *I* can't even believe it.

But Jill isn't here anymore. She was always the one. Before her it was Mom.

Sitting here all alone in Murder Central trying to build up the courage to contact someone, I pick the knife back up. Since getting the blade back from Tommy's safe-keeping, I vow to wear this everywhere. It makes me feel like Jill's still with me, keeping me safe, protecting me.

My purse dangles at my waist. After one more long deep breath, I sit the knife on my lap and pull out my cell. With my hands shaking so much, it takes me a few tries just to type a short, simple text.

Me: You out yet?

Tommy: Almost

Hour left

Why

You alright?

Me: Kinda-sorta-not

Might have a heart attack

No biggy

Footfalls sound from the front porch. Then the downstairs front door knob starts turning.

My heart jumps into my head. Shoulders hike up to my ears. My cell hits the floor.

Instead of picking up my phone, I pick up the knife again and look down the stairs.

Clayton, my neighbor. The drunk who caught the killer and the creature on video. I scrabble for my cell, pick it back up and type the quickest possible message.

> Me: Can you come straight to my place
>
> I need help

Clayton has almost reached the top of the stairs when I hear Tommy's text chime. A quick peek at the screen tells me he's leaving now and will be over very soon.

> Me: Waiting in my car

"Sorry for your loss."

Eyes only, I glance up from my phone. He's towering over me like a massive wall of beer gut and former bodybuilder shoulders. Just standing there staring down at me. We had never spoken before he barged into the interrogation room the other day. I never even knew his name before that little meeting.

Why is he just standing there like that?

Oh, wait. He can't pass by with me sitting on the top step.

I stand up and step to the side. The wall side. *Not* the railing side.

Trust—not my thing.

At least I moved the knife out of sight. Don't think he'd stop to say *anything at all* if he saw that in my hand. Though it *is* still in my hand, held flush against my back.

This gal's not taking any chances. He's a fucking house

compared to me. And, yeah, he did capture important information on his phone about Jill's killer, but still...I don't *know* him.

"Thanks," I mumble and glance down at my fidgeting feet. Even though I'm hella nervous, I immediately look back up at him. I keep my eyes on him and my grip on the knife tight.

Slowly, Clayton climbs that last couple of stairs and steps into the hallway. He walks a couple paces toward his place at the far end of the hall, but his footfalls halt abruptly.

Back to me, he's standing in front of Priscilla's door, right before my apartment.

He remains silent.

The air is so thick with tension I'm surprised he made his way that far.

He wants to say something. I feel it. Maybe he senses that I want to say something, too.

Why is it so difficult for me to talk sometimes? I just don't understand.

When I clear my throat Clayton does the same. He turns around to face me. Then we both start speaking at once.

"Hey, could you send me..."

"Sorry about barging in on..."

Uncomfortable laughter follows from both of us.

He glances away. I do the same. We both look back toward each other at the exact same moment.

With a little time to wait for Tommy to arrive, I step closer and force myself to ask about all the details I've been craving but didn't know I was craving until seeing him today.

"That video you took...is there any chance I could get a copy of that? I know it sounds kinda creepy, but..." I glance away as I pull my phone out of my pocket. "Maybe you could airdrop it to me?"

He fumbles around in his jacket pockets. "Oh, yeah, sure, no problem. Let me just..." After coming up empty from his outside pockets, he reaches into an inside pocket. He pulls out his cell, taps the screen a few times, then steps closer to hold it next to mine.

The distinct stench of beer and cigarettes hits me like a wrecking ball. Pulling my head back a bit, I rub my nose and hold my breath for a few seconds. A multitude of dark images flash across my mind: a trap door hidden under a rug, raunchy graffiti on plywood walls, cigarette burns on baby-soft skin, shattered glass dripping blood, hooks and chains and a bag of cocaine. A cringe trickles down my spine and a sick feeling tumbles around my stomach. I shake the intrusive images from my head, try to brush aside my trauma linked to addicts.

Clayton repockets his cell and takes a couple steps back. "You can double check, but I'm pretty sure it sent."

As I check to make sure I have the video on my phone, I dig up a much tougher question.

"That night, besides the killer, did you hear anyone else scream or struggle?"

———

Fifteen minutes later I'm sitting in my car in front of my apartment building, cold bottle of iced tea from my lunch cooler in my hands, waiting for Tommy to show up. His work, Silver Springs Psychiatric Hospital, is about a thirty-minute drive from my place. The orange hood of my Outback stares at me, as though waiting to see how long it will take for me to check all my mirrors again, and how long it will take for me to recheck the locks for the umpteenth time to make sure no one can get to me.

The details from my short chat with Clayton run through my head over and over. I still can't make sense of it. It would be easy to just watch the video again, since I had him airdrop it to my cell, try to see if I can see more details of the killer or the creature now that I've had some actual sleep, but I just can't bring myself to hit the play arrow. Not yet. Not alone.

I really hope Irie can get some information for me tonight from the hospital. If the same image of that black-winged creature was at the cemetery where we accidentally got Shawn arrested, then Shawn *must* know something about it.

That's what I'm counting on, anyway. Might be a longshot but we won't know if we don't try.

A sudden knock sounds on my window. The bottle of iced tea slips from my hand and lands in my lap.

"It's just me." Tommy's voice hits my ears just as I turn and see him.

I buzz down my window. "Damn you, sneaking up on me like that." My words squeeze out through tense laughter.

We both look down at my now empty bottle of iced tea and my wet jeans. I roll my eyes up to meet his, see his crooked smile and that dimple-scar on his cheek. "At least it was almost gone." I grab a bandana off my passenger seat and dab at the wet spot. When I look back up at him, I tell him, "I just can't bring myself to go in alone."

He nods and steps aside for me to open the door and get out. "I understand."

As I click my key fob to lock the doors, he nods toward my hand and the blood speckled paper towels wrapped around my knuckles. "You get in a brawl or what?"

"What." A huff leaks out of me that was intended as a laugh, but I'm just not in a laughing mood right now. "Just my weak attempt at smashing the world to bits. That's all." I shrug and step up onto the sidewalk beside him.

He pats me on the shoulder. "Aha...Didn't go as planned, huh?"

"Nope."

When I unwrap the paper towels, I notice that the scrapes aren't as bad as they first appeared now that I soaked up the blood. I stuff the bloody crumpled up towels into my jeans pocket, look up at my building, and take a very deep breath.

Our walk up the front steps is slow, hesitant, as though we're entering a haunted house.

"Hey, I never meant for you to leave work early for paranoid ol' me, but thank you." I glance up at him beside me.

He places his hand on my upper back. "Anything for a friend."

For some reason, Tommy's touch never makes me flinch.

He pulls open the front door and steps aside for me to go in. Just as I'm almost passed him, he reaches out and grabs my arm, stopping me from entering. He gives a head nod toward the street. My eyes follow his motion. A cruiser rolls on up the street, slowing down as it approaches the front of my building.

"Looks like Detective Landry kept her word." I huff. "Ooh, I feel so safe now." Sarcastic laughter leaks out of me.

Why do I do that? Laugh at the most not-funny times. Is it another tic to add to my oddities?

You can bet your ass the cop in the passenger seat stares us down for an uncomfortable amount of time. But the officer's eyes don't meet mine. They glom onto Tommy. He's with *me*, obviously. He's even holding the door open for me like some old-school gentleman (I didn't know they existed anymore). So, *why* the stink eye?

Well, this officer is none other than…yep, you guessed it, Officer Dickhead.

"What the fuck?!" The only words I can say before the cruiser stops right beside my parked car, directly in front of my building.

The passenger window zooms down.

Before a word escapes the officer, I wave and say, "Thank you for keeping an eye out for me. I feel *so much* safer with you around." The blatant sarcasm in my tone defies my intention at sounding genuine. Wait. Who the hell am I kidding? That sarcasm was intentional and warranted, though completely unplanned.

Whatever.

No way in hell will I let anyone make my friend feel uncomfortable. Though it might already be too late for that. But still...

Officer Dickhead smiles a forced grin and waves, as the cruiser slowly picks up speed and drives away. That racist fucker may not realize it but I can see his face glued to that side mirror, still staring at Tommy.

"For fuck's sake! Doesn't that kind of shit drive you nuts? Damn!" The anger rises to my face in the form of a flush. "How do you keep so calm?"

Tommy just shrugs it off. That signature crooked smile of his emerges again.

Two minutes later, Tommy walks into my apartment with me—*ahead* of me, per my request.

"You're definitely a stronger person than me if you're brave enough to stay here after what happened." He stops short before getting through the kitchen doorway. He looks over his shoulder at me. "Sorry. Did I say that out loud?"

With my foot I nudge him in the back of the knee, give him a fall-down scare. "Yeah, thanks for making this easier for me, buddy ol' pal." A tense laugh leaks out of me. "I really just want to burn this place to the fucking ground." My teeth clench, holding back the waterworks.

With a flick of the switch on the wall I illuminate the kitchen. "No, but seriously, I really don't have much of a choice. It will take time to scout out a new place to rent and save all the money I'll need. Then the bullshit rental application and waiting for the landlord to choose the best new tenant. Shit. It's not like I have family to take me in."

As we move further into the kitchen, my foot lands on something squishy and slippery near the refrigerator. I stop, look down, pick up my foot.

A dollop of old beans and rice and egg.

The food fight.

With Jill.

I can't move. I can't even fucking breathe. With a sickness in my stomach and stinging in my eyes, I crouch to the floor.

"You find something, Dabbler?" Tommy's shadow moves closer until he's standing beside me.

As I try to speak, nothing but a stuttering breath comes out of me. Warmth touches my back. Tommy's hand.

"Are you okay? What is it?" He crouches down beside me.

Forcing words through my suppressed sobs, I manage to say, "Food…We had a food f-f-fight…me and J-J-J…" I can't even…

"Oh, Dory…" Tommy wraps his arms around me and hugs me close. "I'm so sorry."

With my head against his shoulder, I start sobbing.

Dammit! I can't even handle this shit with Tommy here with me. What a fucking mess I am. Why he even wants to be friends with me, I may never know.

Just a quickly as the tears start flowing, I start wiping them away, stuffing them down deep. I've just got to get what I came for and get the fuck out of here.

After another swipe under my eyes with my sleeve, I look up at Tommy. "Let's just get this over with and get outta here."

"You sure you're alright to do this?"

I shrug. "Not much of a choice."

As we stand, we both take in long, deep breaths, preparing ourselves.

A nod toward the open door of my bedroom shows him, "That's mine there." I glance over at the closed door of Jill's room. Tommy sees this, as his eyes follow mine then quickly look back toward my doorway.

He steps toward my room ahead of me, glances back over his shoulder. "I'll check it out first. Cool?"

I nod.

His music note shoelaces catch on the cymbal stand leaning against the doorframe, and it clatters to the floor. He halts, looks down and picks it up.

"Light switch is on the wall to your right."

Laughter erupts from him the instant he flicks on the light. "Holy *shit!* Dabbler?" He clears his throat. "Uh...You really know how to downplay yourself now don't you?"

"What*ever* are you talking about?" I manage a smile and walk into my room behind him.

By the time I pass through the doorway, Tommy's already sitting behind my kit giving the bass drum some triplet kicks with the double foot pedal. He glances around at my walls as he pounds out the rhythms.

A moment later, he abruptly stops the kick drum hits. "Nice sound proofing job. Do it yourself?"

"Sure as shit I did. I sometimes do session work at a local studio for extra dough. I got tips from the pros."

"Looks to me like *you're* one of those 'pros.' Damn, Dabbler!" He laughs. "You really are more than meets the eye." He fingers through my sack of sticks hanging from the kit beside the seat, pulls a pair out. "What's your regular gig anyway? Can't believe I still don't know what you do." His eyes glance up at me through the strands of hair that have fallen out of his ponytail, dangling in his face. "You really *are* a secretive one."

"Drum instructor over at The Drum Shop." I step over to the window, pull the curtain away and look down into the driveway of the neighboring building. No one's out there. After closing the curtain, I turn around and see Tommy smiling bigger than I've seen him smile since that day Irie found us all hiding in the old stairwell at the hospital. I'll never forget that—when those crazy Duster fucks went off the rails at that last group meeting and Shawn and Davey had pulled me out of the madness, and Tommy led us all to that hiding spot.

More hair slips out of his hair elastic as he's shaking his head. A breath later he suddenly freezes and an aha expression emerges. "Hey, why not crash at Irie's until you can find a new place? I know she'd love the company."

"I don't want to get in her way, be a distraction from her studies." Uncomfortable, I turn away. "A burden is the *last* thing I want to turn into for *anyone*."

"What?" Tommy's voice jumps an octave. He huffs. "Don't think like that, Dabbler. Friends are *never* a burden, not *real* friends."

It takes a moment for his words to sink in. When they do, it feels like nothing I've ever felt before. Except with Jill. Well, now that I'm thinking about it, I did get a taste of it with Irie, too.

It's an amazing feeling.

Acceptance.

I smile.

Then suddenly I remember...

"Ok, not a burden...friends...that's awesome, but she works overnights. Last night I was lucky she didn't have to work. But, no, I can't stay there. I'll still be all alone at night, like staying at my own place." A shiver runs through me.

He shrugs. "Well, I was going to offer for you to stay at my place, but I didn't want you to think I was coming on to you or anything like that. If crashing at a dude's place is fine with you... "

An unexpected laugh shoots out of me. "No need to walk on eggshells around me, man. I know you're not some slime-o trying to get in my pants." I punch him in the shoulder. "Thanks for the offer." I nod. "Your place it is." I turn and look at my backpack on the floor, then back to Tommy. "Well, then, I guess I'd better pack some stuff."

"I'll drop Irie a line and let her know the new plan. Maybe she'll swing by during the day in-between her classes when you're not working and check in on you."

As I'm at my dresser grabbing clothes I realize, "I'd better let Detective Landry know where to find me, so it doesn't look suspicious or anything."

While Tommy shoots a text to Irie, I step into the kitchen to make the call.

Detective Landry thanks me for the consideration of calling her to inform her of my situation. Then she says, "Well, Dory, you sure do have uncanny timing once again. I was planning on calling you soon to tell you the blood analysis results came back."

With a knot in my stomach, I hesitate before saying, "Great. What's the verdict?"

First, she assures me she'll amp up police patrol in Tommy's neighborhood and cut back on mine a little. Then she gives me all the blood details. A couple minutes later, we say goodbye. As I hang up, the name she gave me repeats in my head as my cell slips from my shaking hand and clatters in the sink.

A blink later and Tommy's at my open bedroom door, worry on his face. "You alright?"

With my amped up heartbeat pounding in my head, my breath hitches and my shoulders tense up. I just stare past him.

Zoned out and feeling a bit numb, I walk straight past Tommy and go back into my room to pack my stuff.

Tommy spins around and follows me in.

Silence.

Trying to act chill, he sits back behind my drum set, starts thumbing through some rhythms I've written out in one of the many notebooks strewn around my kit. I can feel him waiting for me to speak first.

"It was Snake Girl." My eyes remain riveted on the drawer I'm rifling through for clothes, though I'm not really seeing what exactly it is I'm pulling out and stuffing into my backpack.

"What?" There's that octave jump in his voice again.

"Yeah, that slimy bitch killed Jill. Now, I need to find out what came down from the sky and grabbed her. I have a sneaking suspicion there's something bigger behind all this crazy-ass shit. Just like that Nurse Hatchet—the image that was in her place on the camera. It has to be connected *somehow*."

I slam clumps of clothes into my pack as I'm talking. As soon as nothing else will fit in, I fling the pack over my shoulder. "Let's get the fuck out of here. I need to talk to Irie about getting more than just that contact info tonight."

A look of curiosity washes across Tommy's face as he moves out from behind the kit. Readjusting his ponytail, he steps up beside me, nudges my shoulder with his arm. "Whatta you got brewing in that mysterious brain of yours?"

CHAPTER 20
BACK TO THE NUTHOUSE

"Shit. Fuck. Shit." Clyde frantically mumbles and hair-fusses while pacing around the group counseling room. Several folding chairs have already been set up in a circle to accommodate the number of people expected for group. He's rounded the room five times when he suddenly halts. At the rack containing extra chairs, he peers between the folded seats hanging from the metal rod.

"I don't know," he says while staring into the dark crevice between hanging chair legs.

One of his sweaty hands rubs down his face. He shakes his head. "No. No. No! It's not like that. I told her, 'No dusting.' I told her it would get us busted. I fucking told her!"

Swaying side to side from one foot to the other, he focuses intently. He nods. "Yes, I understand. Don't worry. I won't say a thing, no matter what happens during questioning."

He nods again, staring into the darkness.

A *click-squeak* sounds out.

"Hey, hey. Whatcha say?"

Forehead beaded with sweat and shoulders hiked up to his ears, Clyde spins on his heel.

Slug Man glances around the circle of chairs. "Good. I'm the first one here. So, what's the news? Did you find a way to get the job done, or what?"

"Or what." Clyde goes over and sits in his usual spot, with his back to the wall and facing the front curtained window-wall beside the door. He makes no eye contact with his friend, the only other person in the room.

The door gets locked immediately after Slug Man glances out into the hallway. He rushes over and sits beside Clyde. In a hushed voice he says, "Wha-does that mean? Is the bitch dead or what? What happened?"

The doorknob starts jiggling. Someone's trying to get into the room.

Eyes only, Clyde glances at the moving doorknob. "Oh yeah, a bitch is dead—two bitches actually." He's up on his feet now. Before heading over to unlock the door to let others in, he looks over his shoulder at Slug Man. "The *wrong* bitches."

Slug Man's mouth drops open. Eyes bulging.

Chattering patients start sauntering in through the door while Clyde holds it open for them. After the last person expected enters, he pops his head out the door, looks both ways down the hallway, then shuts and locks the door again. He pushes the blind on the door aside and peeks out the window one last time. When he pulls away and closes the shade, he locks the door again.

The first thing he says to everyone once he's back in his seat — "This may be our last meeting, everyone. Now, it's time for all of us to prepare for questioning."

All chattering ceases.

"What the fuck is that supposed to mean?"

The newest guy, Darren, isn't shy. After his recent initiation-dusting, he's been quite vocal about his excitement at joining the group. "I just got started here. I need to know more. I need to know how to go about getting my own angel dust. You can't just send me out on my own with this new addiction with no knowhow on scoring some for myself." He finger-combs his long, red undercut mohawk out of his eyes as he says, "Shit. You all got me into this fucking group. It can't just end without any kind of warning."

Clyde jumps up out of his seat. His metal folding chair flips back and clatters to the floor. He storms across the circle and stops dead in his tracks right in front of Darren. He leans down, places his hands on the guy's knees, squeezes hard. He leans in close, nose to nose with the newbie. "Just because you didn't rat doesn't earn you brownie points with me. Consider this your *official* warning. I don't have time to hold your fucking hand and walk you through this, not when a detective is coming here later to talk with me about why one of my former patients has gone missing soon after her release. I'm quite sure this detective is going to ask me about what goes on in this here counseling group of mine."

Clyde pauses, glances to the side and cocks his head as though confused. When he turns back he looks Darren directly in the eyes and grabs a fistful of his t-shirt. "Who the fuck told you to call it 'angel dust' anyway? It's from fucking humans, not angels, you idiot. And angel dust already exists, you fucktard!"

"Yeah, well I'm no fool. I've been to the cemeteries. My crew parties in the cemetery *often*. I know about the graffiti. I know about the angels."

Clyde laughs. He releases Darren's t-shirt and stands back upright. "You really are a fucking idiot." He smacks the new guy upside the head, sending his long red mohawk flipping into his face, then heads back toward his own seat while saying, "You can bet your ass those images are *no* angels." He takes a deep breath, calms himself, looks down at his fallen chair.

Slug Man scurries to stand the chair back up for his friend.

Clyde sits, takes a couple more very deep, exaggerated breaths.

Darren's laughing and finger-combing his hair again as he says, "Whatever, Old Man. What the hell else has wings and frequents cemeteries, genius?"

Clyde fixes Darren with a stare so sharp it could sever his skull. "Your choice of wording should help you answer that for yourself, *newbie*."

The creepy calm of Clyde's voice makes Slug Man fidgety.

A huff escapes Darren just before he turns to his right. The middle-aged woman beside him, the one with scars all around her wrist bones and running up her outer forearm, is nudging him with her elbow. Out of the corner of her mouth she's repeating in a loud attempted-whisper, "Demons. Demons. They're pictures of demons."

"Sherry!" Clyde yells. "Keep your trap shut, or the *angels* will come for *you* next."

Slug Man shoots Clyde a worried look. "Is that what you were trying to tell me earlier? Is that what happened to Snake Girl?"

Clyde whips his stare toward Slug Man. "What do you mean? I never said anything happened to Snake Girl. You have no idea what you're..." Another deep breath. "Snake Girl is the one who has gone missing. That's all I know. Now, let's just get this meeting over with." There's that creepy-calm tone in his voice again.

Clyde's tone doesn't fool anyone. His flush face and fierce expression say it all.

Clyde is fucking pissed.

For someone who knows him a bit better than the rest of the group members, Slug Man can tell there's a little more going on here. He detects a lot of fear in Clyde's eyes. That look has never been witnessed by Slug Man before, not on Clyde, which is why he notices it so easily.

Clyde looks back out into the center of the room. "You all need to know what to say and what not to say once the questioning begins. And it's coming soon...*very* soon." He glances around the circle at all the confused and worried faces. "Are we ready?"

Like the heads of one giant monster, they all nod in unison.

Clyde leans forward, elbows on his knees. "All right then. Let's begin."

CHAPTER 21
ANOTHER CRAZY PLAN

Her house keys dangle from my finger as I approach. In Tommy's driveway and ready to head to work, Irie's leaning against the side of her purple Jeep in her janitor attire: black Dickies, white button up shirt, black leather non-skid shoes, dreads pulled up into a fat bun on top of her head.

"Thanks for meeting me here instead." I toss the keys into her outstretched hand.

"No problem." She looks at my pack slung over my shoulder. "I wouldn't be able to stay at your place now either. Happy to know you're staying with my dad."

Tommy holds the door to his house open for us. It leads straight into his kitchen. "I suggested your place, but..."

"No *way* do I want to stay alone at night while you're working."

"Yeah, I hear *that*." A shivery shakedown creep-out-dance straight to the fridge follows her words.

I flop my pack on the kitchen table and my ass in a chair. "So, tonight. You really think you'll be able to get that info for me?"

"Easier for me to try during the overnight shift than for Dad during the day when all the docs and counselors and whatnot are floating around." She pops the top off a bowl of leftovers, leans against the sink and starts munching.

Without hesitation, I fill her in about the phone call with Detective Landry back at my apartment.

With a mouthful of leftover pasta, she almost chokes at the discovery.

Tommy steps over and pats her on the back. "Easy now. Don't choke on that info." He looks over at me. "Guess we're not the only ones shocked by the news." Walking across the kitchen, he slips off his thin jacket, hangs it on the back of a chair, and then he leans against the counter opposite from Irie.

"Did that Snake Girl *just* get out? I thought I heard something about that not too long ago. Now that I'm thinking about it—I haven't seen her around the hospital. But then again, I do work overnights, so what do I know?" She shovels another forkful of pasta into her mouth. A few chews go by before she adds, "I was never one to listen to much of the chit-chat around that place, but ever since this whole mess with the Dusters I make sure to listen to *everything*."

"Yeah, well I appreciate *anything* you can find out, especially if you can 'overhear' anything about that mysterious disappearing Nurse Hatchet. I was telling your dad I think someone or some*thing* much bigger is behind this whole crazy Duster cult."

Then I remember the call with Detective Landry earlier. I hadn't even told Tommy about that yet. So much is happening so fast, I haven't had the chance. I fill them in with the details.

Silence follows as both Tommy and Irie shake their heads.

Tommy speaks first. "Just like my Kaya." He looks down at the floor.

"Those psychos need to get what's coming to them once and for all." Irie jabs the fork at the pasta so hard it *clanks* against the bottom of the glass bowl over and over.

"I completely agree. Now, what do you guys think that white powdery stuff might be?"

Still staring at the ground, Tommy says, "If not drugs, I have no freakin' idea."

Another moment of silence.

"Hey." Irie addresses her dad. "Have you met the new nurse yet? Nurse Freyja? Or does she only work nights?"

Tommy rolls his eyes up, as though looking into his mind for a memory. A blink later an amused smirk suddenly emerges. "Oh, you bet I've seen that new nurse. She's even hotter than Nurse Hatchet. And when I say 'hotter,' I'm talking goddess quality hot." His long ponytail is hanging over his shoulder. He slips the hair elastic out and shakes his long locks free. "I'm sure I don't need to tell you two, but that horndog Rick ogles her like he's a worshiper at her feet. And man, she eats that attention up like it's her sustenance, her power source."

He glances off in thought.

In that moment, as I watch him, waiting to hear more, I realize that I've never seen Tommy with his hair down before. Those long, dark shaggy locks hanging down over his shoulders remind me of a soft, warm blanket to wrap up in.

He looks back toward Irie and me, ready to say something.

My eyes reflexively look away. Thoughts scramble. I can't even remember what he was saying a moment ago.

With a furrowed brow, he cocks his head. "Wait a minute. I thought I'd mentioned her to you two before. Maybe I'm mistaken, but I know one thing for sure—She dishes the attention right back out on Rick. And he drinks every drop of that right up like he's her lapdog. He's completely gaga over her, just like the las..." His words stop short as a concerned expression washes over him. "Hmm...Is it just me or does this look like a weird pattern? Two hot nurses, both all over force-a-fat-roll Rick, and it's all going down during this Duster nightmare?"

Sitting up straighter, I'm at attention now. "Oh, hell yeah, I see the pattern."

Wide-eyed and nodding while forking up more food, Irie displays her total agreement.

"I wonder if *this* one is in the system?"

They both glance at me questioningly.

"Remember? Dr. Headstrom had never even heard of Nurse Hatchet. She *somehow* flew right under the radar of the higher-ups who can actually do anything about anything. Now *this* new one's there?" I look at Irie as she chows down more pasta. "Maybe that's something else you should check up on, *if* you get the chance. If you find what I suspect you'll find, that may lead us to Nurse Hatchet as well. Or..." A shiver runs through me before I finish my thought. I shake it off as best I can. "It may lead us to finding out *what* they are."

Irie nods enthusiastically, then gives me a thumbs up with her fork yielding hand.

Suddenly I realize I'd forgotten something crucial from earlier. I pull my cell out of the pocket of my zip-up hoodie and place it on the table screen up. "Damn! Tommy, I forgot all about this—I ran into my drunk neighbor right after I texted you earlier. He airdropped that video footage to me."

Both Tommy and Irie freeze, eyes bugging out in amazement. The next forkful of food Irie was about to stuff into her mouth falls to the floor.

"Well, holy shit, Dabbler. That's quite a big thing to forget." Tommy sits at the table, scoots his chair over beside me, eager to see the evidence. Irie follows his lead. I'm sandwiched between them at the table, cell in front of me. After shaking off a shiver and a de'ja'vu vibe, I open the video.

We lean over the phone and watch intently.

Immediately following the distinct sound of a woman screaming, the night sky over my building quickly sweeps across the screen in streams of star-smothering city lights. On the fire escape outside my apartment window there's a woman —Snake Girl—swatting at a huge black winged figure hovering in the air. The wingspan stretches wider than I've ever seen before—in real life anyway. A gasp later, the creature rises into the night sky with Snake Girl dangling in its clutches.

I play the video a few more times before we all sit back, trying to process it. Even though I've watched the video at the police station, it's still difficult to imagine such a creature even existing, let alone seeing it right outside my apartment window. The crazy sight still takes my breath away with shock and confusion. There's so much in this world that no one knows about, so much no one understands.

Silence.

Tommy shakes his head, running his fingers through his hair. "Just like you said—I can't help but think of that image on Dr. Headstrom's camera from when we set up Sheila and got her busted." His eyes glance over at me. "But *that* thing," he nods down at my cell, "is fucking huge compared to what we saw on the Doc's camera. And you're right—it does look kinda like a gargoyle. I just wish we could see its face more clearly."

"I know. Right? But the other strange thing is, at that moment when Sheila was in my room that night, I saw Nurse Hatchet in the room with us. She was in the corner near the bathroom door." Trying to recall all the details, I have to look away. "And I heard Sheila talking to someone before she attacked me. Then—*poof*—that winged skull-faced image suddenly appeared behind her. It was almost like..." I shake my head, still not believing what my own eyes had witnessed that night. "...like whatever it *was* had control over her, or was guiding her, or some crazy shit."

More silence.

"I wonder *how* it picked Snake Girl up. Does it have talons like a gargoyle, too? Maybe that's how her blood was found on the fire escape." Irie says, while periodically glancing at the clock on the stove. The sky outside the kitchen window is dark. It's just about time for her to head to work for her overnight shift. "Can you zoom in to see more of what the creature looks like?" Another glance at the clock. Another forkful of pasta gobbled up.

"Nope. Nothing. Already tried at the station on Landry's laptop. Plus, Landry also told me her tech people tried, but she said all it does is blur the image unrecognizable." I shrug. "Maybe because it's so dark?" I drag the video time strip back to where the creature is about to grab Snake Girl and zoom in. Nothing. Just as I already knew, it doesn't help at all.

Both Tommy and Irie nod.

Then Irie abruptly stops nodding. "Maybe it won't *allow* us to see it more clearly."

We pause. Give it some thought.

"Suppose it could be possible, for all we know. If it's an unearthly creature it could likely have unearthly powers. Makes sense." All this feels so unusual. I keep feeling like it isn't real, like this is someone else's conversation that I'm listening to from a movie or a book or something.

"What I wonder is...why? There must be a connection to what Snake Girl did to Jill and that creature taking her. But what? Is she dead? Did it kill her?" Tommy looks at me. "The detective told you she found Snake Girl's blood, but how much of her blood was found? Enough to kill her?"

"She didn't say. What she did say is Snake Girl—Roxanne Kyser is her real name—hasn't been seen since. And no remains have been found. She's now listed as a missing person." I play the video one more time. Then it hits me.

"Maybe because she killed the wrong person? Maybe *that's* why it came for her." I pause. Consider this possibility a bit more.

A bowtie noodle slaps me in the chest as Irie smacks me in the shoulder with her fork-wielding hand. I look down at the red sauce splattered across the white skull of my Misfits zip-up hoodie. In her excitement, Irie doesn't seem to notice the stain she just made.

"Or maybe—consider this—it came to eliminate the weak link, the *connector* link."

With another forkful of pasta in her mouth and eyebrows raised, she glances away chewing thoughtfully.

Tommy snatches the bowl of pasta away from her. "No more. You can't just leave us hangin'. Link to *what*?"

She reaches across the table, tries to get the bowl back.

Tommy pulls it out of reach. "Uh-uh-uh...you get it back *after* you fill us in. What's your theory, Miss Drama?"

Looking at me she says, "Well, you said that Jill was dusted to death."

My breath gets stuck in my chest. I close my eyes, nod.

A hand rests on top of mine, stopping my fingers from scraping the tabletop, which I hadn't even realized I was doing. At least I wasn't scratching my head again. Maybe I'm starting to get a handle on this tic of mine after all.

My eyes open. Irie gives my hand a gentle squeeze. "Sorry to bring it all back, but what I'm getting at is—even if Snake Girl's blood hadn't been found on the fire escape, her DNA most likely would've been found on Jill's body if she was dusted."

Tommy and I both flash her a questioning look.

"I imagine that it would be difficult for one of these Bone Cutters to *not* leave their DNA behind after doing that to someone." She looks over at her dad. "I mean, you know...we tried to get the detectives to look for traces of the killers' DNA from when they did that to Mom, but the lab results were '*mysteriously*' lost and no more was done about it." Her shoulders hike up as she quietly adds, "Maybe if Mom was white that wouldn't have happened." She glances at me. "No offense, Dory."

"No worries. None taken."

Tommy turns away, looks out the window beside him as he mumbles, "Yeah, sure wish they'd done their fucking jobs.

Didn't even help that we'd seen the killers, had given descriptions of them."

Irie now holds one of Tommy's hands as well as mine. "That's my point. These scumbags are not as good at covering their tracks as they might think. Maybe it's because Snake Girl not only killed the wrong person," she nods toward me, "leaving you free to testify against two of their own, but she also left DNA behind. The detective already told you that she traced Snake Girl back to the hospital while you were there, and linked her to that creepy dysfunctional NA group. Link. Link. Link. See what I'm gettin' at?"

Wide-eyed, Tommy and I both sit up, pushing aside the hurt of our losses for the moment.

I feel the jaw-dropped *aha*-expression on my face. "I see exactly what you're getting at. That thing came for her in an attempt to keep this from leading back to that group of Dusters."

They both nod as they listen.

"Maybe..." I hesitate, still forming my new theory. "Maybe they're some kind of recruitment group or collection group or some shit like that. You know—collecting more dust to sell and share, or turning more people into monsters like themselves, or..."

The chair bumps the windowsill as Tommy jumps to his feet and says, "Or all of the above." He pounds the side of his clenched fist against the table. "That's it! It has to be."

Silence.

I cock my head and look up at him, considering what he said. Glancing to my side, I see Irie, brow pinched, doing the exact same thing.

Tommy pulls his chair closer and slowly sits back down. "But still, what the fuck *is* that flying creature? What's *that* link? That's the part I don't understand at all. That video..." He grabs my phone, stares down at the paused video as he speaks. "It's like something out of the *X-Files* or some crazy batshit horror or sci-fi flick. Is it some alien collecting human samples? Maybe to clone us. Create more humans to make their slaves. Or maybe to turn us all against each other, to destroy ourselves, devour one another. Fuck. I don't know." A nervous laugh escapes him. He leans back in his chair, shaking his head in confusion.

A breath later, he sits back up at attention. "Wait a minute. I know we can't see its face clearly, but it sure as hell resembles a fucking gargoyle. And don't forget, ladies—gargoyles protect *against* evil." He looks from me to Irie and back again. "Maybe it came to *eliminate* the evil. Maybe it *killed* Snake Girl for killing Jill." His shoulders hike up for a long, considerate shrug. His eyebrows repeat the gesture as he looks from me to Irie and back again.

Turning away for a moment, I consider this new idea. I sure hope the creature killed that slimy bitch for what she did to Jill. But we still don't know for sure.

Irie snatches the bowl of pasta back while her dad stares at the ceiling in deep thought apparently engrossed in his epiphany.

"Well, Dory has an idea about how to find out more on that unidentified creature and its link to the Dusters. If all goes well for me tonight, we'll hopefully know more very soon." Through a mouthful of pasta she adds, "Fingers crossed Dad is the one who's right and it's on our side."

Grave Robberies and Graffiti at Church Street Cemetery

With four people arrested and out on bail awaiting trial for the Hill-crest Cemetery gravesite desecration in Sokokis, more grave robberies occurred last night at the Church Street Cemetery in Edgerton. Suspicious activity was reported by a local man out walking his dog after arriving home from his nightshift. Unfortunately, by the time police had arrived on the scene, those guilty had already fled the area. Again, this cemetery was covered in similar graffiti as the other graveyards that have been affected by this slew of robberies across the state. An image of a black-winged creature of some sort was spray painted on a number of headstones, on a sarcophagus, as well as on all four walls of a family mausoleum. Police are asking for anyone with information about this Edgerton grave robbery, or information about any of the other grave robberies, to please call the State Police tip line: 1-800-555-7686.

CHAPTER 22
CRACKING AT THE NUTHOUSE

Seemingly alone behind the closed door of his office, Clyde paces and feverishly finger-combs his hair. After a couple circles around his desk he stops, out of breath, in front of the wall behind his chair and just stares.

After a few moments, he speaks in a stuttering voice. "W-what do you w-want me to tell them? W-what sh-should I say?" With a shrug of his shoulders, he leans one ear closer to the wall. He appears to be waiting for someone to reply.

His brow furrows. He throws his hands in the air. "How the fuck am I supposed to know? I'm *here* all day, not out *there*."

His pacing commences. "Shit. Shit. Shit! This wasn't the plan. This wasn't in the cards." Hands waving around, he keeps jabbering about how everything has turned into a fucked-up mess.

Meanwhile, Slug Man speed-walks up and down the hallway outside his room. Spittle flies from his mouth as he also jabbers to no one. Maybe himself. But it seems as though he's addressing someone. Maybe someone in his head.

"How was I supposed to know cops would end up here? I did what I was *told*. He wanted more recruits. *Always* more recruits."

He paces back and forth, back and forth.

"Fucking Clyde, that slavedriver. Even gave me some magical powder—'To help you out, man, make it easier.'" His hands keep waving around just as fast as his lips keep flapping. "Huh...easier. Right. Where the fuck did he even get that shit anyway?" He stops, stares up into the buzzing fluorescent light in the ceiling above his head. "Yeah, newbie will probly run his stupid fucking mouth. Shit." He shakes his head and continues speed-pacing. "Pissed off cuz group's ending? Fucking goo-goo boy can't figure out how to get the goods on his own? Too fucking bad! *I* learned on *my* own. Shithead can fend for himself like the rest of us had to for so long."

He stops outside his closed bedroom door. "Fuck!" He screams and punches his door open at the same time.

Two husky male psych techs round the corner and head in the direction of the sound. Neither of them saw what happened.

The tall one says, "I'd recognize that gravelly voice anywhere."

"Yeah, good 'ol Lou," the other adds as he slips his key bracelet around his wrist, prepping for an anticipated restraint or escort to the padded room.

———

Detective Landry and her partner, Detective Morris, follow behind Dr. Headstrom as he guides them through the large locked double doors of the adult unit of the hospital. With his white coat flapping like a cape, the doctor leads the two to the large counter at the T-intersection of the two hallways.

Rick, the head psych tech for the shift, stands leaning with one elbow on the half-door of the nurse's station. He keeps glancing over his shoulder at the two out of place arrivals.

"Yes, she *is* on the schedule," Nurse Taylor says to Rick, though she's looking past him. She leans closer to him and whispers, "Are those *cops*?"

"Detectives," he whispers out of the corner of his mouth, still staring toward the counter.

"Detectives?"

"Yeah, the suits...Cops wear uniforms." He dons a smug smirk.

Nurse Taylor bops him in the shoulder with the end of her pen. "Yeah, I know *that*. What I mean is why are *they here*?"

"Not sure, but I have my suspicions." He turns and glances at her. "So, you said she's on the schedule, but where *is* she? The shift started three hours ago."

She shrugs and tosses her pen on the counter. "No idea. No call, no show." A huff later, she adds, "Guess she's not too serious about *keeping* this job. Can't say I'm surprised. That one's a bit too squeamish around blood to make it in this field."

Rick appears only half listening as their eyes remain riveted on the detectives. Dr. Headstrom, glasses perched on the tip of his nose and a tablet in his hands, is introducing Landry and Morris to a few of the psych techs behind the counter. He periodically looks down at his gadget and swipes across the screen a few times as though looking for something specific.

Nearby, just around the corner from the nurse's station, Irie stands outside the open door of the janitor's closet, gloved hands clutching the handle of the cleaning cart, box of trash bags and various cleaning supplies on top. She can hear every word from Rick's conversation, and she takes it all in. As she listens, she also watches the doctor and the detectives at the counter, wondering if she'll ever get her chance to search the hospital files for that contact information and also thinking, *Another vanishing nurse—doesn't sound like a coincidence to me.*

She hangs around longer, fiddling with the supplies on the cart and adding more from the tall shelving unit just inside the janitor's closet. No more supplies are needed, but more time to listen and watch is definitely needed.

"So, your suspicions?" Nurse Taylor nudges Rick's elbow off from the shelf of the half door. "Same as mine, I bet."

He glances sidelong toward her. Then, in stereo, they both say, "The NA group."

They're both nodding while speaking.

"Yeah, I've known something's been fishy with those ones for a while, but..." He pauses, looks over his shoulder toward Dr. Headstrom and the detectives. "Let's just say," he says out of the corner of his mouth, "I think the head-doc has been working on cracking that one open." He nods toward Headstrom and the visitors. "And now he's got himself some help." He laughs. "Good. That group has been giving me the creeps ever since what happened with Dory. Oh, shit." He leans over the half door and looks at the calendar hanging on the wall inside the nurse's station.

"What?" She swats at him with a stack of papers she's getting ready to affix to a clipboard. "Get out. Techs aren't allowed back here."

"Just looking..." He points at the calendar. "I've gotta testify in court *next week* for that crazy shit that happened. Damn. Not sure if I'm ready to play 'witness.'" He air-quotes his last word.

"You *were* a witness." She smirks. "Plus, don't you *want* to help psycho Sheila get sent to jail for what she tried to do?"

"Yeah, but just helping set her up got me drugged and sent to the hospital. Shit. I'm lucky I survived. Now this." He shakes his head, waves of his hair-metal mullet sway with his movements. "What if something *worse* happens to me for standing up for Dory in court?"

Nurse Taylor looks at the calendar then back to Rick. "Well, adding to the creepiness in all of this—that court date is the day before Halloween?"

"Yeah, don't remind me. Everything about this weirdo-shit is creepy." He glances back toward the detectives as he adds, "And it keeps getting creepier."

"What do you mean?"

"Nurse Hatchet disappeared right after that setup."

"Yeah, that was weird, but what's that have to do with today?"

"Don't you see the similarity?" He doesn't wait for an answer. "It was a no-call no-show. Same as today." He mumbles the last part, "Well, and Hatchet also left mid-shift, but..." With pursed lips, he cocks his head to the side and slaps the shelf of the half door. "Sure wish Tommy hadn't left early today. He'd definitely back me up right now." He walks off toward the detectives, leaving Nurse Taylor speechless and wide-eyed.

As soon as Rick walks away from the nurse's station, Irie immediately steps into the janitor's closet out of sight and grabs more supplies for her cart that she doesn't need. *Yep. Just as I suspected. That new nurse, just like Hatchet. Can't wait to bring this info home with me.*

Just as Rick makes it over to the large counter, Dr. Headstrom is ushering the two detectives to follow him to his office. "Excuse me," Rick says, catching the doctor's attention.

"Yes, Rick. How can I help you?" Dr. Headstrom motions for Landry and Morris to wait a moment. Then he steps back over to the counter.

"If those detectives are here about that NA group, I have some info they *might* want to know about."

"Well, Rick, any information you have..." Dr. Headstrom glances back at the detectives, then back to Rick. "Yes, just come to my office. We can all talk in there."

As soon as the office door clicks closed, Rick addresses Landry and Morris at auctioneer-speed. "My gut tells me this visit is all about that crazy NA group and now Nurse Freyja is a no-call no-show just like that Nurse Hatchet who pulled a disappearing act right after that incident with Sheila attacking Dory and I think those two nurses have something to do with all this but I just don't kn. . ."

"Slow down, Rick. Take a deep breath...and slow down." As he speaks, Dr. Headstrom mimics what he instructs Rick to do. Then he sets his tablet down on his desk and starts rubbing his forehead, trying to keep up with motor-mouth Rick, who is apparently a bit over excited to help the detectives get to the bottom of this workplace chaos. "Now, please back up a minute with this bit about a nurse not showing up to work. *Who* didn't show up?"

Rick takes a deep breath and puts his shaky hands in his pants pockets. "Yeah, yeah, no problem. Sorry. It's that new nurse, Freyja. She's on the schedule to work tonight but she never showed up. Nurse Taylor told me she never even called in. And I've seen her coming out of Clyde's office all smiley and looking suspicious, just like what used to happen with smiley Nurse Hatchet. Plus, Hatchet was always bringing Dory to that NA group when Dory didn't belong in NA. I find it all very suspicious, don't you?" He turns toward the detectives with his question.

Landry and Morris both nod, but before either of them can say a word, Dr. Headstrom, looking completely confused, jumps in first.

"New nurse?" He leans both hands on his desktop and looks from Rick to the detectives then back to Rick again. In an angry yet hushed tone he says, "Why is there another nurse here that I don't know about? Somehow Nurse Hatchet flew under my radar, and now someone else. You say Freyja is her name?" With a flushed face, he stands back upright and puts his hands on his narrow hips.

A wide-eyed Rick nods anxiously, sending his shaggy 80s metal-mullet swinging and swaying.

Landry puts her hand up, palm facing out. "Hold up. How do *you* know about that NA group being 'crazy'? And how are there nurses *working* here that aren't supposed to be here?"

Rick opens his mouth to talk, but the doctor speaks up first, again. "Rick is the tech who helped us with the Sheila attack on our former patient, Dory. He's the one who was drugged by the mysteriously missing Nurse Hatchet, whom I never had..." he coughs and clears his throat before finishing with, "the pleasure of meeting."

"Looks like it's time to find out about this Nurse Freyja and her relationship with that counselor." Landry looks from Headstrom to Detective Morris and nods, then grabs hold of the doorknob behind her. Before she opens the door, she adds, "Hopefully that info will help us find out more about Nurse Hatchet as well." As her last word comes out, she swings the door open.

Dr. Headstrom leads the group out of his office and straight to the nurse's station, where Nurse Taylor is in the middle of prepping for the patients' medication check-in. A tray filled with tiny plastic cups and a rainbow array of pills sits on the counter in front of her. On the counter behind her sit about twenty different open prescription bottles.

Dr. Headstrom rests his elbow on the shelf of the half-door right beside a pitcher of water and a stack of plastic cups. "Excuse me, Nurse Taylor. I don't mean to interrupt, but do you have Nurse Freyja's contact info readily available?"

Her eyes glance from Dr. Headstrom to Rick, then to Detectives Landry and Morris standing behind them, before setting aside the bottle of meds in her hand. She peels off her plastic gloves as she says, "Sure do. I already pulled it up, with the intention of calling her to find out if she's coming back to work *at all*." She steps over to the computer at the other end of the counter and pecks at the keyboard, illuminating the screen where the information requested appears ready and waiting. "Just never got around to making that call yet."

A moment later, she hands a piece of paper to Detective Landry, who has stepped up to the window for the much-anticipated information. "If you get a hold of her, could you tell her she no longer works here? We need reliable people on staff." Shoulders tense, her lips form a pinched-tight frown. With wary eyes, she glances at the doctor, who gives her a nod of approval.

Immediately, her shoulders relax, showing she now knows she made the right decision.

"Oh, shit!" Rick blurts out. "Oops, excuse my language, but I just realized—Nurse Freyja did the room checks the night that new patient, Darren," he throws a glance to the detectives and adds, "one of the four on suicide-watch—somehow got away with slicing himself open without anyone seeing or hearing a peep. Mary said his door was closed when she found him."

Nurse Taylor's mouth drops open, then she says, "Oh my God, that's right! She *did* do room checks that night. And might I add, she was quite squeamish and not forthcoming with much assistance. Took her a lifetime just to get back with the first aid kit...almost like she didn't want to..." Eyes popped wide, she looks to Dr. Headstrom and whispers, "What is going on here? I'm suddenly not feeling...safe."

Dr. Headstrom steps forward to say something, but Landry puts her hand up palm facing out and says, "Don't you worry. We're about to get to the bottom of this. Thank you for this info." She holds up the slip of paper Nurse Taylor gave to her. "You've been very helpful. You can go back to work now."

Before Nurse Taylor has time to slip on new gloves to finish setting up for med management, Detective Landry already has her phone to her ear, awaiting Nurse Freyja's answer. Within seconds, Landry huffs and pulls the phone down. "Phony number. Out of service." She starts clicking on her phone. "Looks like we'll need to pay her a visit once we're done with our questioning here," she says to Morris.

All five, Nurse Taylor included—though she tries appearing as though she's fully engrossed with her own task at the nearby counter—wait anxiously for what the detective finds.

A pinched line of frustration emerges on Landry's lips as she pockets her phone. "Well, if this address is correct, it looks like our Nurse Freyja—if that really *is* her name—lives at the Church Street Cemetery in Edgerton."

Curious expressions spread across every face present, all

looking from one person to the next as though someone might have the answer to the unspoken questions on everyone's minds.

Who *are* these mysterious nurses, and what's up with *both* of them disappearing after NA group issues?

Landry glances down at her partner Morris and nods. "You thinking what I'm thinking?"

"You know it." A crooked half-smile appears after his reply.

Landry turns to Dr. Headstrom. "Doctor, that NA group—cancel it *immediately*." The doctor nods in agreement. "Now, could you please bring us to speak with that group's counselor, uh, Clyde. He's got some serious explaining to do."

———

Red-faced and sweating profusely, Clyde slowly opens his creaking office door. The instant he sees Detectives Landry and Morris standing there, panic fills his eyes.

"Hello, Clyde. I'm Detective Landry and this is Detective Morris. We have some questions for you. May we come in?"

Clyde swings the door open so quickly it slips from his hand, flies wide open with the doorknob banging into the wall. He winces at the sound and walks to the other side of his desk. Before Detective Morris gets the door closed, Clyde starts rambling and hair-fussing and pacing all at the same time.

"Look, I know you're here about Roxy but I can assure you —I don't know why she did it she never displayed a violent tendency while she was here she seemed completely ready for release with no indication that she was angry or had it out for anyone or anything like..."

Landry silences him, stopping him with a simple hand gesture. "Hold up there, Clyde. *What* did you not know Roxy was going to do? Why do you think we're here to talk to you? What do you know?"

"I told you I don't know anything!" Clyde pounds his

clenched fists on his desktop, then immediately starts hair-fussing again. In a quieter and forced-calmer voice he tells them, "I have no idea why she killed Dory's roommate. When both were here, she seemed like she liked Dory. Roxy didn't seem angry at all before release, and I haven't seen her since she got out. I have no idea why she did it or where she is."

Landry and Morris make brief eye contact. Then they both step in closer, each on opposite sides of the desk. Morris eases his jacket aside and reaches toward his back, as Landry says, "Well, Clyde, it seems you know a hell of a lot more than you should. We never told anyone that Roxy *did* anything illegal, especially not that she killed someone. All we told Dr. Head-strom was that she's gone missing and is merely *suspected* of having committed a crime." She glances at Detective Morris. He nods.

In the time it takes Clyde to blink and drop his mouth open to possibly defend himself, Morris is beside him and has the cuffs locked around one of his wrists. Morris moves in close and says in a low, deep tone, "You're under arrest. Time to come with us for some more questioning."

Taken by surprise, Clyde tries to tug his cuffed hand away, but Morris takes control. He may stand much shorter than Landry, but Morris is a well-built machine with tremendous strength. He yanks Clyde in close, flips him around and then face down on the desk with his hands cuffed behind his back. He places his hand on Clyde's head, pinning him down so he can't move. The reckless idiot that he is, Clyde still tries to wiggle free. That move only succeeds in making Morris lean down onto Clyde's back to hold him down tighter with his weight on him.

Landry steps in close, leans down near Clyde's ear, quietly says, "Now, we can do this the clean and easy way or the rough and bloody way. Take your pick. And, hey, if you pick correctly, we'll allow you to save a smidge of respect—we'll hide the cuffs from your co-workers as we lead you out of here and on your way to the station with us. What do you say? We got a deal?"

As best he can, with his face smushed into the desktop and Morris practically lying on top of him, Clyde nods his head. Then Morris begins reading him his rights.

———

Detectives Landry and Morris walk past the counter at the T-intersection of the hallways in the adult unit, following very closely behind Clyde. Five psych techs are sitting behind the counter. Rick and Dr. Headstrom stand watching from the psychiatrist's open office doorway. Nurse Taylor and Mary stand in front of the nurses' station. Irie slowly wheels her cleaning cart back toward the janitor's closet. Every person witnessing the apparent escort has their eyes riveted on Clyde's walk of shame. He keeps his head held high, while his jacket hangs over his cuffed hands out in front of him.

Clyde must feel everyone's eyes on him. He turns toward the counter and then to the nurse's station and says, "No worries. Just helping these fine detectives find a missing person. I'll see *you* all tomorrow." He throws them all a wink. He doesn't look at Irie. It's as if he doesn't see her at all.

Dr. Headstrom rushes over to unlock the doors to the adult wing. As Detective Landry holds the double doors of the unit open for Clyde and Detective Morris, sniggers and whispers sound out from behind them as they exit.

Once those double doors shut and Clyde is gone, Irie goes into the janitor's closet and shuts the door behind her. With her hand over her mouth, she starts laughing.

What an idiot. Does he really think anyone believes him?

A chuckle later she has her cell in her hand, texting the news to Tommy and Dory.

CHAPTER 23
SEEING A MAN ABOUT A THING

I hope my guilt and shame stay hidden away once we're face to face.

Irie got the contact info we needed. Now we're almost there, and I *still* have no idea what to say to him. The unexpected news Irie gave us when we all met up at Tommy's still has my mind reeling.

"You're *absolutely sure* he was arrested?" The dream come true seems too much like that—just a dream.

I see Irie, dreads draping down toward the center console, in the rearview mirror. She's wedged between the two front seats, leaning into the front from the back of my car, nodding as she speaks. "Clyde may have thought the jacket draped over his bound wrists hid those cuffs, but I'm not a naïve little girl." She shrugs and smirks. "If it wasn't for the detectives showing up and taking Clyde away, I may have had a much harder time getting the address. Everyone was so engrossed in gossiping it was a piece of cake."

"So, I guess I should thank Detective Landry for bustin' Clyde and lending you a helping hand." As I smile at Irie in the rearview mirror, I realize the distraction tactic going on. Asking questions about last night helps me keep my mind off what's waiting for me at the end of this car ride.

"Bustin' that slimeball is all well and good, a step in the right direction and all, but what *isn't* sitting well with me is the disappearance of another mysterious nurse." Tommy starts thumb-drumming on his knees, staring out the passenger side window, appearing deep in thought.

"Yeah, the timing...come on...It's too obvious they're connected to this psycho-shit-show somehow." When the heavy sigh-laugh comes out of me, I finally realize how quick and shallow my breathing has been. I take a long, deep breath. Then another. I need to calm myself. The camera image of what should've shown Nurse Hatchet in my room that night we set up Sheila pops into my head. Instead of the red-haired hottie that should've been there, it showed her long flowing hair morphed into red-wings, with a flaming-eyed skull-face. It wasn't near the bathroom where I had seen the nurse—It was directly behind Sheila at the moment of the attack.

Maybe all those counselors do have a good point about deep breathing. It sure does help clear out some of the brain fog.

"Who *planted* them there to get involved?" Irie's dreads sway side to side as she looks back and forth between Tommy and me. "They *had* to have been planted there by *someone*."

"I think the bigger question is—what the hell *are* they? I can't get that camera image from the night Sheila attacked me out of my head. Maybe they planted themselves there."

Tommy faces me, head cocked. "Wait. Maybe what we saw wasn't the nurse, but rather what she had *summoned*."

Irie says, "Or, like I said already, maybe it was who, or what, planted the nurses there to begin with."

Silence.

The atmosphere in the car swirls with the energy of our deep thoughts, thrumming. I don't hear the thrumming; I feel it, like when the drums and the bass guitar fall in the pocket together, blasting from the PA speakers, vibrating through your entire body.

We drive at least another mile before anyone says a word.

Then comes the big question.

"So, this gargoyle thing...if Shawn *does* know about it and can help us figure some of this crazy shit out, how is any of *that* going to help with the revenge we all want so badly? Did you two plot-devising ladies give much consideration to *that* yet?

Eager as a wolf pouncing on a kill, Irie pops her head between our seats again. "I think if it's on our side, maybe we could somehow lure it to more of those slimy bone dust junkies. And if it's..."

"Wait. Lure it? You think we'd know more about finding these junkies than a creature from some other fucking world?" A cynical laugh shoots out of Tommy. "No offense, Sunshine, but I imagine a creature like that *must* have supernatural powers, powers well beyond what any of *us* can do."

Iries punches him in the shoulder. "Hey, don't rain on my parade, Mr. Negative Nancy. Do you have any better ideas?"

He cocks his head to the side and shrugs. "Hey, just callin' it like I see it...or imagine it."

"Hey, you two, no arguing." My eyes remain on the road ahead. "I just hope like hell it's on our side. Maybe if Shawn *does* know about it, he can tell us if it has any supernatural powers. That's a very crucial piece to all of this, whether it's on *our* side or *theirs*. Let's just wait for more planning once we know more about this thing. Sound like a plan?"

They both nod. Silent, they each turn to look out the side windows as the trees zip past. Again, I feel the thrumming of their deep thoughts.

This is all so fucked up and confusing, it feels like my head might explode with the overload of ideas and various theories.

Before anyone says another word, we start driving down the last street on the GPS directions. It's a small neighborhood on a dead-end street.

Oh, lovely, a dead-end. That only means one thing—

No way out.

I sure do hope this unexpected visit is received well.

The house is larger than I expected. It has a separate three-car garage with either a large entertainment room or an in-law apartment above, and a white fence stretching around the perimeter of the backyard where a built-in swimming pool sits as centerpiece. It all resides at the far end of a cul-de-sac in the town of Scarborough about fifteen minutes outside the city.

With the sun quickly sinking behind the tree line surrounding the neighborhood, I sure hope Tommy and Irie aren't noticeable sitting in my Outback. No way in hell was I coming here alone. But I don't want all three of us knocking on Shawn's door, freaking him out. There's no telling what state of mind he might be in when he answers my knock–*if* he answers my knock.

What if he's in a bad way—like Jonesing or high or some other who-knows crazy shit?

Thankfully, Tommy was able to use a few hours of his personal time to get out of work early for this. Irie straight up called out, refusing to get left out. As she keeps reminding her dad—this is her fight, too.

We've all lost someone to these psycho bone-chiseling freaks. Now it's time for us to help find out what the fuck is *really* going on. Can't trust leaving such an uncanny case up to conventional law enforcement to figure out on their own. If we did that, the truth would never be discovered.

Well, here goes nothing.

The first step up toward the front door—shit, this isn't easy.

Why am I so hesitant? Shawn saved my ass back at the hospital. Twice. Not just from Sheila, but from that whole psycho NA group when they all went nutty—nuttier than normal.

Though nothing about that group is normal.

Good thing Detective Landry cracked that nut to pieces.

But Shawn's been using again. Or at least trying to use, hence that cemetery incident.

Is he even going to welcome me? Will he talk to me at all?

Leaning down, I fiddle with my pant leg to make sure Jill's boot knife stays secure and well hidden.

Nothing to see here. Just checking my shoelace, fixing my pants.

All's good. I'm still armed, you know, just in case. But still...

Uncertainty is a bitch, debilitating at times—like now.

Here goes. I can do this.

Yeah, I'll just keep telling myself that.

Okay. One last deep breath, maybe that will make me push that damn doorbell. It's right there, staring me in the face. *It won't take much effort, Dory. Just press the fucking thing already. If you just stand here looking all suspicious and stuff, he probably won't even answer the damn door.*

One last look over my shoulder. Yep, can barely see Tommy and Irie at all.

Without looking back to the house, for fear it might make me cower, I reach out and press the buzzer beside the door. I perk up as soon as it sounds out.

Jimi Hendrix's signature opening guitar riff for "Voodoo Chile" rings out loud and clear. A smile spreads across my face. Drums may be my life, but damn...

I can't believe I'm actually smiling, considering what I came here for.

The whole song intro plays.

No one answers.

I press the doorbell again and listen to some more Jimi, while tapping my foot to that sweet, sweet riff.

Still, no one answers.

The music has made me a bit more relaxed, though. But if no one's here, that doesn't really matter much.

I reach out to ring the bell again. Just before my finger

touches the lit-up blue light of the buzzer's button I hear a window slide open on the second floor of the garage.

"Dory? Is that you?"

Such a distinct voice. I don't even have to look to know it's him. Ever since I first heard him speak in that counseling group, I've wondered what makes his voice sound so strained and sort of squeaky.

When I turn toward the garage, I see Shawn with his face practically smushed against the screen. I yell up to him before he falls through that window to get a better look. "Yeah, it's me."

With a head nod toward the back yard, he says, "Come on up the back stairs."

I give him a thumbs up then start back down the front porch steps. After hearing the window slide shut, I glance up to make sure he's not still watching, then I look back at Tommy and Irie to make sure they see where I'm headed. I point a thumb to my chest then to the back yard, and I glance up toward the garage apartment. They both give a nod of understanding.

Climbing this tall set of stairs proves a bit easier than climbing the couple of steps on the front porch a moment ago. At least now I know he welcomes my visit.

The back door at the top of the stairs stands ajar, with no one there to greet me. Easing it open I knock while slowly entering, expecting to walk into a sort of bar or game room or maybe both.

What I see before me is completely unexpected.

Displayed on the wall of a lit-up hallway straight ahead of me are five electric guitars, all hanging by their headstocks from wall mounts, shimmering under spotlights. These beasts are not your generic beginner axes. They are all top-of-the-line models from the likes of Gibson, Paul Reed Smith, and Fender.

How the hell can Shawn afford this kind of gear, this sort of house? And why is he hanging out in what looks like an apartment above his garage?

Damn. I didn't even know he was a musician.

Beside the opening of that hallway, in an oversized black Lazy Boy recliner with the footrest stretched out, sits Shawn, black and gray medusa tattoo—with the Duster-scar masked by her snake hair—peeking out from under the leg of his long black cargo shorts. Dark, puffy circles appear under his eyes, making him look like a depressed bloodhound.

Now, can this bloodhound help me sniff out some clues?

"Hey, stranger," I say as I shut the door behind me. "I hope you don't mind me just popping in unannounced like this."

A hand wave toward a matching recliner to the left of the door is all I get for a response.

A man of few words. All right. I understand. I can relate.

I sit in the chair offered.

Silence.

We're muted in the dim shared-light surrounding us in this room, since the only lights turned on in the place illuminate that gear-filled hallway.

Hey, if I owned gear that nice, I'd want a spotlight on it at all times, too.

If I'm seeing correctly, it looks like there's a kitchen at the other end of the hall. Though most of that room sits to the right side of the end of the hallway where I can't see any appliances, it has a white ceramic tile floor common for kitchens, and I see the back of what looks like a kitchen table chair. There's a closed door on the opposite side of the hall from the guitars. Maybe a bedroom? We're obviously sitting in the living room but there's no TV. It appears like this place *is* actually a full apartment. Not a bar. Not a game room. Not even a simple jam space.

After scoping out the place I realize I have no idea what to say, where to start. Why I'm here. I look back at the guitars. With a nod toward the lit-up display I break the silence. "Sweet guitars! I had no idea you played."

What better way to break the ice than with a compliment?

Plus, I'm not so good at striking up conversations. Compliments are usually my go-to.

"Thanks. Started when I was about six or so. My dad insisted I play music and I *don't* hate him for it." Shawn squeaks out with his pre-teen-boy voice. With every word that comes out of him, the veins in his neck bulge out like a network of bursting-at-the-seems rivers. That strain could be why he's a man of few words.

"Sweet! I'm a drummer. I teach at The Drum Shop."

He perks up a bit. "I had no idea *you* played." He chuckles under his breath. "Between the two of us, we've got half a band."

Normally the idea of starting a new band would excite me, but I can't forget why I'm here to begin with. "Yeah, right? Food for thought."

For some reason he's now sinking back into that cushy seat. I hope he doesn't think I'm blowing him off on the band thing.

A heavy sigh rushes out of me. "Okay, look, no bullshitting around. Starting a band would be great and everything, but the reason for my visit is pretty fucking strange." I hesitate, wondering how to describe the why of my visit.

Hopefully he'll forget to ask about the how.

Leaning forward, elbows on my knees, I dive right in. "I'm here to see what you know, if anything, about some giant flying creature that *may somehow* be connected to those crazy Duster fucks back at the hospital. Last weekend..."

Shawn slams the footrest shut and sits up at attention. "How do you know about that? Have you seen it?" As he talks, his eyes move side to side, scanning the place.

Does he think someone is listening? Watching?

My words have obviously put him on edge.

Shoving my hand into the pocket of my hoodie, I reach for my cell to show him the video.

Before my hand wraps around my phone, Shawn jumps to his feet and yells, "Wait! What are you reaching for?"

I ease my hand back out and hold both up, as though under arrest. "No worries. It's alright. I can wait to show you. Just sit and listen."

Though he hesitates, he sits back down. After seeing him out of that chair, I realize he looks a few pounds heavier than when we were in the hospital together. That's a good sign. Maybe he *isn't* using. Or at least isn't using regularly.

Revisiting what happened to Jill doesn't thrill me, but I tell him everything that happened, including the video my neighbor recorded that I want to show him on my phone. He settles back in while I'm talking, kicks the footrest back up.

"Holy shit!" Shawn takes in a deep breath and holds it for more time than seems possible. He turns away, as though processing everything I just told him. Or maybe he's got something he wants to tell me but doesn't know if he should. I don't know. His reaction is difficult to read.

It may be a lot to process but I can't wait. His reaction shows me he knows something.

"So, have you seen this...this flying creature? Or maybe you've heard about it, or seen some of the graffiti the detective told me about? It kinda-sorta resembles a gargoyle, but I haven't seen its face. Though some of the graffiti, I've been told, resembles an angel."

He remains turned away from me. I can't tell if he's going to answer me or not.

"It's just that...remembering that creepy image on Dr. Headstrom's camera from that night back in the hospital, I can't help but wonder...Hell, I can't help but *assume* this creature, whatever it is, is somehow behind those crazy-in-deep-Dusters. Like the ones you and Davey told me and Tommy about—those long-time users and how they go a bit nutty and seem to have uncanny abilities. Getting into people's minds and whatnot. Remember? *You told me that.* Come on. They could *smell* me bleeding. They knew where my wound was when it wasn't visible. Am I onto something? Or maybe it *really is* a gargoyle and it's trying to get rid of those evil fuckers? Is that it? What do you know? You must know something. *Anything. Please...*"

He puts his hand up, palm facing me. I shut my mouth, give respect.

It's the least I can do after getting him arrested. Hopefully he never finds out about that little detail. I have a hard time living with that knowledge myself. I don't want him hating me for what I inadvertently did to him.

"Listen, I don't know much, but I *do* know this..."

Whether or not he's trying to make me sweat or he just makes a habit of creating a dramatic effect stands as a detail yet for me to discover.

Instead of finishing his sentence, Shawn quickly kicks the footrest of his chair shut again, jumps up onto his feet and starts pacing the living room. He pauses to make sure the curtains on both windows conceal the room completely, leaving not even the slightest sliver of an opening. He even walks down the hallway to the other side of the apartment and does some shuffling around. I assume he's closing whatever curtains might hang from the other windows back there.

Hopefully he didn't open them and look outside, maybe accidentally see Tommy and Irie hiding in my car.

Remaining quiet and patient, I wait for him to come back and finish his sentence.

When he finally does come back, he completes one more go 'round with pacing the living room, then he stops right in front of my seat and stares down at me. "Every Duster I know has either mentioned that *creature*, or has asked questions about it, like you are now." He turns away, steps back over to his seat, and plops down. The footrest does not get kicked up. There is no resting now. "Yes, I've seen the graffiti, too. But, no, I've never seen that thing, not for *real*. But you say you've got that video from your neighbor?"

"Yeah, I got it right here." I reach back into my pocket and pull out my cell. "You wanna see it?" After I pull the video up on my phone, I hold it out, arm stretched across the space between my chair and his. The phone rests right on my palm, waiting for him to take it. The huge play arrow sits in the center of the video, waiting for him to press it.

He does neither.

Leaning forward with his elbows on his knees, he stares at it. The longer he stares, the more tension rises in his chest and shoulders. It looks like he's not even breathing. Eyes wide and getting wider.

A minute or so passes before he finally sits back and looks away. "No. *Nope.* I don't need to see it to know it's real." He releases a heavy sigh. "Honestly, I'd rather *not* see it. Better that way. I already have a hard enough time sleeping." He leans down towards his feet, reaches under the chair and pulls out what looks like a journal of some kind. Leather cover with a metal clasp.

A dream journal maybe?

I act nonchalant about it, wait to see if he wants to share more. His dreams are none of my business.

"Yeah," I say as I pull the phone back and repocket it. "I understand that all too well. I have both court dates coming right up, and now I'm dealing with this crazy shit...and Jill..."

"Hey, yeah, your court dates. Not sure if you know or not..." He looks back at me now. "Davey and I have been subpoenaed. We're witnesses against both those chicks that attacked you."

I perk up. "Really? I had no idea. Sorry you're being made to testify, but I really do appreciate anything you can do to speak *up* for me and *against* them."

"Damn, Dory, I think these cases are both a slam dunk for you, even without us as witnesses. Hell, you got the big guns in your court with Dr. Headstrom."

"Yeah, but he didn't *see* Toodles slice me open during our mad escape from that last crazy NA meeting. So, again, you need to know how thankful I am for you and Davey coming to court on my beha..."

Ding

A text notification chimes on my phone at the same instance that something is stomping a fucking stampede up the back porch steps.

We both freeze.

I don't think either one of us is breathing now, but we both jump to our feet and rush to the window beside the door. I get there first. Through the tiniest opening in the curtains, I can see what's making the noise, though I have no idea why. Before Shawn gets to the window, I pull the curtains shut, turn to face him.

"Wait. Before you look. I didn't come alone. I brought Tommy and Irie with me just in case you didn't take my visit well."

He halts just a foot in front of me. "What? Really? Why would you worry about that?"

"No offense, but I had no idea how you've been doing since getting out. What if you were using again? What if *you* turned into one of *them*—one of those crazy fuckers? What if..."

Bang! Bang! Bang!

Pounding on the door truncates my sentence.

Shawn flings the door open.

Out of breath on the back porch, Tommy doesn't enter. He looks as though he's ready to bolt back down the stairs any second. But not before he dives into frantic rambling.

"Hey, Shawn, good to see you, but no time for chit-chat." He looks back and forth between Shawn and me and continues at auctioneer speed. "We all gotta get out of here. Now! That *thing* is coming. It's almost here." He points his thumb over his shoulder at the expanse of orange and purple painted sky behind the backyard. "Let's go." He grabs my arm and I don't brush him away.

"Why didn't you wait in the car where it's safer?"

"Couldn't trust our lives to technology or your response-time to checking your texts. Now, let's get out of here!" I don't resist as he ushers me toward the stairs.

Shawn doesn't immediately follow.

Tommy halts and repeats, "Shawn, we gotta go. Now! Come on. We're not leaving you here to find out what that thing wants. Let's go!"

"I just need to grab something, dude. Just a sec."

Tommy shakes his head. "Hurry up, man. Get it and let's go!"

After stepping down the first couple of stairs, I glance back over my shoulder past Tommy and see Shawn rush to his recliner and grab his journal. When I turn back around toward the stairs to make sure I don't miss that next step, I see the creature in the distant dusk sky. Its wingspan is massive. And it's flying straight in our direction.

No time to wait.

But I do have time to yell. "Hurry, Shawn!"

CHAPTER 24
ANOTHER UNINVITED VISITOR

I make it to the driveway a lot quicker than I'd expected.

Taking cover stands as top priority. Anyone left outside under the open sky when that thing gets here—who knows what'll happen. Since we're not the bad guys in all this, I imagine it's not here to eliminate evil, as Tommy thought.

I jump into the driver's seat of my car and immediately lean across the center console and fling open the passenger side door. The back door on that side is already open, with Irie inside waiting for Shawn or her dad to jump in beside her. Every second we can shave off our escape gives us a better chance of survival.

"Where's Dad? Shawn? Why aren't they with you?"

"I don't know. Shawn said he had to grab something."

"But what about Dad?"

I shrug, shake my head. "I have no idea. He was right behind me."

I look at the garage to see where the guys are. They haven't made it into the driveway yet.

Where are they?

Thudding footfalls suddenly sound out as they're running down the back stairs. Relieved, I slam my door shut, though I still don't see them.

"Thank goodness. I hear them coming. I already called 911." Irie is leaning far into the front between the seats. "Hopefully the cops will get here soon."

"Not soon enough." I'm almost kissing the windshield, looking up at the expanse of wide-open sky behind the house and garage. That damned creature is flying fast! It's already zooming toward the backyard fence.

A blink later, Shawn skids around the back corner of the garage into the driveway. One hand is tucked into the front pocket of his hoodie. It looks like he's holding something so it won't fall out while he's running. Must be that damn book he needed so badly for whatever reason.

Another blink later and Tommy appears at his heels.

I smile.

He waited for Shawn. My new friend wouldn't leave anyone behind.

Shawn scurries around the flung-open back door just as the creature glides down toward the driveway. The darkening colors filling the sky play tricks with my eyes. It's difficult to see the features of this thing clearly. One moment it looks like it has leathery skin. But as it gets closer, I notice spikey-spotty fur or feathers. One thing I know for sure—it's blacker than black, if that's even possible. Now that I realize how much of it I can see, I notice how close it is behind Tommy.

Shit. Shit. *Shit*! I don't know what to do.

I yell, "Come on, Tommy! You can make..."

Irie leans even further into the front seat, grabs my shoulder and screams, "Dad, hurry!"

We exchange quick, terrified glances, then look back at what's to come.

CHAPTER 25
PUDDLE OF BLOOD

That creature grabs hold of Tommy with some sort of massive claws on its feet. It clamps him by the shoulders with those lethal talons, though they look more like a cross between scythe blades and Arabian Scimitar blades.

Tommy starts thrashing around and kicking with all the vigor he's got. One of his shoulders gets free of the creature's hold. An enormous flap of its vast wings spins them around, as it appears to get another hold on his shoulder. From this angle it's difficult to tell for sure what's going on. But now I can see there's a line of coarse red hair or fur or feathers running from the creature's head down its back, like a mohawk, between its wings.

Fuck this! I can't just sit here and watch this shit go down. That man is the *only* one who believed me in the hospital. He saved my life!

Time to return the favor.

Jill's boot knife is in my hand by the time my feet hit the pavement. Irie is already half out the back door when I turn to her and say, "I'm armed, you're not. Stay here. He'll *kill* me if you get hurt."

Her face is smeared with running mascara as the tears stream down her cheeks like coal-colored rivers. All I hear from her is "Dory, please, he's all I've got!" as I charge toward the back of that giant demonic creature—whatever the hell it is.

It must stand twenty feet tall. How does it not have Tommy up in the sky by now? Maybe it's not used to its victims struggling. I have no idea, but I run with all I've got, knife out and ready. As soon as I get almost close enough, I wonder how I can possibly stab at anything other than its wings from down here. It's so huge! And the fucking wings keep flapping, trying to take flight.

How the hell am I supposed to do this?

I notice a bench sitting against the side of the garage not too far behind the creature. One leap up onto the bench, then I push up off the seat with all the strength I can force out of my runner's legs. And I'm there. Up on the back of this thing, with its mohawk, spikey and itchy, poking through my clothes. With a fistful of that coarse red fur puncturing holes in my palm, I hang on as best I can. With pent-up anger filling my insides, I immediately start stabbing at anything and everything I can. A hellacious screech rends my ears with every stab and slice of the blade through its leathery flesh. Black blood spurts out all over me and runs down the demon's veiny, tough-skinned back.

Gunshots blast through the air.

One. Two. Three. Four.

The fifth shot rips through the sky so loudly it tears at my eardrums.

The creature lets out an ear-piercing screech. Then, all at once, it drops Tommy and whips its wings back, tossing me to the ground. Before I can clear my hair from my line of sight, the demon takes flight, fleeing the onslaught of gunshots now firing at it in rapid succession.

The only thing it leaves behind is a puddle of black blood between Tommy and me.

CHAPTER 26

OBSIDIAN DAZE

I scurry over to see if Tommy is all right. He's lying supine and facing away from me, jacket bloody and shredded. I reach out and gently touch his blood-soaked shoulder, careful to avoid his wounds.

"Tommy, are you okay?"

He slowly lifts his head, looks over his shoulder at me. He glances around and sees that the creature is gone. I look around with him. Not only do I also want to confirm the monster is gone, but I also want to see where the shots came from.

Two cruisers are parked on the side of the road in front of the house. Four heads are poking up from the far side, guns still aimed up toward the sky. Parked behind the cop cars a black SUV's motor rumbles, with two more heads poking up from behind it, also with guns aimed at the sky.

I turn back to Tommy.

His hand is on top of mine, clutching it. He gives it a gentle squeeze. "Dabbler, you saved my *life*. You know that, right?" A shimmer twinkles in his dark chocolate eyes. Blood droplets are splashed across his cheeks.

I shrug. "It's the least I could do."

"Least?" He shakes his head and laughs. There's that signature crooked smile and dimple scar. "Shit. Downplaying really *is* your specialty."

That crooked smile makes me smile.

This time I help *him* up to his feet. Before I realize it, he's got me wrapped in a sudden hug, warm and fierce and quite bloody. Against my cheek I feel the pounding of his heart so hard I'm surprised it's not protruding from his chest with every thump like a cartoon character.

Shawn and Irie, along with Detective Landry and two unknown EMTs rush to our sides, breaking our embrace. Irie gets to us first. Sobbing, she immediately hugs her dad. Everyone is talking at once. The two EMTs are on Tommy like gauze pads on bloody wounds. They have to pry him from his daughter's arms. He looks back and forth, from one to the other, and starts pointing to his injuries on and around his shoulders.

Shocked and shrouded in disbelief, I just stare.

First Tommy. A bloody, sweaty, tattered mess of a man with the biggest heart I've ever known.

Then the sky. Darkening shades of burnt orange and violet and indigo streak through gossamer wisps of clouds. The black of night encroaching. No demon in sight.

Suddenly I'm assaulted with hugs and *Thank yous.*

Irie.

"Holy shit, Dory. I have no idea how you did it, but you did. You saved my dad." She pulls back. Still holding me by my shoulders, she looks me straight in the eyes. "I will be forever grateful and I will *never ever* forget." She hugs me so tightly I can barely breathe. Side to side she rocks us.

I remain silent. Whatever the hell just happened seems so unreal. I feel like I'm having some kind of out-of-body experience or something, like this is all happening to someone else and I'm just a spectator. Even all these hugs. Are they really meant for me?

Irie releases her hold on me and wipes her tears on the

sleeve of her jacket. Black mascara smears across the turquoise fabric.

An instant later, I'm getting jostled around. Someone is shaking me by the shoulder.

"Dory, can you hear me? Are you okay? What's all over you? Are you bleeding? Do you need medical attention?" It's a new voice. Not Irie.

I turn and see Detective Landry. She's standing on one side of Shawn. Irie now stands on the other side.

So much is going on, I don't know what to say. I don't know what to think.

I look from Irie to Landry and back to Irie. "I think some of your *thank yous* should go to *this* woman," I say as I nod toward Detective Landry. "After all, it was the gunfire that finally made that thing let him go."

Movement and voices sound out from the other side of the house before anyone can respond. All of us turn toward the sounds.

Out in the side yard on the far end of the garage, I see Landry's partner and all four police officers running toward the back yard.

What are they doing?

Where are they going?

Shawn and Irie are talking and pointing in the direction of the running officers. Whatever they're saying, I have no idea. So much is going on I can't focus.

I look at Detective Landry. "I'm not bleeding, I don't think." I shake my head. "Where's Detective Morris going? What's going on?"

"Are you sure you're not hurt?"

"Yeah, I'm pretty sure." I look down to inspect myself and see a wet sticky substance all over me. I reach down to feel what it is. My hands come back up covered in black inky goo.

"Well, that creature—between you and your knife," with a head-tilt-of-questioning Landry looks at the boot knife on the ground beside me, "and the gunfire, it might be dead or at least severely injured." With one fluid motion, she sweeps her hair over her shoulder and points out to the field beyond Shawn's backyard. "All four officers swear they saw the creature drop somewhere beyond the tree line back there. We might have something to bring back to the lab after all." She looks back to me and adds, "besides all that oil or ink or whatever it is all over you."

"That crazy-ass demon *bled this out* when I was stabbing it." I try wiping my hands off on my jeans, only to come back with complete obsidian palms.

Irie leans closer, examining the strange substance, while Landry lies an interrogatory look on me. "I find your word choice interesting, Dory."

"Word choice?" I'm confused. Did I say something wrong?

"Demon. You called the creature a..."

"Hey, look at that stuff." Irie reaches, index finger out, toward my palm.

Quicker than a blink, Landry jabs her hand out and grabs Irie's arm. "Don't touch it."

Wow! Quite the reflexes. And eyesight—Landry never took her eyes off me. She grabbed Irie's arm without even looking at her.

Practically jumping out of her Mary Janes, Irie pulls away. "Sorry. I just couldn't help but notice...Doesn't that remind you of something?" She points to my palm. "Look closely. Dory, turn your palm a bit, you know, side to side." With her hand out, she mimics what her words told me and slightly tilts her up and open palm left to right.

A beam from the light-sensor flood light on the garage hits my palm just as I angle my hand back toward myself and the building. My palm starts shimmering. The black demon blood, or whatever the hell it is, it's shining. Even as dark as it appears it actually *reflects* the light, making the darkness look shimmery and alluring.

I wobble my hand a bit more, finding a rhythm in my movements, making the light dance across my palm. Before I realize what I'm doing, my whole body is swaying to the rhythm of the mesmerizing light. It feels almost magnetic. I can't seem to pull my stare away.

"Oil?" The quizzical creases in Landry's forehead twitch and move, as though reaching to find the answer Irie is looking for.

"Not quite. Oil shows colors." Irie leans in closer. Her fingertip gets so close to my skin, I can feel slight heat and a little thrum of electricity emanating from her. "Obsidian. It looks like melted obsidian. Maybe if it hardens..." She grasps my arm, falters my mesmerized swaying.

My rhythm skips a beat.

Scratching sounds hit my ears.

I halt.

Confused, I shake my head, then look at Irie and Detective Landry.

A notepad is in Landry's hand. The scratching of her pen racing across the page knocked me out of my trance-like state. I can't see what she's writing.

"What? Did you figure something out? What did she say? What's going on?" It feels like I just woke from a dream or something. I'm a bit foggy. Disoriented. Like I missed something. Dozed off for a minute and just missed something.

Don't tell me I'm now narcoleptic. Shit. Not another disorder. No more labels, *please*.

Landry huffs, shakes her head and says, "Hardly figured any of this uncanny shit out." She catches eye contact with me. "This is just an extremely unusual case. But I *do* know *one* thing for sure—the attack on Roxanne was targeted for some reason. And I fear that someone here may have also been a target."

A pause.

I can't speak.

I've lost my breath.

Who was it after?

"And that thing, well..." Landry glances out back past the house, past the garage and the luxury fenced in yard with built-in swimming pool, past the wide-open field, all the way to the tree line. The border of the dark woods beyond appears to stretch on for miles. "Obsidian—just got me thinking of where we might look to find this creature's origin. Maybe there are more like it out there?"

Shawn steps up. "I can guaran*tee* you *won't* find that crazy fucker's from any part of *this* world."

Landry turns as slowly as a sloth toward the eloquent-speaking man in the Goatwhore hoodie. "Excuse me, but if you know more about that creature, it could *really* help this case." With her notebook at the ready and her pen aimed like a gun at the page, she stares at Shawn. "Please, tell me everything you know. Go."

Shawn reaches into the big front pocket of his hoodie. The band's huge Goatwhore logo image on the front of the sweat-shirt of a gun-toting goat demon wrapped in snakes and standing on what looks like a winged creature nailed to the ground screams for attention, especially after what we all just witnessed. As he pulls his hand out, I see he's holding that black leather book, what I thought was his dream journal. He holds it up in front of his chest, leather strap and metal clasp facing Landry. "This right here is all I know." Outstretching his arm hesitantly, he offers the book to Landry. "Now that I know the demon *is* real, I also know what's in this book is real—*not* just a myth."

Irie intercepts the offer, grabs the book and says, "What could possibly be so important that you risked my dad's *life* to go back for this?"

"I'm wicked sorry." Shawn glances away for a moment, clearly distraught. He looks back at Irie. "I had no *idea* he was going to *wait* for me." He pauses. A look of sympathy washes over his face as he softly says, "He stayed behind for *me*." His eyes begin glistening, tears teetering on the edge, threatening to fall.

"What *is* that, Shawn? I thought that was your dream journal?"

He shakes his head.

"Okay, *okay.*" Landry snatches the book from Irie. "Miss, I need this book, *whatever* it is. You guys can all yell at each other or thank each other or whatever, but the book..." She glances down at what's now in her hands. "Yeah, Shawn, what *is* this?" Her fingers grasp the clasp and unlock it.

"Open it. See for yourself."

The book is made of a soft-looking wrinkled black leather, with worn marks all around the edges. No title appears on the cover. No author listed. No cover image. It may not be Shawn's journal, but it certainly looks like *someone's* journal.

I step a bit closer to Landry, trying to see what she's about to see.

She flips open the front cover, like opening a door. The binding creaks like old rusty door hinges. The first page is empty, but the next two pages have a two-page illustration, like a centerfold image, in black ink of that flying demon, wings outstretched. Even in this picture the face of the demon appears shadowed and hard to discern. As Landry flips to the next page, it looks as though those huge wings are about to wrap around us and pull us into its grasp, pull us into that book, transport us to another dimension.

The next page displays a handwritten title in loopy cursive. And, well...

It's in English.

As ancient as the book looks this close up, I was expecting to find some foreign language. Maybe Latin or something much more ancient. Horror movies always have this sort of thing in Latin for some reason.

Shit. Maybe I shouldn't get my demonic information from horror movies.

As I read the title to myself, Landry reads it out loud. "*The Poison of Addiction: Devourer of Souls.*" She cocks her head, and repeats, "Devourer of Souls?" Then she looks over at Shawn. "Does that thing eat souls?"

The subtitle I see on the page gets ignored.

Banishment to the Dark Realm

Before Shawn answers Landry, I blurt out, "What I want to know is—where is this *Dark Realm*?" Nervous laughter leaks out along with my next words. "Don't tell me my *drunk* neighbor was right *all* along. That thing is a fucking alien?"

"Not quite." A flatline smirk follows Shawn's words.

Landry fans through the pages, stopping here and there to read a bit, as Shawn goes on.

"It's a demon. The demon of addiction and disorder. It weakens and consumes souls. The Dark Realm is Hell, or a section of Hell, or someplace *like* Hell." He shakes his head. "Somewhere in there the demon is referred to as a 'soul-sucker.'"

Landry slams the cover shut and glares over at Shawn. "*Where* did you get this? *Who* wrote it? Is this even *legit*?" She smirks.

Shawn's mouth opens to speak, but instead of hearing his voice. . .

A blood-curdling scream erupts from beyond the house, beyond the backyard, beyond the line of black where the tree line meets the wide-open field.

Another scream. Different person. Same location.

It all pours forth from the deep darkness of the woods beyond.

CHAPTER 27
REFUGE

After the extensive questioning session we each had with Detectives Landry and Morris, Tommy had been patched up at the ER and ready to head home and rest. We were all relieved he didn't get admitted. Though the ER doc did suggest he stay overnight for observation, Tommy adamantly refused.

Tommy's place sure feels like a welcoming refuge from the demon attack. I want to kick back on that oversized, cushy sofa —my new bed as of lately—so badly, but my nerves are still all tied in knots. I've been trying the deep breathing ever since we picked Tommy up from the hospital, but it isn't working to calm me down yet. I'm really trying my hardest to finally relax, but after what went down earlier with that demon, I predict my near-future, maybe even my not-so-near future, doesn't feature much relax-time.

Maybe I could relax more if I didn't try so hard. Isn't relaxing supposed to be, well, what do you call it...relaxing? My muscles are still tense and achy. But dammit, at least I'm trying.

I take in another deep stuttered breath. And another. And another.

Nope. Still not working.

Shawn walks through the front door and steps over beside

me and the sofa. "I can't believe that detective wanted the journal as evidence."

"Don't forget, she has my drunk neighbor's video as evidence, too."

"Well, she *did* say this is the most bizarre case she's ever worked. Might leave her with no other leads to go on." A shirt-less Tommy, with his shoulders bandaged up in gauze that is starting to look bloody and in need of changing already, double checks the locks on his front door, then goes around the living room closing all the curtains before finally easing down into his recliner to rest. Just like when he refused to get admitted to the hospital, he keeps insisting he's fine.

I can't help but notice, as odd and inappropriate as it is to think about this right now, how fit and in-shape he is for being old enough to be Irie's dad. I wonder how old he is. I've never asked. He definitely doesn't look old enough to have fathered a college-aged child. He doesn't look much older than me. Maybe thirty-five or so.

Then I see Irie, her flawless caramel skin and eye-catching beauty. Even with her makeup all smudged she's a head-turner.

Definitely a good line of genes in that family. Kaya must have been a beauty, too. Come to think of it, I'm surprised I haven't noticed any pictures of her displayed at Irie's or Tommy's. The memory must be too painful, I imagine.

"Dad, aren't you cold without your shirt on?" Irie holds out a throw blanket for him.

"Sunshine, I've been sweating ever since that demon sunk its talons into me." He huffs and hesitantly adds, "Plus, putting any sort of weight or material on my shoulders doesn't feel so good right now."

"Well, you just stay put. Try to relax." Irie steps over to recliner and wraps the colorful woven throw blanket over his legs and feet. She tucks it up high under his arms, leaving his shoulders uncovered.

Exhaustion tugs me onto the couch. I plop down in the

corner with a heavy sigh. Shawn takes up the other corner. Elbows on his knees, he keeps tugging at the strings of his hood while tapping out some catchy little funk rhythm with his feet on the hardwood floor. The music from his feet doesn't appear to soothe him.

"Now that an officer is dead and another is injured because of that creature or...demon or ...what*ever* the hell it is, I think she's willing to use just about anything to find out what makes that thing tick." Taking a seat on the cushion between Shawn and me, Irie opens a drawer under the coffee table and pulls out a piece of paper. "Thank goodness it's dead and in the lab."

Faster foot tapping comes from Shawn as he says, "Dead? Not sure if that's even possible. Banishment back to its own realm, *that's* what the journal describes. What if that's the only way?"

Tommy's crooked smirk appears before he says, "Man, we all saw them bring it out of the woods and load it into the back of that big rig's trailer. It wasn't resisting. It wasn't *moving*." He chuckles. "No offense, but maybe that journal doesn't have it *all* right. Who knows what's true?" He winks and finger-points at Shawn when he adds, "That, my friend, is what the detectives are for."

A slight laugh comes from Irie. "I can't believe how big it is...or was. Calling on an eighteen-wheeler just to transport it to the lab. Shit." She shakes her head. "I hope they have room for it at the lab."

Shawn's eyes bulge and his forehead furrows. "Yeah, *quite* massive. Nothing I want to ever see again—that's for sure. Man..." He shakes his head, rubs his sweaty brow. "I don't know what to think anymore. What I *do* know, and not just from that journal, is that this thing has some weird connection to those lowlife Bone Cutters." His lips pinch together a flatline. He nods his head. "Yeah, *I* was one of those lowlifes not too long ago, but at least I never carved into anyone else. Maybe that's why I never really knew about that thing, except through rumors. Maybe it's just the longtime users who also carve *other* people open for their fix. You know..." He nods at Tommy and me. "The ones I told you guys about before—the ones who end up with those supernatural-like abilities. I don't know." Shaking his head again, he adds, "Like when they *smelled* Dory bleeding when her wounds weren't even visible—that sorta shit's *gotta* be linked to that demon somehow."

A moment of silence.

Expressions of deep thought spread from face to face.

Shawn releases a heavy sigh and swipes his hand down his face. "Shit. I don't believe I'm saying this but...I'm kinda glad I got busted the other night at that cemetery. Did I tell you guys about that yet?" He doesn't wait for any replies. "Man, if that hadn't happened, I would've been back on that bone dust crap again, and I don't think I would've made it out of that world alive. Damn. It's like someone was watching out for me or something, you know? Trying to stop me from using again." Another head shake. "Yeah, I know, that sounds crazy, but I can't help but think..." He punctuates his partial sentence with a sigh.

Tommy and Irie and I share a knowing look while Shawn is rubbing his face and shaking his head. He's still quite fidgety and shaken up from the night's events.

I understand. I'm not sure if it shows, but I feel on the inside how he appears on the outside. Everything that went down with that creature feels quite surreal, almost like it never really happened, or like it happened to someone else or on screen or some crazy not-associated-with-me sort of shit. It's all very difficult to grasp, difficult to rationalize at all. I think I'm partially in denial. And now that Shawn brings up that whole cemetery incident...shit, all that just went down earlier tonight had cast a complete shadow over that other mess. I'd almost forgotten about it...

Until now.

"Cemetery?" Tommy kicks the footrest of his recliner down,

locks it in place, and leans forward with a groan. "What, like those cemeteries that've been all over the news with grave robberies and graffiti and shit? You got into that?"

Phew. Tommy comes to the rescue. I'm obviously dumb over here, without a damn idea what to say. I feel stupid enough that the absence of intelligent thoughts *must* visibly show on me somehow. Am I drooling?

I wipe the corners of my mouth.

Following Tommy's lead, I lean forward, trying to appear in awe of what Shawn might say next, like I had no idea he's been anywhere near a cemetery lately.

"The Joneses were getting to me big time. With everything that happened at the hospital, I was released before my treatment was done—a protective measure to keep me safe. But as bad as I wanted the dust, I just couldn't hurt anyone else, and there was *no way* I was carving myself open again. That shit sucks! I don't know how the damned donors do it. There are some sick fuckos out there. Shit. I don't even know how users do it. Many of the sickos actually enjoy it. It's like their wiring gets all wacko after using so much. Anyway, once you use the dust, regular drugs, they just don't do for you what the dust does. It's fuckin' weird. When I heard others had gotten a fix from the dead, and then some Dusters I knew asked if I wanted in on hitting up a grave, I figured, *What's the harm in it—they're already dead?* But I guess some neighbor called the police." A tense laugh tumbles out of him. "Neighbor? More like my guardian angel. Like you, Tommy. You waited for me. Thanks, man." He looks at Tommy. Smiles.

Tommy smiles. Nods. Then he groans as he reaches his arm out, palm up, waiting for Shawn to slap him five. "I leave no one behind."

Shawn slaps Tommy's outstretched hand. Tommy winces. "Sorry, dude," Shawn says, through gritted teeth.

Tommy waves it off.

"Those Dusters who were with you at the cemetery, did any

of them mention that demon at all? Do they know about it?" Legs stretched out and stocking feet kicked up onto the coffee table, Irie follows her dad's play-dumb footsteps.

"If they *do* know, no one mentioned it. But I did see something like that creature spray painted on a nearby tomb. And now that I know this flying demon nightmare is *real*—The Joneses have packed their shit and moved the fuck out of my head, that's for damn sure!"

"I'm confused. You've never carved someone else, you've been clean a while, you're not a rat, so...Why did that demon come after us? We're not users or carvers or killers, we have nothing to do with their cult." Tommy fidgets a bit, adjusts the gauze pads on his shoulder wounds. "It just doesn't make sense. Landry says one of us was a target, like Snake Girl was. But *why*?" He settles back in his seat again, as nervous laughter escapes him. "I was *so* fucking wrong with my gargoyle stopping evil theory. That's for damn sure."

Uncomfortable silence.

We all nod in agreement.

I hear paper crinkling. Irie, with her knees now pulled in close to her chest, is absentmindedly flipping through a takeout menu beside me. The trifold pamphlet blocks Shawn's face from view. The cover of *Pompeo's Pizza, 999 Court Street* stares me in the face.

Then it hits me.

"Court...it's next week." I yank the menu down so I can see Shawn. "It doesn't want us going to court."

They all shoot me confused expressions.

"Come on—don't you see? Getting Sheila and Toodles busted not only takes two Bone Cutters out of commission, but it could also lead authorities to this demon's involvement—*if* it really *is* connected to the Bone Cutter cult. And we all know *Evil 101*: evil likes to remain hidden and always tries to stop good. *Maybe* it wants to eliminate any non-user that knows about it and could lead others to it."

"Yeah, but why did it go to Shawn's? How did it know we were going to be there right then?" Asks Irie, as she stares up at the ceiling in deep thought.

Before I have time to speak, Shawn, with an *aha*-look on his face, chimes in, "I was subpoenaed. I have to be in court, too." A look of terror suddenly washes down his face. "It was coming for *me*."

"*No way*. Don't think like that." I'm shaking my head. "Plus, we're *all* going to court. Tommy and Irie are also coming as my witnesses" I pause, give it more thought.

Before I'm able to think too deeply about it, I blurt out, "Don't forget—we're dealing with an *unearthly* creature. That journal calls it a demon. It probably has telepathic ways to find out where we are, or maybe it sniffed us out. Who knows? Not being of this earth could mean it has numerous abilities we have no idea about, abilities we can't even imagine."

Tommy kicks the footrest down, slowly sits forward again. "Unearthly. Demon. Guys, I can't help but wonder..." He looks from me to Irie and then settles on Shawn when he finishes with, "What if there are *more* of them?"

No one moves.

No one says a word.

The air is a lead blanket.

Crushing.

Confining.

A text chimes from my hoodie pocket. I pull out my phone. Before I light up the screen, a thud sounds against the roof of Tommy's one-story house. My shoulders hike up to my ears and my finger freezes above the screen.

We all look around at one another, but only with our eyes. None of us move.

We all remain quiet.

A couple moments of silence pass. I now dare switch my focus long enough to check my phone. The words on the screen sink into my mind just as I hear scratching noises move across the roof.

I glance up from my phone. I look from Tommy to Irie to Shawn. In a hushed voice I tell them, "Landry." I shake my head, as I relay her text. "It's not dead. It escaped the lab. There have been numerous sightings around the city already. So many that she wonders if there's more of them, or if this thing is just that quick—searching. She wants to know where we are. She thinks it's coming for us again."

A low, deep scratching sound scrapes slowly across the roof.

Tommy rubs his forehead with his tatted hand. L-I-V-E stares back at me as he says, "Tell her—

"It found us and—" He glances up at the ceiling.

"It's here."

CHAPTER 28
BACK FOR THE ATTACK

Swirling lights and screeching sirens surround Tommy's small bungalow before Irie can say, "Takeout anyone?"

She sure does have an unusual habit of calling out for comfort food.

Not much can comfort this crew right now, especially not food.

Just as I jump up to look out the window, hurried scratching scrapes across the roof of the house. The sound freezes me in my tracks before I make it out from behind the coffee table. I hesitate to go any farther. Before I decide if I dare move again, Shawn jumps up and blasts past me, brushing against my arm.

I don't flinch.

I look to the couch behind me and see Irie looking up at the ceiling, though her hands are pushing against the cushion as though she wants to get up and rush to the window, too. When I turn back around, Tommy kicks the recliner's footrest down and starts sitting up, gingerly. That's all Irie needs to see or hear to make her get up.

Just as Irie unfolds her legs and places her stocking feet on the floor to stand, the window behind the couch erupts in a hail storm of shattering glass. An ear-splitting screech rends through the air as the creature reaches its front foot through the window, dagger-sharp talons grasping for anyone.

Irie ducks and falls forward against the coffee table, trying to scrabble away.

"Sunshine!" Tommy's voices bellows as he tries to jump to his daughter's rescue. He winces in pain as his hand slips off the side of the chair's arm. Sean rushes over to help him.

I lunge for Irie. As I grab her arm and pull, I kick the coffee table out of the way. Falling to her knees, she kicks out with her feet, trying to grab purchase on the slippery hardwood floor. Another mind-numbing screech sounds close outside the broken window.

It's trying to get in.

Just as Irie kicks out again to try to help me move her away, the creature reaches for her leg. A talon catches on her fuzzy sock and tugs it right off her foot. Blood bubbles to the surface of her skin on the top of her foot as I pull harder and slide her across the floor toward the opposite side of the living room.

A multitude of gunshots blast from the city street out front, peppering the roof of Tommy's ranch. Another unbearable screech rips through the night as the creature yanks its leg back out of the window. Hurried footfalls pound and scrape across the roof, moving all around as though in a frenzy.

Just as I pull Irie up onto her feet, she rushes to her dad's side.

"Holy shit! Dad, are you alright?" She starts checking his bandaged shoulder.

"I'm fine, Sunshine. Really." He wraps an arm around her shoulders and hugs her. "I'm so thankful *you're* okay. How's your foot?"

"No worries. Just a scratch." She doesn't even look down to check.

"Shit!" Tommy's eyes widen as he glances over her shoulder toward the front window right near them. He shifts them further away.

Shawn and I are standing between the two front windows. Just as I take a chance and pull the curtain aside on the closest window to see how much help has arrived, more gunshots blast through the air. I jump and drop the curtain.

"What the fuck!?" I yell.

Tommy turns toward me. "Dory!"

"I'm okay. Just scared the shit out of me." The moment I pull the curtain open again an ear-splitting screech sounds out from overhead. Multiple cruisers line the street and several officers are shooting up toward the roof.

"The whole fucking cavalry's out front," I say, glancing over my shoulder.

"Holy fuck!" Shawn shouts as he looks out the other window.

Irie looks at her dad and shrugs.

Tommy doesn't stop her as she escorts him over to the window next to Shawn.

No one speaks.

We all stay glued to the window.

"This doesn't feel real," says Irie.

"Maybe we should take cover, move away from the windows." Tommy looks to Irie beside him, then over to me at the other window.

"And miss the action?" Shawn's nose is practically pressed against the glass. "No way."

More gunshots are blasting up toward the creature. I see detectives Landry and Morris shooting from behind their black SUV a couple buildings away from Tommy's house.

A moment later, Landry ducks out of sight. Good timing on her part.

The creature swoops down, screeching, toward the onslaught of gunfire. A spattering of black rain sprinkles all around as bullets blast all over its body. The demon doesn't appear fazed. Nothing slows it down.

Suddenly it sinks its talons into an officer and throws him

down the street. The policeman crashes into the windshield of a parked car. Glass shatters and concaves. The instant he hits, another officer gets thrown like a doggy chew toy, then smashes through the picture window of the house across the street.

Two residents inside rush to the huge hole in their living room and look outside. Expressions of horror fall across their faces. They look down at their floor, where I assume the officer landed. Then they immediately duck out of sight, which is probably what we should do.

We all remain glued to the windows.

Cops are getting tossed around like they're the demon's playthings.

One officer's head cracks into the lamp of a streetlight as she flies from the demon's taloned throw. Darkness engulfs that section of the sidewalk, shadowing where the officer lands.

Another officer, while reloading her gun, gets raked across the head with the demon's monstrous talons as it leaps over her to get to a line of police shooting at it incessantly. Half her face and one side of her skull are torn open. A large clump of skin and hair hang down, swaying, as she stumbles and falls behind her cruiser.

If it wasn't for all the city lights spotlighting the carnage, this gruesome scene would be left up to our imaginations. Maybe it would be better that way. This brutality, these graphic images will no doubt scar the psyche of any spectator and participant. I already sense it all coming. Instant replays will reel through everyone's mind, whether asleep or awake, for years to come. So much for a restful night of sleep ever again.

Out on the street the demon rips through a group of officers. A few of the bodies get tossed around. One of them slams down on the windshield of a parked cruiser, spiderwebbing the glass and cracking open the back of the officer's skull. Blood gushes from under his head and spreads through the multitude of fissures in the windshield. Other officers are shredded. With one rake of the demon's claws down an officer's chest and abdomen, guts and intestines spill onto the street just before his body crumbles to the ground, landing in a puddle of his own blood and innards.

I reflexively turn away.

In a building diagonally across from Tommy's place, some teenage-looking chick is leaning out her open window capturing the slaughter with her cellphone.

Rather than taking cover she wants to document everything instead? No doubt she'll post that clip all over social media before the bloodshed is even over.

Lovely.

What the fuck is wrong with people?

Then I glance at the four of us glued to the windows. Well, at least we're not documenting the bloodshed with our phones.

I turn around toward the sound of a pain-filled scream. One of the demon's massive clawed feet has grabbed another officer. Its talons pierce straight through his body. He whips his head back and bellows to the sky. The creature throws the blood-drenched cop across the street. His body slams into the side of an apartment building. He hits the same building with the chick and her cellphone, right next to her open window. She retreats inside and ducks down. The officer's mangled body—limbs distorted and bent in all the wrong directions, bloody holes riddled through him—drops to the roof of the porch below. A large, dripping dark spot left behind at the point of impact on the side of the building. A blink after the thud of his landing sounds out, the chick pops back up in front of the open window, leans out again, looks down at the poor guy's dead body. His head dangles over the edge of the front porch roof. Blood gushes down to the walkway below, pooling in front of the stairs.

The sick and desensitized crazy bitch, phone still glued to her fucking hand, captures the whole gruesome affair.

Screams of terror dance around with the multitude of gunshots ripping through the air. Before every officer in that line of shooters gets completely ravaged, Detective Landry runs out from behind her SUV with something long hanging from her hand.

A shotgun?

An automatic rifle?

As she nears the creature from behind, a beam from the streetlight reflects off what she's carrying. It swings back and forth with the motion of her arm as she runs.

"A fuckin' machete?" Tommy blurts out.

I knew that bitch was a take-charge chick, but...damn. I wasn't expecting to see *that* in her hand.

An officer's arm, its hand still holding a gun, flies up over the demon's head and almost hits Landry. Sidestepping the near collision, she jumps up onto the hood of a car. Now she's running across the line of parked cars, up over roofs and across hoods and trunks, toward the demon. Its huge head ducks low to the ground toward a female officer fleeing. When the creature turns its wide-open jaw, massive fangs ready to devour, toward the escaping cop, we finally get a glimpse of its once illusive face.

Just like the image on the camera from that night in the hospital, its eyes glow red like flames. Though it doesn't have a skeleton-like face, it looks like part of its face has been torn off, revealing a glimpse of the bones under its leathery skin. Besides the torn off flesh, it does resemble a gargoyle, but something seems different, though in this fleeting moment I can't quite place it.

The demon clamps its mouth full of dagger sharp teeth around the fleeing officer's body. With one sinking chomp, the woman's head and feet drop from the monster's mouth. Then it chews and spits out her gruesome remains.

As blood rains down from the monster's mouth, Landry jumps, with her machete held high, from the roof of a truck beside the demon. As she comes down, the machete slices across the back of the creature's neck. Landry continues to slice and slash repeatedly. It screeches so loudly the windows rattle in their frames. Black blood showers Landry as she swings her blade with the rage of an alpha wolf protecting its pack.

None of us say a word. *All* our noses are now pressed against the glass.

Another window-rattling screech erupts from the demon. I pull back from the window a bit just as it flaps its huge wings and quickly shifts its body, trying to stop Landry and fling her to the ground. Gasps shoot out of all of us as Landry tumbles across its back. Just before I think she's about to fall off and hit the pavement, she grasps a chunk of the creature's long, spikey red mohawk and holds on. She manages to pull herself back up. Then, she quickly raises the long, curved blade of her machete and swings at the neck again as though chopping down a tree.

Detective Morris and the last four officers left standing rush out from behind their vehicles, guns aimed out in front of them. They head toward Landry. Before anyone gets close enough to assist her, the demon's severed head falls from its shoulders and tumbles to the ground. Its body soon follows, landing in the middle of the street with a thud so heavy it shakes Tommy's whole house. The massive wings blanket several cars on either side of the street.

The demon doesn't move. Minus its head, it's certainly dead this time.

Painted black by the demon's blood, Landry pulls herself up off the street where she tumbled, chest heaving, beside the lifeless creature. Morris and the officers surround her, patting her on the back, making sure she's all right. Morris hugs her.

Shawn is the first one at the door. With his hand on the doorknob he says, "All's clear. I'm going out. Who's with me?"

Speechless, we all follow.

As we're standing on Tommy's front porch watching the aftermath, we hear the distinct jackhammering sound of a big rig's Jake Brake. I don't think this trucker's getting any noise ordinance fine tonight. The eighteen-wheeler pulls up at the top of the street. One big, burly bearded guy and a chick just as burly–minus the beard–jump out of the cab and head toward the back to open the doors of the trailer. As they pull down a loading ramp, a white lab van pulls up behind them. Two techs in white lab coats, the same man and woman we saw at Shawn's earlier in the night, get out and walk over to examine the creature, heads shaking. Landry and Morris go to them, talk for a minute, then turn and walk back down the street. The lab techs, continuously shaking their heads in disbelief, walk around the demon's carcass and snap a few crime scene photos. Then the two truckers step up to assist them with cleaning up the remains to somehow load into the truck.

With the machete still in hand and swinging by her side, Landry walks with Morris down the sidewalk toward Tommy's house. Drops of black demon blood trail behind them as it drips from the blade. One knee of her pants is torn open, with her bloody knee cap protruding with each step. The left shoulder of her jacket is ripped and dangling down her bicep. As they get closer, I see a bunch of puncture holes, tears, and blood peppering Landry's body. No doubt the result of the demon's red spikey mohawk.

We meet them at the bottom of the stairs.

"Bet you've never seen a showdown quite like that one, huh?" Landry's wide-eyed and shaking her head as she speaks. Black demon blood is smeared across her face and splattered all over her clothes. She looks like a fucking warrior.

This certainly bumps her up from *take charge* to *kickass*.

We shake our heads *no*.

"The *X-Files* live on our city streets. Great takedown, Mulder." Thumb up and a wink, I smirk.

A smile emerges under the black streaks of demon blood as she nods, proud.

Shirtless and shivering from the chilly October air, Tommy laughs. He steps up to Landry and points down at the machete.

"That doesn't look like department issued weaponry there, Detective."

Her proud smile turns a bit sly. "You can bet your ass it isn't."

Everyone laughs.

Morris pats her on the back, pulls her in for a side hug. "Thanks to her survivalist way of thinking, you can all rest assured that the beast is *not* getting back up and coming after you again this time."

Shawn steps up a bit closer and into the beam shining down from the nearby streetlight. "If *that's* true, those lab techs best just *burn* the remains."

Morris laughs. "That certainly won't happen. They need to figure out what it is, so we can figure out if there are more like it out there."

"To hell with science. Burn that fucker! For all we know, it will morph back together and escape again. Dammit! It's a fucking demon, for fuck's sake! *Nothing* about it is logical. It doesn't follow the laws of your science. Don't you *realize* that yet?!" Eloquent speaking Shawn doesn't sugarcoat anything. He is definitely making this victory less celebratory. If it truly is a victory.

Smiles withering and eyebrows raised, both detectives look stunned.

"Hey, man, calm down. It's alright." A voice of reason and reassurance. Tommy shivers with every word. "These brave detectives saved us *again*. Let's give them the thanks they deserve and save the demon search and worry for another day. We *need* this victory right now. Let us enjoy this. At least for tonight."

A reluctant Shawn nods, reaches out his hand. "Yeah. I guess you're right. Thank you, detectives, for saving our asses *again*."

The smiles return, for everyone.

The handshakes and *thank yous* go around our group before

we say goodnight to the detectives and retreat back to the comfort of Tommy's welcoming abode.

CHAPTER 29
NEW BEGINNINGS

"Ah, shit. Sunshine, don't just *tear* them off! You might rip out a stitch."

"It's better this way, Dad. Trust me. If I try to pull it off any slower, it would hurt a lot worse."

Tommy's bare chest heaves as Irie changes the bandages on his shoulders. When we all got back inside from watching Landry slay that demon, his bandages were a lot bloodier and losing their stickability from all the sweating and hopped-up adrenalin. It may be a chilly October night in Maine, but after watching all the chaos outside Tommy's house, we're all quite sweaty now.

Damn. Even after going outside and then coming in and taking off my hoodie, my t-shirt is still sticking to me. Irie, after double checking her own bandage covering the demon cut, pulls her long dreads up off her sweaty neck and wraps them into a huge bun on top of her head. Shawn looks sweaty too, with strands of his hair sticking to his forehead.

Shawn notices me looking at him. I tug at my shirt a few times, "I feel like I just finished running a fucking marathon." He nods, laughs, and wipes his forehead as I look over at Tommy. "You got a fan in here? I'm drenched."

As soon as I finish talking, I realize I'm a bit out of breath too. My adrenalin's still amped right up. It's so damn hard to believe everything that's gone down tonight.

Irie answers me since Tommy's too busy moaning and groaning after she tore off the bandage on his other shoulder. "I can get you one just as soon as I put the new bandage on."

"Thanks." I turn back to Shawn. "So, that journal...Does it say if there are more of those demons out there? I don't want to be even more anxious than I already am, worrying about the next attack. But still...better to be in-the-know. You know?"

He hesitates to answer my question.

Tommy, Irie and I share curious looks.

"Well, to be honest—I never actually finished reading the journal. Every time I'd open the cover to find out more, I'd get the overwhelming urge to use again. I read quite a bit, but not enough to answer your question."

"In what I've heard about demons, there's always more." Tommy says through a wince as Irie places the last piece of tape on his bandage.

"I wonder if this one was the big demon. *You* know—like the boss or the demon in charge, and maybe the one you all saw on Dr. Headstrom's camera is one of its worker bees. You know what I mean?" Irie tosses the roll of bandaging tape into the bag of first aid supplies on the coffee table.

I shrug, mulling it over. Tommy cocks his head to the side since shrugging will probably hurt him right now. Shawn remains dead silent.

His silence makes me a bit nervous.

I sure hope Irie's right. I hope Landry got the big boss, but...

A disturbing thought hits me.

Before I have time to think it all through, I blurt out, "What if *it was* one of the worker bees and the big boss is still out there?"

We all exchange fearful glances.

Irie walks over to a small cabinet under a tall, narrow book-shelf built into the living room wall. She pulls out a fan and sets it up on the end table on Shawn's side of the couch. "Well, for right now..." With a glance and a smile to her dad, she comes over and plops down between Shawn and me and kicks her stocking feet up onto the coffee table. "Let's all try to relax, take comfort in knowing that the demon that took or killed Jill's murderer..." She places her hand on top of mine, the one that's fidgeting on my bouncing knee, twirling the threads hanging from the hole in the knee of my jeans. "...and tried to kill my dad..." She glances at Tommy again and smiles. "...is dead." Looking back at me she adds, "Thanks again, Dory...not just for saving my dad, but for saving me too."

I smile as best I can. The corners of my mouth twitch.

Tommy, with his twinkling eyes on his Sunshine, smiles and nods, as he gingerly sits back and sinks deeper into the recliner as though a load has lifted from his wounded shoulders.

Still silent, Shawn's eyes roll up, as though in deep thought, and an unreadable smirk spreads across his face.

When Irie releases her hold on my hand, I look down and go back to twirling the threads hanging from the hole in my jeans. At least now, since I felt her touch, my knee has stopped bouncing. My other foot immediately starts tapping out a rhythm on the floor. Come to think of it, with all the crazy shit that went down tonight, I haven't scratched my head at all. My eyes glance at the people in the room with me. As much guilt and pain as I feel and as much as I will *always* miss Jill, I realize that I *do* still have friends. Tommy and Irie, and now Shawn, all three of them—they know I'm quirky, they know I'm an anxious ball of nerves, and they *still* want to be around me. Hell, Shawn even mentioned starting a freaking band together.

Feeling accepted for the fucked-up person I am is quite an amazing feeling. It's such an unusual sensation for me that I can't even begin to describe it.

I smile to myself. My bottom lip splits open. Guess I'm not just smiling to myself. And, man, my mouth is so dry it's cotton.

"My throat is sandpaper. I'm gonna get some water. Anyone

else want a glass?" I'm already up and heading toward the kitchen before anyone answers.

At the doorway I stop and turn, waiting for replies. The nods from the couch confirm. Tommy is out of his seat, following me to the kitchen.

While I'm filling a pint glass from the filtered water faucet, Tommy steps up beside me. "Let me give you a hand." He turns toward the fridge on the other side of him and grabs the ice tray from the freezer, then sets it next to the three other glasses on the counter.

"Thank you, but you *really* should be resting. I can get this. Don't worry."

He steps a bit closer, plops cubes in each glass, then holds a glass out toward me to fill next. Not looking, I reach for it. My hand wraps around his.

Well, this is quite awkward.

I freeze, turn toward him, pull my hand away. "Sorry. Guess I should pay closer attention before I break something."

Stupid. Stupid. *Stupid* me. Why do I always say the dumbest things?

There's that crooked smile, dimple-scar, and those twinkling dark chocolate eyes. "No need for apologies." He leans across in front of me, places the glass in the sink under the faucet. When he stands back upright, he reaches out and gently swipes his thumb across my lower lip. "Looks like you did get a bit roughed up when you saved my life tonight. Or maybe that's from saving my daughter's life. You're lip's bleeding."

Heat rises to my cheeks. I glance away, back again. "No, nothing exciting like that. Just chapped. That's all." Stupid me strikes again. At a loss of what to say or do, I turn back toward the sink, start filling the next glass.

He leans down, brushes my hair out of my face and gently kisses me on the cheek. When he pulls away he doesn't go far. So close to my ear I can feel his warm breath on my sweaty skin, he says in a breathy whisper-soft voice, "Dory, *you* are a lifesaver. Thank you for coming into my life, *our* lives. You're an absolutely amazing woman."

Chills run through me. I turn partially toward him, look at him sidelong and smile.

His smile widens. He grabs the two filled glasses, turns, walks away.

I turn back, still smiling, and fill the rest of the glasses. Unable to process what just happened, I hold tight to the warm feeling surging through me right now. There goes my jackhammer heartbeat racing again, though this time not provoked by fear or anxiety.

Back in the living room, waters and *thank yous* all passed around, I plop back onto the couch with Irie and Shawn.

As I take a deep breath and settle back into my cozy corner, I notice that silence has settled around us.

At the same instance that I look up from my lap to see what everyone is doing, why they're all so quiet, the silence is interrupted by the sound of crinkling paper beside me.

I glance over at Irie.

Yep. Just as I suspected.

With a takeout menu in hand, she says, "I know what we *all* need right now—comfort food. Who wants to order some takeout?"

Tommy and I share a look, start laughing.

Shawn looks over, appears confused.

"She's going to order food whether you want something or not, so you might as well tell her what you like." Tommy chucks a throw pillow at his Sunshine, knocks the menu out of her hand. It lands on Shawn's lap.

"Hey! Doesn't look like your shoulders hurt so bad now, huh, Daddy-O?" She jumps up off the couch, squeezes out from behind the coffee table, pillow in hand, goes over and bops him in the face.

Laughter fills the room.

With a shrug, Shawn starts flipping through the takeout menu, checking out food options.

I pull my legs up onto the couch, spin on the cushion and sit cross-legged facing him. "So, Shawn, are we gonna start a band or what?"

———

Silence fills Tommy's house. Everyone headed home about an hour or so ago, and Tommy went right to bed. He'd dozed in the recliner. Irie had to wake him up and help him out of the chair before she left.

Now, lying under a colorful hand-woven tribal print blanket, I face the back of the couch, trying to block out the streetlights' invasion through the windows. Though the extra weight of the big blanket feels like a comforting hug, I'm unable to fall asleep. Even with all the craziness that has taken place, I can't stop thinking about Tommy.

I have no idea how to take what happened, the kiss, his words. After saving someone's life, I understand how someone might shower affections on the one who saved them. Is that all it was? Extreme appreciation for saving him from that demon? And saving his daughter as well? I take a deep breath and try not to obsess about it.

Excitement about Shawn saying yes about starting a band with me pushes into my thoughts. He hasn't even heard me play yet. For all he knows, I might suck. But he said yes, and that's killer! I need more music in my life. Shit. Wait. I also haven't heard him play. What if he sucks?

Ah…whatever. Right now, I don't really care. I've got a new goal. And I've got new friends. I can't believe someone as sweet and as smart as Irie actually wants to be my friend. And Tommy and Shawn…

A jolt shoots through me. Heat rushes to my face. My eyes pop wide open.

Do they really want to be my friends, or is this just the short-lived behavior of people who went through a traumatic experience together? A shared-trauma response?

Dammit. I bet as soon as the court cases end and the craziness settles, we'll all drift apart slowly over time, leaving me to wallow in my miserable life alone. After all, why would anyone want to hang out with a stressed-out ball of taut nerves like me?

I brought Tommy and Irie back into the Bone Cutters crosshairs. Tommy almost got killed because of me. Irie too. The demon went to Shawn's place hunting us down, and I bet it's because all of them are testifying against those two crazy bone chiseling freaks. This is all my fault, and once they all have time to realize that, they'll leave just like everyone else. That might be what they have to do to stay safe.

What Shawn said about that demon, about the journal, even if they do walk out of my life, they may still have to live in fear, constantly looking over their shoulders—all because of me, fucked up Dory. And though looking over my shoulder all the time is nothing new for me, the thought of needing to watch the sky for new attackers, huge unearthly monsters, certainly roadblocks my chance of falling asleep tonight.

Good thing Irie left the fan going. I'm drenched in sweat. I throw off the blanket, roll over and sprawl out on my back, allowing the cool breeze to blow across my overheated body. Refusing to open my eyes for fear it will make it harder to fall asleep, I fidget around, trying to get comfortable. When I sit up to unwrap the blanket from around my feet, the fan oscillates, and the breeze blows against my moist face. It feels so good, until I wince in pain when the wind hits my head. My eyes shoot open from the sensation. The light leaking through the windows from the streetlights outside illuminates the blood all over my fingers and hands and the strands of hair sticking all through it.

What the hell? When was I scratching?

Oh, how wonderful. Those two court dates are zooming

right up, and crazy me has gone and scratched the shit out of my head again. I wonder how sane I look now?

Easing myself up off the couch, trying not to make too much noise, trying not to disturb Tommy, I notice the throw pillow is covered in blood. Great. Now I've not only ruined his and his Sunshine's lives, but I've also ruined his fucking pillow. Probably the blanket too. I don't bother checking before I head to the bathroom to assess the damage to my scalp.

What greets me in the mirror above the sink looks like it came straight out of a fucking horror flick. Fabulous. No chance for me winning in court. They'll probably lock me back up in a freaking psych hospital again as soon as they see me.

Yes, the bald spot is back and bloody and as visible as a highway billboard sign. But my face. It looks like an abstract painting, all splotchy with blood trails down the right side of my face and blood smears spread all around the rest of it. My eyes sting. A sniffle later, and the tears don't just fall, they pour down in bloody rivers, crashing down all around, splashing a sickly red-fading-to-pink all over the white porcelain sink.

My thoughts start to uncontrollably spiral into an abyss of negativity.

No one wants *this*. No one wants *me*. Why the hell would Tommy ever be interested in unstable Dory? Unattractive me? Why would Shawn and Irie ever want to hang around with this trainwreck? The one always a bloody mess, always needing help. The fucked-up chick who can never get a grip on herself. The one always fucking everything up. Fucking up my own life. Fucking up everyone's life who tries to get close to me.

A shimmer from the corner of my blurry vision catches my attention. Sitting in a mug on the counter of the sink, Tommy's stainless-steel straight razor glistens in the overhead lighting. I take in a stuttered breath, unsuccessful at calming myself down. I reach for the razor with a shaky hand. Unforgiving metal against soft fingertips. I hesitate.

Looking back in the mirror, I wipe my eyes.

Maybe a new story starts for me now. New people. New friends. New band. Maybe this time…

No.

Who am I trying to convince?

Not me. I know better. No more delusional Dory.

Every time someone has saved me, the pain has always come back intensified. Why should I think things will work out any better this time?

Turning away from my black-rimmed eyes and blood-smeared face, I search for that shimmer of hope. That shiny promise of relief.

Tears flow faster as the cold glistening steel of the blade touches the heated skin of my forearm.

CHAPTER 30
SO MANY BONES, SO LITTLE TIME

Six Months Later

With all this tree coverage blocking any views from nosy neighbors, Slug Man feels confident Rose Cemetery was the right choice. The small town of Brooks, with a population just over a thousand people, was a no-brainer of a choice, but picking just the right cemetery to hit is crucial for getting away with the goods. Add in the town's lack of having its own police department and it all seemed worth the nearly two-hour drive at the time they'd planned this grave robbery.

But in the dark of the new moon night with the only partner he could find willing to help him, Slug Man wonders, as he sweats and grunts and digs more and more, if this was such a great idea after all. Yeah, such a small cemetery in such a small town equals a low likelihood of cops staking the place out. But with this Mouth-All-Mighty beside him wielding a shovel, Slug Man's every last nerve gets put to the test, as does his "master plan to hit small town cemeteries up north." Though it is still a much safer route for getting a fix than the alternative, especially since bone-chiseling crimes have plastered the news for the past few months. Plus, with dead bones there's no need to wait for drying time to crush it into dust.

Slug Man tries hard to hold onto the positive aspects of this gig.

"Mother! Fucking! Rocks!" The tip of the spade driving into the rocky dirt punctuates each of Darren's words. "They're bustin' my balls in here, dude. Fuck!" Darren's words fly past his snarling lips so loud and so fast they hit Slug Man like boulders from an avalanche.

Teeth clenched and face caked in dirt, Slug Man tries his hardest to *not* backhand his partner across the face. "Seriously, man, suck it up already. You begged for someone to show you the ropes. Well...This is it—*He who wants the junk must swing the shovel*. These are the days we're livin' in, man. Like it or not." As his gravelly voice shoots out of his mouth, he heaves another shovel full of dirt and rocks over his shoulder from where he stands up to his waist in the third open grave of the night. Pausing, he throws Darren a glare as he quietly adds, "And keep your fucking voice down or you're going to get us busted."

"Busted? Ha! In this tiny town?" Darren huffs and shakes his head, sending his long, red mohawk swinging and swaying. "Just tell me this is the last one, dude." He wipes a hand across his sweaty forehead, leaving a smear of mud, then hauls the shovel back for another swing.

Slug Man just shakes his head, says nothing, keeps digging while wishing Big G wasn't still in jail. With his strength and his jonesing attitude, this third grave would've been done an hour ago and they'd be long gone, headed back south with their goods in hand. But here he is stuck with the desperate newbie who *needed* someone to show him how to score some dust.

Well, Slug Man's quite desperate as well, hence his reliance on the newbie for help. But now he wonders if he should've come alone and stuck with digging up only one grave for the night.

Damned jonesing sure does push a user to do stupid shit. Never enough junk.

A jarring metallic *clang* rings out as soon as Darren drives the tip of the spade into the dirt again. Another rock. A big one. "Fuck me runnin', mother of fuck!" The shovel gets slammed to the ground, then he reaches for the water bottle sitting on the edge of the grave's perimeter beside the flashlight that's aimed down into the grave.

With gritted teeth Slug Man halts, drops his shovel, and snatches the bottle before Darren's able to grab it. Shocked and speechless, Darren just stands there staring at him. With his free hand, fist clenched, Slug Man hauls back and punches him in the mouth.

"Do I fuckin' stutter? Shut your fucking mouth already. If you get us busted, man..." Unable to think of what he'll do if that happens, he just grits his teeth in aggravation then takes a long drink of water. After he drinks all that's left, he tosses the bottle back up on the edge of the open grave, grabs his shovel and gets back to digging, not giving a shit about how Darren reacts. In a grave this old, the casket lid isn't much deeper below their feet. One more bag of bones added to the rest of their haul should give them enough goods to last a while back home. He just wants to end this bullshit gig with this pain in the ass partner as soon as possible.

Well, maybe Slug Man should've cared about Darren's reaction.

Pissed off, Darren hauls himself up out of the open grave while spewing blood and obscenities the whole time. "The fuck, man?! Seriously! This is not what I fuckin' signed up for! Fuck you and fuck this..." On and on Mouth-All-Mighty swears up a roaring storm as his bloody lip swells up. Then he storms off, leaving Slug Man all alone in the grave.

Leaning on his shovel, Slug Man winces as he hears Darren pout and curse his way back through the small cemetery amidst the soft glow of solar lamps. When The Whiner only makes it two family plots away before tripping over a ground level head-stone and yelling, "Fuck me!" Slug Man can't help but laugh along with his wincing.

Man, that fucking wuss is gonna get us busted if he doesn't...

The wind and the *whoosh* of giant flapping wings overhead halts his thoughts and rustles his disheveled hair. Standing frozen in the open grave, Slug Man stares in shock and disbelief as a massive gargoyle-like creature flies past him and descends toward the ground only a few yards away. The leathery wingspan spreads across almost the entire width of the small cemetery. The creature's large hind feet reach forward, toes spread wide, as though getting ready for a landing.

If he could make himself move he'd shine his flashlight on the creature for a better look at this uncanny sight, though he knows that would only draw its attention toward him. With such a strong grip of fear seizing him up and fucking with his mind, he doesn't even think to duck down out of sight and *shut off* the flashlight.

As Darren lifts himself back up onto his feet, yelling obscenities the entire time, the huge winged demon swoops down from behind him, silent but for its windswept movement through the obsidian night sky. Before Slug Man can get a word of warning out, scythe-like talons on the creature's hind feet grab Darren's shoulders, pierce straight through each, and lift him right up off the ground. A torrent of blood instantly trails down his body, darkening his light gray sweatshirt and sweatpants. A stunted scream shoots out of him seconds before another long claw from the monster's front foot reaches back and stabs straight through his throat, stifling all sound, returning the night of this small Maine town to its peaceful quiet.

Blood rains down onto Rose Cemetery while a slack jawed Slug Man remains motionless, fear-frozen, just watching in an awe-struck stupor.

As soon as the massive gargoyle creature escapes out of sight with Darren's bloody carcass in tow, Slug Man finally dares to move. He looks down at the shovel in his hand, then at the lid of the old wooden casket peeking through the thin layer of dirt in the center of the open grave where the flashlight shines on it like a spotlight. Not much more to go to get to the goods.

"Fuck this shit!"

Slug Man hauls his bone rack of a body out of that open grave, grabs his two bags of bones and the shovels and the flashlight. Then he books his ass out of the cemetery, glancing toward the crow-black sky every chance he gets. Two minutes later, he jumps into his old beat up El Camino and peels out. In the red glow of his tail lights a hail storm of gravel and rocks shoots out from his rear tires.

By the time Slug Man makes it to the main road out of town five minutes later, a Waldo County Sheriff's cruiser rumbles down the dirt drive leading to Rose Cemetery in response to a townie's complaint about yelling and screaming coming from the graveyard. It won't take long for the officers to find the trail of blood leading to the three open graves and the empty Poland Spring bottle lying on its side.

ACKNOWLEDGMENTS

Thanks to those people and entities who don't even know how they affect my life and my work: Jimi Hendrix, Chris Cornell, Rob Zombie, Clive Barker, Stephen Graham Jones, *Dexter*, *The X-Files*, Kurt Cobain, *Supernatural*; my well of inspiration overflows thanks to all of you.

Though writing remains a very solitary act, there are special people in my life I would like to thank, people who were there for me in various ways during the making of this book, and some people who were there before the idea was born but still found their way into this story through their importance to my life and my development as a creator. Thanks to Tim Hill, my favorite guitar instructor from my teens, for instilling within me the importance of practice and dedication to your craft, and for teaching me that the only person to blame for you not improving at your craft is yourself. Because of those lessons, I now tell myself, "Show up or shut up." Thanks to my mom, for always supporting my love of music and writing and for telling me that if I never give up, I will eventually reach my goals. Mom, I wish you were still here to see what I'm doing now, but somehow, I sense you already know. Thanks to David Simms, for your endless encouragement and for reading an early draft of this and giving me constructive feedback, as well as for the memorable moment of calling me an asshole for killing off your favorite character. You're welcome, David. Thanks to Morgan Sylvia, for being an enthusiastic beta reader and providing me with priceless feedback that greatly improved this book, especially two chapters that turned out much more powerful thanks to her savvy. Thanks to Spring Harbor Psychiatric Hospital, for giving me the experience of working as a psych tech where I learned the ins and outs of how a psych hospital operates. Thanks to Jennifer Lewis-Auger, for inspiring *and* being the character of the news reporter and for offering me assistance with expanding my in-person readings for a mini, indie book tour. And thanks to my husband, Jesse, for the endless support and understanding, for always actively listening to my ramblings about this story, for providing his witty sense of humor along the way, and for assuring our young son, Sandro, that his mom is the one who keeps the monsters away.

ABOUT THE AUTHOR

Renee S. DeCamillis is a horror author and freelance editor, and the author of the psychological thriller/supernatural horror novella *The Bone Cutters*, book 1 in *The Bone Cutters* series. She also has a book forthcoming in 2025, which is a co-author project, called *Try Not to Die: By Your Own Hand.*

Renee's short fiction appears in various anthologies: *Phantoms from the Sky*; *Dethfest Confessions: The Devil's Playlist*; *Horrors of the Deep*; *After the Burn*; *Wicked Women*; and more.

Her poetry appears in the *Horror Writers Association Poetry Showcase Vol. IV.* She is a member of the Horror Writers Association, the New England Horror Writers, and the Horror Writers of Maine.

Renee is the lead singer/songwriter and rhythm guitarist for the punk-metal band Scars Aligned, and she's a tree-hugging hippie with a sharp metal edge. Renee earned her BA in psychology, earned her MFA in Creative Writing, and attended Berklee College of Music as a music business major with guitar as her principal instrument. Renee is a former model, school rock band teacher, creative writing teacher, private guitar instructor, A&R rep for an indie record label, therapeutic mentor, psychological technician, and preschool teacher. She is also a former gravedigger; she can get rid of a body fast without leaving a trace, and she is not afraid to get her hands dirty.

Renee lives in the woods of southern Maine with her husband, their son, and a house full of ghosts.

You can find her online at renees.decamillis.com, as well as on Facebook, Instagram, and Twitter/X

www.ingramcontent.com/pod-product-compliance
Lightning Source LLC
Chambersburg PA
CBHW011414310726
48972CB00011B/2972